# EVERY SINGLE LIE

# EVERY SINGLE LIE

## RACHEL VINCENT

BLOOMSBURY

NEW YORK   LONDON   OXFORD   NEW DELHI   SYDNEY

BLOOMSBURY YA
Bloomsbury Publishing Inc., part of Bloomsbury Publishing Plc
1385 Broadway, New York, NY 10018

BLOOMSBURY and the Diana logo are trademarks of Bloomsbury Publishing Plc

First published in the United States of America in January 2021 by Bloomsbury YA

Bloomsbury books may be purchased for business or promotional use.
For information on bulk purchases please contact Macmillan Corporate and
Premium Sales Department at specialmarkets@macmillan.com

Library of Congress Cataloging-in-Publication Data
Names: Vincent, Rachel, author.
Title: Every single lie / Rachel Vincent.
Description: New York : Bloomsbury Children's Books, 2021.
Summary: High school junior Beckett's life is turned upside-down when
she discovers a dead baby in her small-town high school's locker room, and her
police detective mother investigates while cyberbullies claim it is Beck's child.
Identifiers: LCCN 2020029392 (print) | LCCN 2020029393 (e-book)
ISBN 978-1-5476-0523-1 (hardcover) • ISBN 978-1-5476-0524-8 (e-book)
Subjects: CYAC: High schools—Fiction. | Schools—Fiction. | Cyberbullying—Fiction. |
Criminal investigation—Fiction. | Babies—Fiction.
Classification: LCC PZ7.V7448 Eve 2021 (print) | LCC PZ7.V7448 (e-book) |
DDC [Fic]—dc23
LC record available at https://lccn.loc.gov/2020029392

Book design by Jeanette Levy
Typeset by Westchester Publishing Services
Printed and bound in the U.S.A. by Berryville Graphics Inc., Berryville, Virginia
2 4 6 8 10 9 7 5 3 1

All papers used by Bloomsbury Publishing Plc are natural, recyclable products
made from wood grown in well-managed forests. The manufacturing processes
conform to the environmental regulations of the country of origin.

To find out more about our authors and books visit
www.bloomsbury.com and sign up for our newsletters.

To my sixteen-year-old self, and to every teenage girl
who needs to hear this: Better times are ahead

EVERY
SINGLE
LIE

# ONE

I drive onto the Clifford High School campus at the end of sixth period, armed with a slim jim and an ironclad hunch. Jake always parks near the gym, so I bypass the main student lot, then the staff lot, and I continue into the one on the far side of the school, which is reserved for athletes and band members.

Jake Mercer is a baseball player, a liar, and a cheater. As of last night, he's also my ex-boyfriend.

His ancient Camry is in its usual spot at the back of the lot, so I pull into a space in the next row, then I get out of the car and grab my backpack, rolling my eyes at the reindeer antlers clipped onto his front windows. There's also a puffy red "nose" wired to his front grill. Last week, he lost a bet with my brother, so he has to keep his car dressed up like Rudolph until New Year's Eve.

Two and a half weeks to go. Not that it matters to me. I don't have to ride in it anymore.

Shivering in spite of my jacket, I take the small cardboard box from my back seat, along with my slim jim, a flat strip of metal used to pop the lock on a car door.

Jake's Camry is old enough that the rubber window seal is already dry and cracked, which makes it easy to slide the slim jim into his door, hook end first. It takes me a second to feel around in there, but then I snag the latch and give the thin strip of metal a sharp tug.

The lock disengages with a satisfying thunk. I withdraw my tool and pull his front passenger's side door open, but before I can get in, a black-and-white pulls into the lot and stops behind Jake's car. Clifford is too small a town to be able to afford a full-time police presence at the high school, so the patrol officers take turns keeping the peace. I roll my eyes when I see who's in charge of campus security today.

Doug Chalmers gets out of the patrol car and walks around the hood, one hand propped on his duty belt. "Beckett Bergen. Getting a head start on a life of crime?"

"Hey, Doug." I give him an innocent smile. "How's your mom?"

Doug grew up across the street from me. He graduated when I was in middle school and made it through a semester and a half of Clifford County Community College before deciding that higher education—higher than high school, anyway—wasn't for him. So my mom got him a job with the Clifford PD. He's been patrolling our three square miles of small-town glory ever since.

"That's Officer Chalmers to you, Beckett."

He doesn't answer my question about his mother, but that's okay. I already know she took a turn for the worse last week.

"Sorry, *Officer Chalmers.*"

"Isn't this Jake Mercer's car?" he asks, but he knows damn well it is.

A few weeks ago, Doug moved back home to help take care of his mother, who has stage three lung cancer—the inevitable yet tragic consequence of a three-packs-a-day habit. Which means

2

he's seen this Camry, reindeer antlers and all, parked in front of my house on countless occasions.

"You tryin' to steal Jake's car?"

I can't see his eyes through his dark sunglasses, but his arched brows practically dare me to deny it.

"I wasn't trying to steal Jake's car."

Doug pulls off his sunglasses and tucks them into his shirt pocket as his gaze finds the slim jim dangling from my right hand. "You are aware that you're still *holding* the evidence, right?"

"I'm holding a slim jim, yes. But you'd have to have superpowers to leap from there to 'grand theft auto' in a single bound. For all you know, I always carry a slim jim, in case I lock my keys in my car."

"I just *saw* you pop Jake's lock."

Okay, that part's harder to defend.

"What's going on?" an achingly familiar voice asks from behind me.

I close my eyes and exhale slowly, taking a second to compose myself before I respond.

"Hey, Jake," Doug says, and I spin around to find my brand new ex frowning at me, waiting for an explanation.

His backpack is slung over one shoulder, his crimson and white Clifford High hoodie stretched taut across his broad shoulders. He looks good. Not at all like he's upset about our breakup.

"I just caught Beckett breaking into your car."

"I wasn't—"

Jake's focus drops to the tool in my hand, and I give up on my denial. "How do you even know how to do that?"

I shrug. "My mom's a cop."

3

Fact-Check Rating: True, but misleading.

My mother *is* a cop, but she refused to teach me how to break into a car when I decided I needed that bit of knowledge a few years ago. Fortunately, unlike parents, YouTube has never once disappointed a mischievous seventh grader.

Doug crosses his arms over the front of his uniform. "In the state of Tennessee, entering a passenger vehicle without permission from the owner constitutes burglary."

"But, Officer, I haven't entered his car." I spread my arms to emphasize that I'm still standing in the parking lot. Outside of Jake's beat-up old Camry.

Jake snorts. "Looks like your slim jim entered my car."

Doug nods. "That counts."

"Actually, it doesn't, unless I entered the vehicle with intent to commit a felony, theft, or assault. And since I had no such intent"—I shrug, and my tool bobs with the motion, drawing their attention again—"no crime has been committed."

Jake groans. "Tell me she's wrong."

"Well, technically . . ." Doug scowls at me. "What the hell were you doing breaking into his car, if you weren't going to take something?"

"I was going to leave something."

"You were gonna—?"

"Here, hold this."

I hand my slim jim to the nice police officer, and he accepts it out of misplaced courtesy a *second* before it occurs to him that he's now holding the tool of my criminal trade. I'm pretty sure that counts as tampering with evidence. He really should have known better.

Before he can object, I pick up my cardboard box. "Jake and I broke up last night—"

"She dumped me."

"—and I was just returning the things he left at my house."

I hand the box to Jake, who takes it because it's evidently human nature to take whatever someone hands you, before you think better of it.

Doug glances into the box and coughs to disguise a laugh. "Is that . . . ?"

"Jake's copy of *Sex for Dummies*? Yes."

It was a Dirty Santa gift he stole from his cousin. We spent hours leafing through it, highlighting and laughing at the instructions, tips, and suggestions. Secretly vowing to try them.

Jake's face flames, and I realize this may be the shittiest thing I've ever done to someone, exposing a vulnerable, intimate moment from our private relationship to the light of day. And to Officer Doug Chalmers.

But I can't feel *too* bad about that, because what Jake did to me was way worse.

It wasn't anything sudden or explosive. I didn't catch him in the act. In fact, I'd been ignoring the signs for a couple of weeks, because I just couldn't believe it. I didn't *want* to believe it. But then last night, we were cuddled up on my bed, streaming a cheesy holiday movie, when he got *another* text that made him tense up and swipe the notification away before I could read it.

I'm not one of those girls who demands to see every message her boyfriend gets. But the pattern was unmistakable, and when I asked who the text was from, he got flustered and refused to answer.

He acted guilty.

People will show you who they are, if you pay attention. Ignore them at your own peril.

I can't be with someone I can't trust. Someone I can't believe. Even if—hypothetically—I still love him. I watched my mom go through that, and it almost destroyed her.

Doug clears his throat and barges through the awkward pause, gesturing with my slim jim. Which I find *highly* amusing.

"You can't just go around breaking into people's cars, Beckett. You and your lawyer can argue intent until you're blue in the face—down at the station."

He knows I don't have a lawyer. There are only three of them in town. One's a divorce attorney, one's a public defender, whose time is mostly spent on meth-head repeat offenders, and the third specializes in probate, because there are far more people dying in Clifford than committing actual crimes. Not that many of them leave wills.

"Oh, come on, Officer Chalmers . . . There was no damage or theft. Can't we just call this strike one?"

I can*not* be chauffeured to the police station in the back of a cop car. My mom works too much to notice when I miss curfew or forget to load the dishwasher, but *this* she'd notice.

Doug considers that for a second. Then he turns to Jake. "I'll leave that up to you. You wanna press charges?"

"No." Jake doesn't even hesitate, and my gratitude is . . . confusing.

I dumped him and broke into his car. Why is he being nice to me?

"Fine, then." Doug's focus narrows on me. "Assuming you're not inclined to repeat this particular mistake."

"Cross my heart, Officer." I lay one hand over my heart and give him a completely unconvincing wide-eyed, innocent look. "Next time it will definitely be an all-new mistake."

Doug scowls at me as he puts his sunglasses on and rounds the front of his patrol car. "Shouldn't you two be in class?"

"I have study hall," Jake says.

"I took a college day."

As a junior, I get two of them, and seniors get four. We're supposed to use those days to take tours of prospective universities, but the local community college isn't really worth the trip, so the CCCC college day basically functions as a mental health day that doesn't count against your attendance record.

"Well, then, stay out of trouble." With that, Doug gets back into his car with my slim jim and drives off, leaving Jake and me mired in an uncomfortable silence.

"You really broke into my car to embarrass me?" he says at last, holding up the sex manual.

No, the box full of his things was just my cover. "I was looking for something."

"For what?"

I consider an evasive response, but I'm already caught, so . . . "Proof that you're cheating."

A misplaced earring. Empty condom wrappers. A bra kept as a souvenir. Anything that will confirm for my head what I know in my heart. That he cheated. That I wasn't imagining the signs. That I wasn't *out of my mind* when I broke up with him last night. Because I don't know how to reconcile my suspicions of betrayal with the guy who just opted not to press charges against me, when I damn well deserved it.

"Beckett." Suddenly Jake looks very, very tired. "For the thousandth time, I'm not cheating on you. But if you have to look, just look." He gestures at his open passenger's side door.

"No."

He's right. Whether or not he cheated, I went too far this time. "I'm sorry."

Maybe I can get out of here with a sliver of my dignity intact.

"It was important enough to you that you broke into my car. So just look."

He's practically daring me. Which means that even if he *was* cheating, I won't find evidence in his car. So I shake my head and pull my backpack higher on my shoulder.

"Beck."

He reaches for me, and I let him pull me close, because my body doesn't care about what my head knows. My body cares about *this*. The familiar fit of his hands at my hips. The comfort that his smile brings. The memory of hundreds of hours spent curled up on my bed, sharing a set of earbuds while we watch movies on my hand-me-down, second-gen iPad.

"What can I do to convince you that I'm not lying?" he whispers, his breath on my earlobe, his chin grazing my cheek.

"You could show me the texts."

"I couldn't, even if I wanted to. I deleted them." Jake exhales, clearly frustrated. "Beck, they have nothing to do with you. With us. Why can't you just trust me?"

"I don't know." I wish I *did* know.

"We could just start over." He lets me go, but I can still feel the ghost of his hands on my hips. "Pretend last night never happened."

We could. We really could. If I could just move past the unnerving certainty that something has changed between us. If I could just trust him without proof, one way or another. But I can't. Because what if I'm right? What if he cheated on me and everyone knows it? What if they're all talking about me behind my back? Again?

I *have* to know.

"I can't."

I can't trust that he's telling me the truth, but I can't trust that I'll be able to resist him either. Not while he's standing so close.

"I'm sorry about your car. Really." Then I turn and run for the building, my backpack bouncing against my spine, because as much fun as breaking into Jake's car and almost getting arrested has been, this is the end of my semiofficial skip day.

While today's seventh period French test is open-dictionary, the makeup exam will not be. So I don't dare miss it.

I head into the gym through the double doors and pass the closed snack bar in the lobby on my way onto the basketball court, which is deserted, because the PE classes have been given a week-long reprieve in study hall to accommodate the "update" of the girls' locker room. I'm halfway across the gym when a group of guys comes in from the other direction, headed for the boys' locker room.

Basketball players. Jake's friends. They're laughing, and I wonder if they know we broke up. That I took most of the day off so I wouldn't have to see anyone.

I still don't want to see anyone, so I veer to the right and duck into the girls' locker room, hoping they haven't spotted me.

The heavy door squeals as it swings shut behind me, the rusty hinges having obviously been overlooked in the renovation. I haven't been in here since freshman year, when I took my mandatory PE class, and the sweaty, mildewy odor I remember has been temporarily overshadowed by the sharp scent of fresh paint—a caustic smell that swells my sinuses shut and triggers a pounding deep in my head.

No one's supposed to be in here for another two days, while the paint fumes dissipate, but I'm not going back out there until I'm sure Jake isn't in the gym telling his friends that I broke into his car. That I almost got arrested.

That I've lost my mind.

I sink onto the nearest bench and set my backpack on the floor, prepared to wait out the rest of sixth period. My gaze lands on the freshly painted red wall—Cougar Crimson!—then slides down to the white metal lockers in front of me. *Huh.* These are the same dented, beat-up lockers we used when I was a freshman. Beneath my feet, the concrete floor is still cracked and chipped in places.

Some renovation.

Over the summer, the boys' locker room was updated with new lockers and benches, upgraded showerheads, and a slip-resistant floor treatment. Jake talked about it for weeks. But it looks like all the girls' facilities got was a new coat of paint.

Oh. And shower curtains. Three stalls stand at the end of the main aisle of lockers, and their new white vinyl curtains are notably missing the greenish mottling of mildew at the bottom that kept everyone out of the showers when I was a freshman. So at least there's that.

A smear of red catches my eye on the floor of the left-hand shower. Paint dripped on the tile.

No, wait. It's thin and watery, and entirely the wrong shade of red.

I head down the aisle, and when I squat in front of the empty shower stall, I realize the paint isn't paint at all. It looks like blood, diluted when someone tried to wash it down the drain. Which is still dripping . . .

What the hell?

Another red drop catches my eye, to the left of the shower. Then another. I follow the trail until I round the end of the bank of lockers to find a duffel bag lying abandoned on the grimy concrete floor, in the aisle not visible from the locker room door.

The main cylinder of the bag is crimson, with "Cougars" written in blocky white letters along both sides. The ends are white, and they each have the school's emblem screen printed in crimson in the center: the silhouette of a cougar's head, its maw open in a roar, with the words "Clifford High School" forming a ring around it.

There's something sticking up out of the open duffel. I step closer, then I stumble to a shocked halt.

It's a hand. A tiny, *tiny* little red hand.

And it isn't moving.

# TWO

The locker room door squeals when I shove it open. My shoes squeak on the gym floor.

The basketball guys are still standing there, right outside the guys' locker room, and now Jake is with them, but my gaze skips right over them this time.

"Coach Killebrew!" I shout at the only other person in the gym.

The guys all turn, startled. The girls' basketball coach looks up from her clipboard, and there must be something on my face—something in the stunned echo of my voice across the empty space—because she takes one look at me, then she follows me into the locker room at a run.

"Back there." I point.

She rushes around the end of the bank of lockers, clearly aware that whatever she's going to find will be bad. But she can't possibly know *how* bad. If she did, she wouldn't be in such a hurry to see it.

She gasps, and I hear a thunk that can only be her knees hitting the concrete floor.

I head down the aisle again until I can see around the end of the lockers, where Coach Killebrew is hunched over the duffel bag. She turns to me, and she looks . . . broken.

"It isn't breathing."

I know.

"We're too late."

I know that too.

"Beckett?"

Jake bursts into the locker room, but he stops in the threshold, his right palm holding the door open. Behind him, several other guys are on their toes, peering over his shoulders.

"What happened? Are you okay?"

"Out!" Coach Killebrew shouts as she steps into the main aisle again, holding her phone. "And keep the rest of the students back."

I don't know if there's anyone else out there, other than Jake and the basketball guys, but there will be soon. The bell ending sixth period is about to ring, and seventh period is optional, so all the athletes and band kids will be traipsing through the gym on their way to the far parking lot.

Jake backs out of the locker room and lets the door swing shut, as Coach Killebrew dials.

"Nine-one-one, what's your emergency?" the voice on the other end asks.

"This is Angela Killebrew, up at the high school. One of our students found a baby in a duffel bag, in the girls' locker room. It isn't breathing."

The shock of her words—of hearing it out loud—snaps my focus back to the open gym bag, where it snags on a distinctive white blotch marring the crimson on the right side, near the bottom. I dig my phone from my pocket and open the camera app. I don't understand what I'm seeing. I don't know whose baby this is, or why it isn't moving, or why the hell someone would leave it in a duffel bag in the girls' locker room.

13

But I know who that bag belongs to.

I tap the camera icon, and my phone clicks as it takes a photo.

Coach Killebrew doesn't hear the click. She's still talking to the 911 operator, and by the time she rounds the lockers again to pull me back from the duffel bag, I can hear the sirens.

Clifford is only three miles across. You can get anywhere in town in under eight minutes, even without sirens.

Officer Doug Chalmers is the first one on the scene, because of course he is.

---

I expect to be asked to leave the locker room so the cops can do their job, but a crowd has gathered in the gym, so Doug asks me to sit on the bench near the door instead. Most of seventh period passes in a blur of blue uniforms and low-pitched voices. Quiet procedure and whispered outrage. No one wants to speak very loudly, even though there's no chance of waking this baby.

I want that not to be true. I want to hear the baby cry, offended by the indignity of having a gym bag for a cradle. But any distant hope of that happening fades when the county coroner shows up, his job title printed on the back of his jacket, to officially declare the poor infant dead.

A few minutes later, Doug introduces me to his direct supervisor, John Trent, the patrol sergeant, who is the first to ask me questions and write the answers in a little notepad.

Several minutes after that, my mother arrives. I'm not really surprised that she's the investigator in charge. Clifford PD only has two of them, and I can *almost* understand why Chief

Stoddard might assume a case involving a dead baby and a bunch of high school students should go to the "lady detective."

"Okay, somebody catch me up," she says as she pushes her way into the locker room wearing a tailored blue button-up and a gray blazer, her badge clipped to her hip. "And Doug, you and Robert Green get out there and start asking questions." She points through the closed door at the gym. "Take all their names, and send anyone who didn't see anything home, but let them know they might need to give a statement later. School's over, isn't it?"

"It's still seventh period," I say, and my voice sounds like there's a frog in my throat.

My mother's gaze lands on me, and her brows dip. "Beckett? What are you doing here?"

Doug's hands are propped on his duty belt again. "Julie, Beck found the . . . um . . . body."

She exhales. Then she points at the closed door again, without ever looking away from me. "Go, Doug. Question teenagers."

He heads into the gym, and my mother's assessment of me deepens, like maybe everything she needs to know about this case is hidden somewhere on my face.

"Stay put," she says at last. "I'll be right back."

Then she gives Coach Killebrew a pat on the shoulder on her way down the aisle and around the first bank of lockers, to See What We're Dealing With.

That quiet look of unflappable resolve is a Julie Bergen classic. It's the same one she wore when she marched calmly into the kitchen to see why my little sister Landry was screaming, only to discover that she had chopped off the tip of her middle finger, along with the end of a carrot.

Silence descends from the other side of the lockers, and in that silence, my mother's heavy exhalation echoes like a distant roll of thunder.

A heartbeat later, she starts talking. "John, call the state police and let them know we need to borrow a couple of lab techs."

Because while the Clifford PD is perfectly equipped to collect evidence, it lacks the manpower and facilities of a larger police force. At least, that's what my mom told me when that meth lab blew up half the Dogwood Village trailer park last year.

"I want the security footage from any camera that faces the locker room door. Has anyone touched anything in here?"

"The coach said she touched the baby, to see if it was breathing," Officer Trent says. "But no one's touched anything since."

"What about the bag? Do we know whose it is?"

"Coach says that duffel bag is available to any school athlete with twenty bucks to spend, so it could belong to a couple hundred different people."

"Yeah, my son has one just like it," my mother says. "So do all his friends."

"The school secretary is putting together a list of everyone who bought one in the past three years."

"Okay. I'm going to have Coach Killebrew walk me through this, while you call State, then I want you to take her to the station to submit prints and DNA for exclusion, just in case."

"I'm on it." Officer Trent appears in the main aisle with his phone pressed to his ear, and a second later my mother follows him.

Nothing fazes Lieutenant Julie Bergen. Nothing. Yet she looks a little pale as she waves me up from the bench.

"You okay?"

I nod as I sling my backpack over my shoulder.

"Did you touch anything?"

"No." I should tell her I know whose bag that is. And I will. But not yet.

"All right. I'm going to have Robert escort you to the library, where it's quiet. I'll be there to take your statement in a few minutes." She frowns, still studying my face. "You sure you're okay, Beckett?"

"I'm fine. I just . . . Why would someone leave a baby in a gym bag?"

"I promise you, we're going to figure that out."

———————————

Officer Robert Green seems uncomfortable in the library. He keeps pacing, like he's afraid that if he sits still for too long, one of the books will sneak up on him.

I want to assure him that literacy isn't contagious, but he doesn't seem like the type who uses humor as a coping mechanism. Which means we basically have nothing in common.

We're alone in here, since the librarian retreated to her office and everyone who doesn't take seventh period has gone home, to work, or to some kind of extracurricular practice.

Officer Green stalks past the table where I'm sitting, and for the dozenth time, he stops to stare at me for a second. He clearly wants to ask me something, and I can't blame him. But my mom told him she'd be the one to take my statement.

Finally, the library door opens and she comes in. She doesn't sleep much, and she eats too much junk food at work, but neither of those have anything to do with how tired she suddenly looks.

It's the dead baby.

She sits across from me and sets her phone on the table, open to the audio recording app. "Okay, Beckett, I need to ask you a few questions, and I'm going to record the whole thing, so I can refer to it later."

"Are they going to let you do this?" I ask, and she looks confused. "I mean, shouldn't they take you off this case, since your daughter is involved?"

"You're not 'involved,' Beck. You're a witness. And Andrew"—the other investigator—"is busy with that copper theft out at the substation."

Yet I can't help noticing, as she taps the RECORD icon on her phone, that she lets Officer Green stay as a witness.

While the app records, my mother states her name and rank, then she announces me as a witness and gives my full name, birthdate, and address. Then, finally, she looks at me. "Okay, Beckett, so tell me what happened."

"I went into the locker room and noticed a drop of blood in one of the showers. Then I saw the duffel bag. When I realized what was in it, I ran into the gym and got Coach Killebrew. She called 911."

"What were you doing in the locker room? Coach says it's supposed to be off-limits for a couple more days, because of the fresh paint."

I glance at Officer Green as warmth floods my cheeks.

"Beckett?" My mother frowns. "You're not in trouble. Just tell me."

"I was kind of . . . hiding. I broke up with Jake last night, and I took a college day today because I didn't want to see anyone.

18

Then I remembered that I can't miss that French test, so I came to school just for seventh period. When I saw a bunch of his friends in the gym, I ducked into the locker room so they wouldn't see me."

Fact-Check Rating: True, but incomplete.

My moment of cowardice was as much about my near arrest as about our breakup. But I don't think that matters so I don't feel bad about leaving that part out.

Much.

"And did you touch the baby, or the bag, or anything in the locker room?"

"No. I already told you that."

"It's for the recording." My mom nods at her phone. "Did you see anyone else in or around the girls' locker room?"

"No."

"Do you know of anyone at Clifford High who is or was pregnant? Students or teachers?"

"Yeah. Mrs. Torres, my precalculus teacher, is pregnant, but she's not showing yet. She's left class to throw up twice this week, though. And Lilly Copeland. She's a senior. She's about to pop."

"Okay." My mother writes down both names. "Did you see anything else out of the ordinary in the locker room, other than the blood and the duffel bag?"

"Yes. There was a distinct lack of mildew."

Another frown. "Beck . . ."

"No. Nothing else out of the ordinary."

"Great. Thanks, Beckett, you've been a lot of help," she says as she stops the recording.

The words feel like professional courtesy. More like Lieutenant Bergen than like Mom.

"I have to ask you not to speak to anyone about what happened today. About what you saw in the locker room. Out of respect for that poor baby and its family. And for the integrity of the investigation. Do you understand?"

"Of course." I stand and sling my bag over my shoulder, assuming I'm free to go. "What's going to happen now? What are you guys going to do?"

"Well, while we wait for the results from the coroner, we're going to try to find the baby's parents."

"By questioning students and teachers?"

"By *interviewing* them, yes. And by analyzing the evidence at the . . . at the scene."

"The blood and the duffel bag?"

"And whatever the baby was wrapped in. And any security footage we can find. Though it turns out there are no cameras facing the locker room door."

"What will you do when you find them? The parents?"

"Maybe nothing more than offer counseling. We don't know that any crime was committed. It's possible the baby died of natural causes."

"It's premature, isn't it? That's why it was so small and red?"

"I think so. The coroner will be able to tell for sure." My mother finally stands and signals to Officer Green that he can go. "I'm sorry about Jake," she says as the door closes behind the other officer. "What happened?"

I shrug. "We're teenagers. We get bored."

My mom wears skepticism like a second badge. "Well, I'll be home tonight, if you want to talk about it."

"Sure." But we both know that isn't going to happen, even if she does make it home before I go to bed. I tug the strap of my backpack higher on my shoulder and head for the door.

"Beckett," my mother calls. I turn, and the way she's looking at me now is all Mom. "I know that couldn't have been easy. Finding the baby. I'm so sorry that . . . Well, I'm just sorry. I hate that you had to see something so sad."

Again.

She doesn't say that part out loud, but I know she's thinking it. Because I am too.

*I miss you, Dad.*

In the parking lot, I start my car, but before I head home, I text Jake.

come over. now. i found your duffel bag.

# THREE

My dad's truck is in the driveway. It's my brother's truck now, but it always takes me a second to remember that, even seven months after the funeral.

Before my dad died, Penn and I shared the car I drive now—a ten-year-old Corolla with a dented rear bumper that Dad always said he was going to pound out with a rubber mallet. But he never got around to it.

I run into my brother on my way into the house. He's wearing sweats, running shoes, and a Clifford High hoodie.

"Hey," he pants, jogging in place on the front porch, and I can see from the sheen of sweat on his forehead that he's already done the first part of his workout, which was probably a million push-ups, or something equally insane.

"Hey." I let the screen door slam behind me as I head through the living room and into the kitchen.

A second later, the door slams again as he follows me back into the house.

"Where's Landry?" Penn asks from the kitchen doorway, and now he seems to be jogging in place just to annoy me.

"Isn't she here?"

"Beck, you were supposed to pick her up."

"Oh shit."

Mom never gets off work in time, so Penn and I take turns driving half a mile to the middle school after seventh period, and he's right. Today was my day.

"I forgot." I close the fridge door—we're out of sodas anyway—and text my little sister.

sorry i'm late. on my way

It's after four o'clock. She's been out of school for more than an hour, probably sitting on a bench out front, all by herself. Why didn't she text?

Her response comes almost immediately.

kitchen window

I pull back the curtain hanging over the sink, and there's my little sister, waving from the kitchen window of her best friend Norah Weston's house, next door. Norah's sister, Anna, is a senior. I think she has a couple of classes with Penn.

I call Landry.

"Hey. Anna brought me home when she picked up Norah," she says the second she answers her phone. "She said something went down at the high school today and she saw a cop take you into the library. You okay?"

"I'm fine."

I hesitate with the rest of it, because even though she isn't exactly a little kid, at thirteen, Penn and I still think of her as one. But if Anna Weston hasn't already heard what happened in the girls' locker room, she will soon, and even if she isn't the one to tell our matched set of eighth-grade sisters, *someone* will. At least if Landry hears it from me, the information will be accurate and firsthand.

"I . . . um . . . I found a baby in the locker room at school."

"*What?*" Penn's exclamation drowns out our sister's reaction.

I hold up one "wait a minute" finger at him without turning from the window, where Landry's still staring at me through both panes of glass and across the strip of side yard separating our property from the Westons'. "Someone left a dead baby in a duffel bag."

"Oh my god," Landry breathes, and I can feel Penn's stare like the focused burn of a laser beam on the side of my face.

"Mom told me not to talk about it, because they're investigating, but she's pretty sure no one hurt the baby. That it just . . . died."

Fact-Check Rating: Unproven. But no thirteen-year-old needs to hear that the baby I found in the locker room *may* have been killed and abandoned by its mother.

"So, Mom got the case?" Landry says.

Norah appears in the window next to her, pressing her white-blond head against my sister's dark-haired one with the phone between them, trying to hear what she's missing. Norah can't *stand* being left out.

"Yeah, and she'll probably work late," I say. Which would be true even without the new case.

"Can I stay here, then? It's the weekend, and Norah's mom's ordering pizza. She said I could stay the night."

"Sure." I don't really want her here when I confront Jake again anyway. "Don't forget to thank Mrs. Weston."

24

"I won't. 'Bye."

Landry hangs up, and she and Norah disappear from the window.

"What the hell?" my brother says when I slide my phone into my pocket. "You found a dead baby?"

"What part of 'Mom asked me not to talk about it' do you not understand?"

Penn just waits. He knows I'll spill, because Mom only meant that I shouldn't gossip or, like, call up CNN in Jackson and give them an interview. I tell Penn just about everything, eventually, but I can't tell him everything about this. Not yet, anyway.

"There isn't much more to tell." I shrug as I brush past him to stare into the fridge, even though I know there are no sodas. "I found a baby in the girls' locker room. It was tiny and red, and it wasn't breathing. Mom's investigating. End of story."

"End of—?"

"Don't you need to go run laps around yourself, or something?" I wave one hand at his workout clothes. Which are practically all he wears these days. "Isn't your big test next week?"

"It's the Candidate Fitness Assessment."

I know. The CFA is all he talks about, other than to stress about his grades in calculus and physics. Which means it offers limitless potential as a change of subject.

"Is that not a test?"

"It's West Point's way of assessing my athleticism."

I know that too. He has to do timed sets of exercises and a one-mile run (child's play, for Penn). And he has to be able to throw a basketball, like, around the globe. From a kneeling position.

I'd collapse halfway through any one of those, but Penn will kill it.

"I'll be glad when this is over. For your sake," I tell him, thinking back to his nomination interview with our congressman. Penn was so nervous that he sweated through his shirt.

"Some people have already been accepted, but most of us won't hear back until April," Penn says as he sticks an earbud into his left ear, jogging in place again now. "So it could be a while."

Four more months of watching him stress over every test and run himself into the ground. Which will only get worse when baseball season starts up.

I think he's lost his mind. I mean, yes, Mom and Dad both served in the army. But West Point is something else entirely. I've looked at the brochures he leaves lying everywhere. He'll have to wear a uniform to class and go on long runs with a twenty-pound backpack, while upperclassmen yell at him. And that's just the tip of the iceberg.

No thanks.

But Penn's convinced the only way he can afford college is if he gets into West Point, because his four years there would be free, in exchange for a service commitment. Because according to our guidance counselor, only 41 percent of the kids who graduate from our school go on to college, and even fewer of those finish a bachelor's degree. And most of those who do wind up with a ton of student debt.

I look up when I realize Penn's staring at me. "What?"

"Your junior year's half over, and you haven't even taken the ACT yet."

"So?"

"So, time's running out."

I roll my eyes at him. "Just because you have every minute of your entire existence already planned out doesn't mean the rest of us should."

"No, but you should plan *something*. You don't want to be stuck here for the rest of your life do you?"

I shrug. "It was good enough for Mom and Dad."

Penn looks thoroughly disappointed in me. "Fine. I'll be back before dinner," he says as he jogs through the doorway into the living room.

"Mom and Landry won't be home, so make yourself a sandwich!" I yell after him, but I can't tell whether or not he can hear me over his music.

A second later, the front door slams shut.

My phone buzzes with a text from Jake.

on my way

———————————————

"I'm not even sure why I'm here." Jake sinks into the wobbly chair in front of my desk.

That's new. Before we broke up, he always flopped onto my unmade bed.

"I don't care about the stupid duffel bag. I just wanted to make sure you're okay. Everyone's saying you found a dead body."

He frowns when I close my bedroom door, because we're the only ones in the house. But I don't want to be overheard if my mom or my brother comes home early. Or if Landry changes her mind about the sleepover.

"What's going on, Beckett? Did you actually find a dead body?"

"You really don't know?"

I study his face, looking for a lie in features I know as well as my own. We were together for nearly a year. I would never have gotten through what happened with my dad—not just his death, but all the crap that led up to it—if it weren't for Jake. In fact, he slept over three nights in a row after the funeral, when it all really hit me, and Mom was so out of it that she didn't even notice.

That's why it hurts *so much* to know he was cheating. But this . . . The baby in his gym bag . . . That's something else entirely.

"I only know what I've heard. What am I doing here? Where's my bag? I hadn't even realized I'd lost it until you texted."

"That's your story? You're going to go with 'I lost it'?"

"What's going on, Beck? Why would that be a story?"

I watch dawn fade into dusk in his eyes, and suddenly I realize what this moment is for him. He thought I wanted to start over, like he suggested in the parking lot. He thought his duffel bag was just my excuse to get him over here, and that light dying in his eyes . . . that's the death of hope.

It hurts me to see him in pain, even after what he's done to me. Even with the worst-case scenario of how he might be connected to the dead baby swimming around in my soul like a shark waiting to take a huge bite out of me. Because it isn't simple, Jake and me. Love, betrayal, forgiveness, truth, pain . . . they don't all carry equal weight. We were messy from the get-go, and my dad only made that worse.

Jake made that better.

And now I feel bad for hurting him, and I'm confused, because I can't think of any other way for that baby to have wound up in his duffel bag. It has to be his kid. But if he thought the bag was just an excuse to get him over here, then he really doesn't know where I found it. Or that this has any connection to what happened in the girls' locker room.

"Beckett."

His frown deepens, and now Jake's looking at me the way he used to when my dad was "sick." Because Jake thinks I've lost my mind. That I'm about to ride a dark, dark spiral into nothing.

He stands, like he might reach for me, but then he thinks better of it. "Say something."

"Something." The word comes out on its own, and my bark of laughter is an awkward self-defense against the sob clogging my throat. That stupid joke doesn't work now, because we aren't curled up in my bed, exploring a silence that got too comfortable.

I clear my throat and start over. "Your duffel bag is in police custody. Because I found a dead baby in it."

"You *what?*" He blinks, and I can see him trying to put my words together like a puzzle, waiting for the image to make sense. "I— *What?*"

"I did find a body in the locker room. It was a baby. And it was in your duffel bag."

"Oh my god." He sinks back into my desk chair.

"Is it yours, Jake?"

"I don't know! I didn't see it."

It takes me a second to understand what he means. "Not the bag. That's definitely yours. I'm talking about the baby. Is it your baby?"

"Of course not!" He pops out of the chair again, and suddenly he's looking at me like he's just figured this whole thing out.

"This is still about last night, isn't it? You're so convinced I cheated on you that you're seeing things that aren't there." He shakes his head, and his astonishment bleeds into a patronizing kind of sympathy that makes my teeth grind together. "Is there even really a baby? Because if there is, it's messed up of you to make that about us. About *you*."

"Don't—" I spring up from my perch on the edge of the bed. "*Don't* do that. I'm not crazy, and I'm not making this up. Look." I pull my phone from my pocket and open the most recent photo, then I shove it at him.

He starts to refuse to take it. But then his focus drops to my screen, and he goes so still it's like someone tapped the pause button. I'm not sure he's even breathing.

"Oh my god, there *is* a dead baby." He takes the phone and sinks into my desk chair again. "That's *so* fucked up." He frowns up at me. "Why would you take a picture of it?"

"Look at the bag."

Still frowning, he uses two fingers to zoom in on the image. "It's a CHS duffel bag. Every athlete in school has one. They even sell them to the golf team."

"Look at the bottom of the bag, on the left side."

He zooms in again, and I can tell the instant he sees the stain. He keeps blinking while he stares. "Bleach." Finally, he looks up. "Okay, that doesn't mean anything. I mean, it's creepy, because that's definitely my bag. But I already told you. I lost my duffel."

"You said you hadn't *realized* you'd lost it until I texted."

"I hadn't. But that doesn't change anything. I have no idea how it got there, and I have nothing to do with that baby." He shoves my phone at me. "Is my bag really in police custody?"

"Yes. They don't know it's yours yet, but—"

"You didn't tell your mom?"

"I wanted to ask you about it first." Because I had to know. And because I felt like I owed him that, after everything he did for me after my dad died. Night after night of holding me while I cried myself to sleep. Calming me down after nightmares. Riding out emotional outbursts I couldn't even explain. He was so *there* in those moments. So *present*. Which is why I can't understand how things changed. Why he's lying now. Hiding things. Unless . . . "You're sure that's not your baby?"

His gaze hardens. "Of course I'm sure."

"Is there any way that could be your baby without you knowing it?"

"No!" He stands and runs one hand through his hair again. "What are you now, a cop?"

"You look scared."

"Of course I'm scared. If you don't believe me, why would the police?"

"When they figure out that's your bag, they'll take your DNA and run a paternity test. If the baby isn't yours, you'll be cleared. But if it is . . . Well, lying about it now is pointless."

"I'm not lying!" He takes a deep breath, and I can see him trying to calm down. "Since when am I just a suspect for you to interrogate?"

"Since you started getting texts you don't want me to see!" I don't expect to read his messages, but the fact that he's actively hiding something—practically lying right to my face—is a humiliation I can't just ignore.

If he's cheating, I *can't* be the last to know.

"Beckett, I—" He opens my bedroom door, then he turns back to me, still holding the knob. "You need to get help."

I follow him into the hall just as he stomps past Penn and bumps his shoulder.

Startled and sweaty in spite of the cold, my brother pulls his earbuds from his ears. He glances from me to Jake. "What's wrong?"

"Your sister's lost her mind." Jake disappears into the living room. The front door slams shut, then I hear his car start. His tires squeal as he backs onto the street way too fast.

"What the hell?" Penn says. "I thought you two broke up."

"We did." And I'm sure that's awkward for my brother, because he and Jake have been friends since long before Jake and I got together.

"What was he doing here?"

Instead of answering, I go back into my room and close the door.

Penn follows me in without knocking. "Beckett. What happened?"

"The bag is his." I flop down on my bed and stare up at the ceiling. "The duffel."

"Whoa, seriously? Are you sure?"

"I recognized the bleach stain on the bottom left side. He swears he doesn't know how his bag got there and that the baby isn't his, but if it isn't, what the hell was it doing in his duffel?"

Penn shrugs, leaning against the door frame. "Maybe someone stole it."

"He says he lost it."

"Okay, so maybe someone found it."

"And held on to it, just in case they needed somewhere to put a dead baby?" I sit up so he can see how skeptical I look.

"That's probably not *exactly* how it played out."

"If he did cheat on me, maybe he doesn't *know* he had a baby. Maybe he left his bag at the girl's house, and she just kept it."

"Is that why you broke up with him? Because he cheated?"

I shrug. "He denies it. But something went wrong between us, Penn. He's been hiding texts from me."

"And obviously that could *only* mean that he's cheating."

I sit up to frown at him. "I can't tell whether you're playing devil's advocate for the hell of it or defending him because he's your friend."

Penn doesn't answer, and I can see from the dip in his eyebrows that he's moved on. "Does Mom know? About the bag?"

"If she does, she didn't find out from me."

"Are you going to tell her?"

"I think I have to. There's no reason the police should have to spend time and money finding out something I can tell them for free."

Mom complains about the Clifford PD's budget almost as often as she worries about ours.

"But . . . ?"

I flop back on the bed again, my arms tossed over my head. "But . . . as mad as I am at Jake, telling Mom about the bag still feels like betraying him."

Penn lifts one brow at me, in this way he has of saying a lot without saying anything at all.

"Yes, I'm aware that it sounds like I still care about him. But that's irrelevant."

"You caring about him is irrelevant to your relationship?"

"He cheated, Penn. And he won't admit it. I can't forgive either of those."

I can't stop him from hurting me, but I can make sure he does it as my ex rather than my *everything*.

"Okay. But is it possible—just *possible*—that he *didn't* cheat, but now that you've said he did, you can't let yourself be wrong? Even if you're wrong?"

"No."

Penn snorts. "You're not right all the time, you know."

"I know." But I'm not wrong about this.

---

When my mom isn't home by eight o'clock, I make myself a peanut butter and Nutella sandwich and eat it in my room, while I fill out the note card I'm allowed to bring to my chemistry midterm.

My phone beeps with a Twitter notification, and I hardly glance at it. Then my phone beeps again, and I turn off the notifications. They're probably questions about why I was escorted into the library by a policeman during seventh period, and I can't deal with that right now.

I'm halfway through my sandwich and a third of the way through the formulas I'm printing as small as I can when Penn knocks once on my door, then bursts in without waiting for a response.

His hair is still wet and he smells like shampoo.

34

"Have you seen what's going down on Twitter?"

"I turned off notifications. Why?"

I open the app, and a string of new @ mentions scrolls rapidly down the screen. There must be at least two dozen of them. The one on top—the one with the most interaction—is from someone I've never heard of, retweeting someone else I've never heard of, with added commentary demanding to know how I could be so heartless.

"What the hell?"

I click on the original tweet and read the username. "Crimson Cryer. Who is that?"

"It was the name of our school newspaper, until it got cut for lack of funding, after my freshman year."

"So then, it's definitely someone from school. Probably a senior. No one younger than that would know about the paper."

Then my focus snags on the image, and shock sucks the air from my lungs. It's a picture of the baby I found in the girls' locker room.

It's the picture *I took* of the baby I found in the girls' locker room. The angle and lighting are identical, though the photo has been zoomed in.

"Everyone's saying someone leaked a photo from the police," Penn says, looking at my phone from over my shoulder. "Or that the Clifford PD was hacked."

It wasn't the police department that was hacked. Fortunately, Penn doesn't know I took that picture. The only person who knows is Jake.

He wouldn't.

"Beckett," Penn says, and I look up to find him staring at me. "Read the caption."

35

**CRIMSON CRYER**

@crimsoncryer · 2hr

Rumor has it someone left a dead baby in the Clifford High School girls' locker room. Rumor also has it the mother is @BeckettBergen, who only *pretended* to find the baby she actually gave birth to.

#CliffordBaby
#Discuss

 56           302           493

# FOUR

When I went to bed last night, the Crimson Cryer account had just over five hundred followers, despite being only a couple of hours old and having posted only that one tweet. Because a picture of a dead baby is evidently destined to go viral.

This morning I slept in, because it's Saturday, and when I woke up around ten, the Cryer had two thousand new followers, including two of the three news stations in Jackson, and it had retweeted two posts. The first is from the Clifford PD (@CliffordTNpd), confirming that the remains of a newborn were found on the grounds of Clifford High School yesterday afternoon, but that no further comment will be offered, because police are still investigating.

The second retweet is of a picture from Lilly Copeland (@LillyPadCopeland), confirming for the world that the #CliffordBaby is not hers, along with a mirror selfie showing her still very swollen belly, in profile.

I spend ten minutes sitting in bed while I scroll through nearly two hundred Twitter mentions of my own, most from people I've never heard of, demanding to know why I would abandon my baby like garbage. By the time I get out of the shower, there are twenty-eight new mentions, all on that same theme. Except one, from someone I've never heard of.

Watch yur back @BeckettBergen b4 sum1 leaves you
ded on the floor like your baby

Wrapped in a towel, wet hair still dripping, I sink onto the edge of the tub and stare at the message in shock. Is that a death threat? A warning?

This can't be real.

I click the button to report the threat for violating Twitter's policies. Which seems like a pretty serious understatement.

I only have two hundred followers, and in my entire two years on Twitter, I've never had more than twenty replies or fifty likes on a single post. This is insane. Yet suddenly, thanks to the Crimson Cryer, I'm "popular" enough to be threatened.

If this is Jake getting back at me for accusing him of cheating—and of fathering the #CliffordBaby—I'm going to kill him. If this isn't Jake, and it *really* doesn't feel like something he'd do, then I have an even bigger problem.

I want to comment and tell everyone that it isn't my baby, but I'm afraid that feeding the trolls will only result in more trolls. So I turn off my notifications again and get dressed.

Mom is in the kitchen when I come out for breakfast. She's staring into her coffee mug like it holds the secret of life, and I can't tell if she's already up or still up.

"You okay?" she asks, and I nod, because whether she's talking about the fact that I found a dead baby yesterday or the fact that I'm now being accused of having birthed and abandoned that baby, the answer is much the same.

Life sucks, but I'm fine.

I drop a Pop-Tart in the toaster and pour a glass of juice.

My mother sips from her mug. The nearly empty pot says it's not her first cup.

"So, I have to ask," she says, and I groan inside. "Is it your baby, Beckett?"

"Seriously?" My temper flares like a fresh log thrown on a campfire, shooting sparks inside me. "Why, exactly, do you need to ask me that?"

"Because if my daughter was pregnant, and I didn't notice, that's on me." Guilt swims in her eyes, and it's uncomfortable for me to look at. "What kind of mother would I be?"

The kind who's never here. But I can't say that. It's not like she stays out late partying. Cops work long hours.

"No, it's not my baby. You saw me in a halter top and black leggings yesterday morning, Mom. Did I look pregnant to you?"

"No, but there are legitimate cases of women who don't show until they're seven or eight months along." She shrugs. "The coroner says the baby was only at thirty weeks' gestation or so. Which means it's unlikely, but possible, that the mother wasn't showing much. Or at all, depending on her body type and clothing choices."

The toaster pops, and I grab my Pop-Tart, hissing when it burns my fingers before I can drop it on a paper plate.

"Did he say how it died?"

"No. That'll take longer. But he said there was no obvious external trauma."

I blow on my breakfast to cool it. "Boy or girl?"

"Girl." My mother refills her mug with the last of the coffee. "Again, though, you can't tell anyone that. I'm trusting you with this information because I feel like you at least deserve a few answers, after what you went through. Finding her and all. And what they're saying now."

I nod and sip juice from my glass.

"Beckett." She puts her hand over mine until I meet her gaze. "I'm sorry. I had to ask."

"I know." I pull my hand free and carefully back away from this tender moment. Detective Julie Bergen may be more observant than the off-duty version of my mother, but she asks fewer personal questions. Which is why I'd much rather deal with the cop right now. "What I did *not* know is that you're on Twitter."

"I'm not, but the Clifford PD has been made aware that an anonymous Twitter account has posted a picture of what may turn out to be a crime scene, and we're obviously interested in finding out who opened that account. And where they got the picture."

"It isn't from you guys? Penn said people think it's a leaked police photo."

I should feel guilty for this obvious misdirection, but I don't.

"We're looking into that possibility too, but unless one of our guys took a photo on a cell phone—which *is* done, sometimes—it isn't ours."

"By looking into it, you mean . . . ?"

"Chief pulled Doug off the street and parked him in front of a computer at the station with a gallon of coffee and a pizza. Until we know there's been a crime committed, we can't justify borrowing a tech guy from the state police. I'm going back in to help him in a few minutes."

"Can you get Twitter to remove the account?"

"Not until it posts something that violates their terms. Unfortunately, hypothesizing on the parentage of a dead baby doesn't do that."

40

"What about the picture? How is posting that okay?" I ask, without saying what's really going through my head: *Yes, I took the picture, but I had no intention of sharing it. And I didn't take it to exploit that poor baby. I just needed to know if it was Jake's.*

"That's not against the terms either. In fact, there are hundreds of images of war victims out there, posted by journalists covering combat zones. This isn't the same thing, though, and we *have* put in a request to at least have the photo removed. But I have no idea how long that will take, or whether Twitter will comply."

"So, what should I do?" I haven't asked my mom that in a long time. "Should I reply? Tell people it's not my baby?"

"That'll just invite more interaction. Delete your account."

"If I do that, I'll look guilty." And I won't be able to follow what's being said about me, as infuriating as that effort will no doubt be.

"I'm not going to tell you what to do. But that's my advice." She takes another sip from her mug while I chew a Pop-Tart that has gone tasteless. "So, what happened with Jake?"

"Am I still being interrogated?" I can't tell her that I think he cheated, because if we do get back together—and I can't seem to let myself rule that out—she'll always have a grudge against him. Whether or not he deserves it.

"Not interrogated. Interviewed. And that's really the only choice I have, lately."

That's not fair. I'm not the one who stopped talking after Dad died. Mom shut herself off for weeks. It was like she spent so much effort on him in the months before he died—so much wasted energy and pointless words—that she had nothing left for afterward.

But I can't hold that against her. Not after what he put her through.

"We just broke up." I shrug. "There wasn't really a specific reason."

Fact-Check Rating: Liar, liar, pants on fire.

---

By that afternoon, the Crimson Cryer's follower count has tripled, even with no new posts. And that's when my cell phone starts ringing.

I have to hang up on three reporters before I realize this isn't going to stop. Some asshole has given out my number. And because my phone won't quit ringing, Penn calls Mom from his.

"Turn off your cell," she says the second she walks in the door, as I'm rejecting the fifth call in as many minutes.

And for about half an hour, that does the trick. Landry comes home and starts talking about this new recipe she just found, but she can't get out anything more than "fish tacos with mango," because that's when the home phone starts ringing.

Mom fields the calls, turning down all requests for a comment. Landry goes back to Norah's house. Penn goes out for a run that turns into a marathon. And I try to distract myself with a new streaming show, but I can't concentrate on it.

By that night, all the Tennessee news stations are running the #CliffordBaby story, even without a comment from me, or from Coach Killebrew or the Clifford PD, and by Sunday morning, the national media has picked it up. I don't think I've ever watched the news, unless you count sitting through that headline channel my dad used to leave on during breakfast, but today I can't seem to turn it off.

The stories all say that a deceased infant was found by a student in the girls' locker room, but other than that, the reporting varies. Some pieces lament the lack of access to birth control in rural, conservative communities, and others offer condolences to the anonymous teen mom and applaud her apparent desire to keep her baby, inferring that from the fact that she swaddled it—they can't tell what it was swaddled *in*, from the photo—and made no attempt to hide its body.

None of the news stations show the picture, and none of them mention me by name, but they *all* keep trying to contact me for an interview. Several of them have come to town, and there's footage of them following my high school principal, asking for a comment. Then they camp out in front of the police station, and Chief Stoddard tells my mom to put out a statement. Live, in front of the media.

On Sunday night, I emerge from my room to watch the press conference on TV, but Landry and Norah Weston are on the couch, arguing about some extra credit project they're working on for their earth science class.

"But the carbon snake is *so cool*." Landry flips her phone around to show Norah a picture of what looks like a gnarled black branch growing from a bowl full of sand.

"Yeah, but I *really* want to build an infinity mirror," Norah whines. "We could use little pink bulbs, and—"

She jumps up from the couch when she sees me. "Beckett! Check out my new boots! Landry wanted to borrow them, but her feet are too big. Aren't they adorable?"

She sticks one foot out and rotates it slowly, so I can admire her white leather ankle boot, with little pom-poms hanging from the ends of the laces.

There's a knock at the door, and I veer that way to open it, but Norah jumps in front of me and throws the door open. Even though this isn't her house.

There's an eighth-grade boy standing on the porch, tugging awkwardly at the zipper of his jacket. Behind him, a bicycle is lying on its side on our front lawn.

"Fletcher!" Norah squeals, then she pulls him inside. "I invited Fletch, because he always gets an A."

"Hey." He regains his balance, then he glances from Norah to Landry, his hands out in front of him, as if he's about to perform a magic trick. "I have three words for you. *Rube. Goldberg. Machine.* I made one in fifth grade, and it won second place in the school's science fair."

I shut the door and try to figure out how to get them out of the living room, so I can watch the press conference without an audience of middle school kids.

"This isn't fifth grade, Fletcher," Landry points out. "We aren't going to get many bonus points for something a ten-year-old can do."

Fletcher's expression collapses like one of those controlled-demolition-implosion videos, where the buildings just kind of fold in on themselves, instead of exploding.

"Fine," he says. "But I am *not* building a potato clock."

When I realize I'm not going to get rid of them, I head into the kitchen and unplug our old iPad from its charger. Penn's earbuds are lying on top of it, so I plug them in and pull up the Clifford PD's Twitter page just in time to click the link for the live video feed.

I watch from one of the kitchen bar stools as my mother

stands in front of the media in a small room at the police department. She says she's going to read an official statement, but that she will not be taking questions, and neither will anyone else from the Clifford Police Department. Then she reads a single paragraph acknowledging that she is the investigator in charge of the Clifford Baby case and insisting that it was just small-town coincidence that her daughter found the baby. And she says, very clearly, that her daughter is *not* the baby's mother.

The Crimson Cryer retweets the video of her statement, and I go to bed Sunday night hoping that when I wake up, my life will be back to normal.

---

People stare at me as I walk down the school's main hallway. That isn't an entirely new phenomenon, but before, they'd at least wait until I passed by to start whispering about me. They'd look away when I challenged them with eye contact.

Evidently "left dead baby in a duffel bag" trumps "father killed himself right in front of her." Even if neither of those is true.

There's no way anyone at school could possibly have missed my mother's statement. The Crimson Cryer's retweet of it got more than a thousand comments debating its accuracy in twelve hours. But no one here seems to believe a word my mom said.

It's a sad state of affairs when the rumor mill is deemed more trustworthy than an official police statement. But that is *definitely* the case at school.

"She wasn't in class on Friday." The whisper comes from behind me, but I can't tell who's talking. "She could totally have spent all day in labor in the locker room, then pretended to find her own baby during seventh period."

"—really think she killed it?"

"Why didn't she just call 911? The poor thing might have lived if it was born in a hospital."

When I can't stand any more of the stares and whispers, I stop in the middle of the hall and take a deep breath.

"Don't," someone whispers as an arm links through mine.

And the next thing I know, Amira Bhatt is tugging me down the hall toward the junior lockers in the math and science corridor.

"Don't what?" I whisper back, but she only rolls her eyes.

"I know what you were about to do."

"You know I was about to pull my waistband down to my hairline and show off my complete lack of stretch marks and postpartum pooch?"

The internet says it takes a while for the uterus to contract to normal size, and mine's never been anything *but* normal size. That has to mean something.

Her full, perfectly arched brows rise. "Okay, that's a little more graphic than I expected, but I knew you were about to make a scene."

Amira used to be my best friend, but we've hardly spoken in six months. We didn't have a fight or anything. After my dad died, we just kind of drifted apart. I mean, she came to the funeral, and for a little while after that, she would drop by and try to cheer me up. But when I wasn't ready to cheer up, she didn't seem to know how to be with me, the way that Jake did. Being at my house made her uncomfortable, and I didn't want to go anywhere else. So she just . . . stopped.

And I just let her.

"It isn't my baby," I tell her as we stop in front of my locker. "And I can prove it."

"I know. But there is *no world* in which pulling your pants down at school ends well. So unless you want your proof to go viral, you should just keep your pants buttoned. Besides, showing people your stomach won't prove much. They've been googling 'pregnancy doesn't show' all weekend, trying to figure out how someone at Clifford could be secretly pregnant, when Lilly Copeland's situation is so . . . obvious."

I did the same thing. It turns out my mom was right; occasionally, and for various reasons, a pregnancy doesn't show until it's nearly over.

"And a belly that didn't have much pooch during pregnancy won't have much pooch afterward," Amira says. "Right?"

I have no idea. But I do not want my soft, winter-pale stomach on the internet.

"Just hang in there and ride it out," she advises while I dial in my locker combination. "Wear tight clothes, so they can see that neither your stomach nor your boobs are any bigger than they used to be, and people will move on to whoever the Crimson Cryer points a finger at next."

"Any idea who the Cryer is?"

"Nope. My mom says that was the name of the school paper before it got canceled." Her mother teaches our one physics class, as well as all the Chemistry I and II sections.

"Yeah, that's what Penn said." I take my history textbook out of my locker and shove it into my backpack, and when I look up, I catch Jake's gaze from across the hall.

He looks away immediately.

47

"Thanks for saving me from myself," I tell Amira as I close my locker.

I've missed her, and it's not like there were a bunch of people waiting to step into her place when she and I drifted apart. My friendship bench is not deep. These days, thanks to my dad, I basically have Jake and Penn.

Wait, no. Just Penn.

"I . . . um. I know we haven't hung out in a while." I clear my throat and stare at the front of my locker. "But if you wanna come over later, we could make spicy pretzels and study for midterms, like we used to."

"Yeah." Her smile relieves a tension that seems to have my entire body in its grip. "I'll bring the pretzels."

"Great." Out of the corner of my eye, I see Jake start to move down the hall. "I'll text you. Sorry, I gotta go . . ."

Then I fast-walk after Jake, hoping that's at least a little more subtle than actually chasing him.

"Do *not* run away from me," I snap when I get close enough.

Jake sighs and turns around. "I was just trying to avoid a scene."

"A scene?" I tug him into an empty classroom and pull the door shut. "You mean like reporters calling your house all night? Strangers calling you names on Twitter? The whole world thinking you gave birth in the girls' locker room and left your dead baby in a duffel bag?"

"I'm sorry about all that. But none of it has anything to do with me."

"So you're not the Crimson Cryer?"

"No!" And to his credit, he truly looks shocked by my accusation. "Why the hell would I do that? Everyone who thinks you're the mom thinks I'm the dad! I'm getting the same weird looks you are."

Maybe. But he isn't getting the calls, and the threats, and the national media onslaught. This is nowhere near as bad for him as it is for me.

"Jake, no one else knows I took that picture."

He frowns. "What does the picture have to—?" Understanding dawns, and his mouth snaps shut.

"You didn't recognize it?"

"I only saw it that once," he says. "I knew the one on Twitter was similar, but the police could have taken a hundred shots just like it, and without anything to compare it to . . ." He shrugs. "But I swear it wasn't me."

Maybe I shouldn't believe him, but I do.

"The police never came for that DNA sample." He's whispering, even though we're alone in this classroom, because that could change any second. It *will* change, once the first bell rings.

"Then they probably haven't figured out it's your bag yet. I didn't tell my mom. The reporters started calling, and suddenly everything was crazy."

He sits on the edge of the nearest desk. "Did your mom say anything else about the baby? Do they know how it died?"

"Not yet, but the coroner said she didn't have any obvious signs of trauma."

"She?"

Jake looks suddenly sad, and I know how he feels. Knowing something specific about the baby made her really *real* for me too. Made her death more jarring. Even more, somehow, than actually seeing her had.

"Yeah." I back slowly toward the door. "You can't tell anyone, though."

"I won't. I swear." Jake clears his throat and slides his free arm through the second strap of his backpack. "Beckett, are you okay? This is all insane."

"Yeah. But I'm fine." I give him a small smile to reinforce my lie. Then, when he stands and reaches for me, I open the door and head to my first period class. Not because I don't want him to touch me, but because I do.

I really, really want that.

———————————

After school, my mother is waiting for me on the couch with her laptop open on the coffee table. She's logged into the @CliffordTNpd Twitter account. My phone is in my pocket, but it's been off all day, in case any more reporters call, so I haven't seen the tweet centered on her screen.

All the blood drains from my face as I read it.

"Beckett," my mother demands. "Did you have *anything* to do with this?"

**CRIMSON CRYER**

@crimsoncryer · 15m

Rumor has it the #CliffordBaby was a ! Sleep well, little ! Rumor also has it that @CliffordTNpd calls her Baby Jane Doe, but she deserves a name of her own. Let's call her Lullaby.

#LullabyDoe
#RIP

💬 83          ⇅ 296          ♥ 1024          ⬆

# FIVE

The #CliffordBaby has a name now, and #LullabyDoe is already trending as strangers all over the country send condolences to our town, and to Clifford High, and to the Crimson Cryer account. Some of those strangers are also sending hate messages to me, which I can see in real time, because my mother has set up a search column for @BeckettBergen. Doug must have helped her with that.

@BeckettBergen I hope you burn in hell
#BabyKiller #LullabyDoe

@BeckettBergen should be ashamed. There's ALWAYS another option.
#BabyKiller #LullabyDoe

Why hasn't @BeckettBergen been arrested???
#BabyKiller #LullabyDoe

@BeckettBergen i hope you cant have anymore kids you dont deserve them
#BabyKiller #LullabyDoe

"Jesus. They're calling me a murderer."

My backpack hits the floor. My bones melt, and I fall onto the couch.

"Don't look at that." My mother closes her laptop. "We've put in a request for Twitter to suspend the Crimson Cryer account, but the chief doesn't think they're going to comply without a court order. Which we can't get, because the account hasn't broken any laws or violated Twitter's user agreement or content guidelines."

I didn't actually read the user agreement or content guidelines when I signed up for my account, so I'll have to take her word on that.

"Can't you ask Twitter who opened the account?"

"They're not likely to comply with that request without a warrant, which we don't really have the grounds to get. So, if you know anything about this, you need to tell me. If it's a student, we stand a better chance of getting his or her parents to delete the account than we do of getting it taken down through legal action. I know you're not the Cryer—"

"Of course not! Why the hell would I do this to myself?"

"—but no one else outside of the Clifford PD knew the gender of the baby, so if you told anyone . . . ?"

"How do you know that? One of the other officers could have told their kids the baby was a girl, just like you told me."

I shimmy between my mother and the coffee table on my way into the kitchen, where I open the fridge and grab one of the sodas Penn picked up after his run yesterday.

"I'm the only one in the department with teenagers."

"Okay, but you don't know the Crimson Cryer is a teenager.

You don't even know that the baby belonged to a student, for that matter. Maybe a *teacher* had her."

My mother shrugs with her arms crossed over her chest, leaning against the framed archway between the kitchen and the living room. "We're certainly keeping that possibility in mind. But the fact is that most teachers—most adults, in general—don't have any reason to keep a pregnancy secret for thirty weeks. Or to give birth in a shower in the girls' locker room, instead of calling an ambulance."

"Is that what you think happened? The baby was really born right there, in the middle of a school day?"

"That's what it looks like." My mother sighs and lays one hand over her heart. "Beckett, childbirth is exhausting, and excruciating, and terrifying. And that's coming from an army vet who had three epidurals. Anyone who gives birth alone, in a locker room shower, must really, really not want anyone to know she was pregnant. And that just doesn't make sense for an adult in a professional career. Like a teacher."

I duck into the fridge again and pretend to look for a snack. "Okay. But that Twitter account could still belong to an adult. A friend or relative of someone you work with. It could be *anyone.*"

Her footsteps cross the kitchen, and she tugs me out of the fridge and closes the door. "It certainly could. But I think there's a reason you've spent the past five minutes arguing for that possibility instead of answering my question. Did you tell anyone about the baby's gender?"

My mother basically interrogates people for a living. I don't really stand a chance of keeping this secret. Yet . . .

"Is the rest of it true?" I ask. "Do you guys call her Baby Jane Doe? Because I didn't know that, so even if I mentioned the gender to someone, I couldn't have said anything about that part."

"Yes, but it's common knowledge that unidentified female victims are called Jane Doe. Anyone could have drawn that conclusion." My mother exhales slowly, holding my gaze. "Who did you tell, Beckett?"

"Jake." I sink onto a wobbly bar stool at the narrow, cluttered island. "But it's not his account. He's getting as much shit from this as I am, because people think that if I'm the mother, he must be the father."

People at school, anyway. His name hasn't come up online. Probably because he's not on Twitter, so there's no one to tag.

"Is that why you were talking to him about the baby? You feel like he's in this with you, because people are giving him a hard time too?"

She looks so sympathetic that I almost hate to admit the rest. But I can't be the reason the police fail to identify that poor baby.

"No . . . there's more."

Silence stretches between us, and I can see my mother trying to compose herself. It's okay to get mad at your daughter, but it's unprofessional to get mad at a witness. Visibly mad, anyway. The fact that I'm both daughter and witness is obviously uncomfortable for her. But that feels fair, because the fact that she's both mother and cop is uncomfortable for me.

"Do I need to record this?" she asks at last.

I shrug. "I mean, maybe? I need to amend my official statement, so I guess so."

She takes another deep breath. Then she pulls her phone

from her pocket and opens the audio recording app and says my name, the date, and the time.

"Beckett, is there something you'd like to add to your original statement?"

She tucks her hair behind her right ear, even though it hasn't fallen forward, and I realize she's nervous about this. She has no idea what I'm about to say, or whether or not it will somehow incriminate me.

But nervous or not, she's going to do this by the book. Which means that Detective Julie Bergen has won out over Mama Bear. At least for today.

"Yes. Sorry. I . . . um . . . I know who the bag belongs to. The duffel I found in the girls' locker room. It's Jake's."

Another heartbeat of silence. "Jake Mercer?"

"Yes."

She sets her phone on the counter between us, still recording. "How can you be sure of that?"

"I recognized the bleach stain near the bottom of the left side."

"Why didn't you tell me this on Friday, in your original statement?"

"Because I wanted to ask him about it myself first. I mean, if the bag is his, I thought . . . the baby might be. And if that's true . . ." I shrug.

My mother ends the recording, because whatever she wants to ask now will be off the record. "Beckett, did your breakup with Jake have anything to do with the baby?"

Translation: Did you dump your boyfriend because you found out he got someone else pregnant?

"No! I didn't know anything about the baby until I found it Friday afternoon. And Jake swears it isn't his. That it can't be."

"So then, why did you break up with him?"

"Mom, that doesn't matter—"

"To the investigation? Probably not. To your mother? It definitely does."

"Fine." I sigh, as if saying this is no big deal. "I thought he was cheating."

She blinks, and I can't tell what she's thinking. She's gotten really good at that, and I don't think it's a skill she learned on the job. I think it's something she picked up from dealing with my dad. From trying to keep the worst of it to herself.

"Why did you think he was cheating?"

"Because he started hiding texts from me. Like, turning his phone over, so I couldn't see the screen. Putting his phone under his leg while we watch movies, so I can't even see if it lights up. And that felt suspicious. And you said that sometimes you have to trust your hunches."

Her guarded expression crumples to expose . . . guilt. "Oh, Beck, that's not . . . You're not a police detective. I was talking about work. About an instinct I've developed over a fourteen-year-long career. You haven't had—"

"You weren't talking about work when you said that. You were talking about—"

*Dad.*

I don't say it out loud, but I can tell that she hears it, because she looks like I just slapped her.

"Beckett . . ."

"You said you could tell something was wrong, and that you had to trust your gut, and you were *right*."

But she was too late. We were all too late.

I can't be too late again.

"Beckett, that's an entirely different situation. Jake isn't your father. Your father wasn't cheating. And you don't know that Jake was either, do you?"

"I can't prove it, but—"

"Stop." Her hand settles over mine on the counter, and she squeezes. "Again, for the record, this is a completely different situation than what happened with your father. But if you're going to take my advice and apply it in ways I never intended, then take this next piece of advice with it, because it's just as important. The *worst* thing you can do in an investigation is to start off with a presumption of guilt. A detective investigates to *find the truth*, not to prove what she thinks she already knows. If you're looking for evidence that Jake cheated, eventually you're going to find something that looks like proof, whether or not it *is* proof."

"So . . . what should I do?"

"You should decide whether or not you trust him, because that's what really matters. If you trust him, you have to believe him. If you don't, then it doesn't matter whether or not he lied—whether or not he cheated—because you can't be with someone you can't trust. And—"

"But you stayed with Dad, and you couldn't trust him."

*We* couldn't trust him.

At first, it was little things. Like text messages he didn't want us to see. So he stopped leaving his phone sitting around. Then the fire station let him go, and we didn't know about that for three days, and once we finally *did* find out—my mother figures *every-thing* out, eventually—he lied about how he lost his job. He said a couple of the other guys had it in for him. That they were telling lies about him to the chief. Dad said those guys were jealous because he was a better fireman, and that he didn't want that job anyway if they were willing to believe those assholes over him.

He said there were lots of other jobs out there for a man with a decade of active duty service and several more years in the reserves. He said offers would start rolling in. He said we would be fine. But those offers never came, and with our household income cut in half, it didn't take long for us to go through our savings. For my mother to start paying for groceries on a credit card. For her to downgrade our internet speed and cancel the cable. To start buying us Walmart-brand sodas, jeans, and shoes.

We weren't supposed to notice any of that. And maybe Landry didn't. She was only in the seventh grade. But Penn and I aren't kids. We understood what was going on.

At least, I thought I did.

The really embarrassing part is that at first, I believed my dad. He railed against the injustice of a soldier being unable to find honest work, and I *believed* the world was out to get him. I thought those other firefighters were jealous, and that the fire chief was a coward who'd fired my dad two weeks before Thanks-giving because that was easier than believing him. Than con-fronting those other guys on their bullshit.

I even called him once. At the end of Thanksgiving break, when my dad was so upset about losing his job that he hardly got off the couch. When my mother had to work over the holiday, to get overtime pay. I went out into the backyard, where no one would hear me, and I called the fire chief, demanding to know how he could be so heartless as to let one of his best firefighters go *right* before the holidays.

He was super polite, but firm about the fact that he couldn't discuss human resources issues with the child of a former employee. And I was *so mad.* In that moment, it felt like everything that was going wrong for us was the chief's fault, for firing my dad, and I *needed* to know why. But he couldn't tell me that my father had been showing up for work late, and high. That he had put other people's lives at risk. That he was a liability to the entire department.

And even if he'd been allowed to tell me that, I don't think he would have. Who wants to say something like that over the phone to a fifteen-year-old girl? So I got nothing from him but repeated, gentle, and humiliating encouragement for me to talk to my parents. Then, suddenly, my anger—my *utter outrage*—fell apart like a cookie crumbling in my fist. And I started crying. Right there on the phone with the fire chief.

I hung up when he asked if I was okay, and the next day, it was all over school, because the chief's son had overheard him tell his wife how worried he was about Kyle Bergen's family. That's when the rumors at school reached a fever pitch. When I started to feel like people were staring at me and whispering behind my back. When—depending on my mood—I started either hurrying through the hall with my head down or making aggressive, confrontational eye contact with everyone I saw. And it all started with my father hiding text messages.

Just like Jake.

My mother exhales slowly. Pain crackles behind her eyes, as

if I've just pried the coffin open and demanded she take another look inside. As if I've disinterred his memory.

"What happened with your dad was different. And much more complicated. Your father and I had an entire life together. Twenty years of history. Three children. And he loved us. Even when things started to go bad, that much never changed. I couldn't give up on him. I couldn't throw all that away. Maybe I made the wrong call, and if I did, I'm *really* sorry. But you and Jake . . ." She lets go of my hand and runs her fingers through her hair, and it's like she's just hit the reset button on this entire discussion. Like she's stricken Dad from the official record. "If you *insist* on investigating Jake, what you should do instead of looking for evidence that he cheated is look for the reason he's acting suspicious. Which may or may not be that he's cheating. *Investigate* the cause. Don't *assume* the cause."

Oh my god, that's what I did. I just assumed he was guilty. That's what Penn was trying to tell me.

My mother watches me as if my eyes are an old-fashioned Polaroid and my thoughts are finally starting to develop. For a second, I think she's going to ask me something. But then she just clears her throat.

"You're sure Jake's not the Crimson Cryer?"

"He says he isn't, and I believe him. He also swears he knows nothing about the baby, and I believe that too."

Does that mean I *do* trust him? Did I just throw away everything we had, for *no* reason?

My mother ducks to draw my gaze up from the countertop. "But you're sure it's his bag?"

"Yes, and he is too. He says he lost it."

61

"Okay, we'll have to ask him about that."

"I know. He was expecting you to show up with a cotton swab and a warrant over the weekend." My mother gives me a look, and I shrug. "Like I said, I meant to tell you it was his bag."

"Beckett. I'm going to say this one more time, and I want you to take me *very seriously*. You cannot talk about—"

The front door squeals open, and my mother bites off the rest of her warning as my little sister comes into the kitchen with two plastic grocery bags swinging from one arm and her backpack hanging from the other.

"Hey, we're home!" Landry calls out. "Penn took me to the Super Walmart in Daley, but they didn't have miso paste, so I had to give up on the miso-roasted mushrooms. We're having risotto and vegetable tian instead."

"What on earth is vegetable tian?" I ask.

"Slices of sweet potato, tomato, squash, and zucchini, baked with cheese melted on top. Like potatoes au gratin, but with healthier veggies."

"You owe me twenty-three dollars," Penn adds as he follows our sister into the kitchen.

"I'll try to stop for cash on the way home." Mom gives him a tight smile, then she turns to Landry. "But next time, submit your budget for approval *before* you shop."

Landry dumps the grocery bags on the island. "You're not staying for dinner?"

"I was going to, honey, but something came up with a case." Mom presses a kiss to Landry's temple, then heads back into the living room. "I'll be back as soon as I can. Save me some leftovers," she calls as she shoves her laptop into her bag.

"I always do," my sister says. But Mom is already halfway out the front door.

For a second, we stand there in the kitchen, looking everywhere but at one another. Then Landry reaches for the nearest grocery bag, and Penn exhales, as if her sudden motion has cut through the tension and made it okay for him to breathe. "I gotta go for a run. Can you help her unload all that?"

I nod and reach for one of the bags, but he doesn't see my reply, because he's jogging through the living room toward the hall.

*Coward.*

"So!" I set a long, green zucchini on the counter, and I manage not to gag at the sight. "What are we having with the risotto and cheesy layered rabbit food?"

Landry has been our designated family chef since shortly after Dad died. She asked for the chore. She says it's because she'd rather make the mess than clean the mess—Penn and I get stuck with dishes—but the truth is that this is how she keeps Dad alive.

He used to cook. And even toward the end, when he basically just sat on the couch all day, he watched hour after hour of the Food Network. Landry watched with him, her feet tucked beneath her on the center cushion, her homework open on her lap. They used to talk about all the fancy meals they'd make together, just as soon as he got to feeling better.

He never got to feeling better. So she cooks in his honor. On a budget.

"French onion chicken." Landry pulls a sealed package of thighs from her bag and shoves it into the fridge. Then she stands there with the door open, staring at the food. "She said she would be here for dinner. That's why I made Penn take me to Walmart."

"She was going to. But—"

"Something came up with her case. I know." Landry closes the fridge and turns back to the island, pushing dark hair back from her face. "It's that baby, isn't it?"

"Yeah."

If she's heard anything about the Crimson Cryer, I can't tell, and I'm not going to be the first to mention it. I don't want her to know what people are saying about me. I don't want her to realize it's my fault Mom went back to work.

For a moment, I think she's going to ask about the case. She's going to make me lie to her, or at least avoid the question. But then she just heads into the pantry with a canister of smoked salt.

"Chicken gets tough when you warm it up."

"Then I'll eat Mom's meat, and I'll save her my veggies. Need some help cooking?"

"Nope. Cleanup is all yours, though."

---

After dinner, Penn unloads the dishwasher, then he heads to his room to do his calculus homework. I hurriedly reload with everything that can go in the dishwasher, and I'm scraping cheese off the bottom of a baking dish when the doorbell rings.

Amira stands on the front porch, holding a bag of pretzels. "I got the sticks instead of the twists. Those are your favorites, right?"

I can't resist a grin as I let her inside. Despite the recent distance between us, it's like nothing has changed.

We grab spices from the pantry, and she preheats the oven while I toss the pretzels in vegetable oil in a plastic bag. But before we can add the spices, the TV comes on in the living room.

We hardly ever use the TV anymore, since Mom canceled our cable. These days, Penn, Landry, and I are much more likely to fight over her old iPad so we can stream a show alone in our rooms than we are to watch anything broadcast on one of the basic networks.

I set the bag of pretzels on the counter and grab a hand towel on my way into the living room, where I find Landry standing in the middle of the floor, staring at the TV with the remote in her hand.

"What'cha looking for?"

"Norah said Clifford's on the national news, but I don't know what channel that is."

"We don't get those channels anymore. Come here."

I head back into the kitchen and unplug the iPad from its dock on the counter, while Landry turns off the TV. She and Amira watch over my shoulder while I search for "Clifford, Tennessee news" and click the first video posted by a network I recognize.

"Tonight, all eyes are on Clifford, Tennessee, a town of fewer than five thousand people near the western edge of the state, where, on Friday, the remains of a newborn were found in the high school locker room."

The camera pans out from the pretty reporter's face to show the Clifford Police department in the background. That shouldn't be a shock, considering how many stations sent reporters to town yesterday for Mom's press conference, but seeing that little slice of our quaint downtown on the national news sucks the air from my lungs.

I didn't realize any of the reporters had hung around.

"Rumors abound online about the identity of the infant, and while there are no answers forthcoming from the local police department, it's clear that the tragedy has really brought the people of Clifford together in their search for answers about the baby, affectionately dubbed 'Lullaby Doe' by the online community. Here to talk to us about how this tragedy has affected their hometown are Clifford residents Marina Tillman and her daughter Claire, who goes to the high school where the baby was found."

Of course she does. There's only one high school in town.

The camera zooms out a little farther as two more figures step into the frame. I recognize Claire; I think she's a sophomore.

"My mom has her for Chem I," Amira says.

But Claire's mother is familiar too, though I can't quite place her.

"Now, Mrs. Tillman, I understand that you're actually a local businesswoman. Is that right?"

"Yes, I'm the owner and florist at Flower Power, just down the street. Lived here all my life, and so have my parents."

Marina Tillman nods in the direction of Clifford's only flower shop. And that's when I remember that she took my order for Jake's boutonniere, for the Fall Ball, back in October.

"And what would you like the world to know about your hometown?"

"We're a real community, out here. Clifford's small enough that everyone pretty much knows everyone else. Or else they know someone who knows 'em. We've been shocked by this tragedy, but it's bringing us together as a community."

The reporter nods, while Mrs. Tillman parrots her own words back at her.

"And we're going to get answers for that poor little baby. That's the very least she deserves."

The reporter turns to Claire. "I understand that you go to the local high school? Tell us what it was like at school today, after the shock of Friday afternoon's tragedy."

"It was weird. Everyone was kinda . . . numb," Claire says. "I was there all day on Friday, and it's weird to think that while I was goin' to my classes, eatin' in the cafeteria, some girl was havin' a baby in the locker room, and no one knew a thing about it."

I know the second I hear her accent that the world will either fall in love with her Southern charm or make fun of the hick from hicksville, depending on which way the wind is blowing at any given moment.

"Really?" The reporter looks skeptical. "It's a little hard to understand, from an outsider's perspective, how in such a small, tight-knit community, a pregnant teenager could have gone unnoticed for so long. There are fewer than four hundred students at Clifford High School, isn't that right?"

"*Somebody* knows," the florist insists. "I mean, somebody *has* to know who had that baby. The girl's boyfriend, or her parents, or someone." She turns to her daughter. "I mean, I'd definitely know if you were pregnant, right?"

"Of course," Claire agrees, as if this is a thing they discuss all the time. "And, I mean, I'm sure her mother knew she was pregnant, even if no one else did, but it's not like she's going to admit it."

"Whose mother?" The reporter suddenly perks up. "Do you know who gave birth to Lullaby Doe?"

"Well, no one really knows, but we all *kinda* know, you know?"

The reporter frowns. "We can't air unsubstantiated rumors—"

"It's not a rumor," Claire insists. "Just because we don't have proof."

"That is the *definition* of a rumor!" I shout at the iPad, and Landry jumps, startled by my outburst.

"I'm just sayin', that Twitter account's been right about everything else so far."

The reporter swings the microphone back toward her own mouth. "You're talking about the Crimson Cryer account?"

"It's a cop. It has to be. Like a . . . a whistleblower. And if a cop says it's the girl who called 911—" Claire suddenly turns to the reporter. "I can't say her name on camera, can I?"

"Our policy is not to broadcast personal information about minors. We also don't air unsubstantiated—"

"Not that it matters," I snap at the screen, speaking over the reporter. "They just advertised that Twitter account on national television. Anyone who scrolls back through the Cryer's feed will see the accusation against me. And I didn't call 911. Coach Killebrew did."

Landry's still staring at the iPad. Amira is staring at me.

"So as you can see, there's plenty of speculation here in town about what, exactly, happened three days ago at Clifford High.

But one thing you can count on is that we're going to be here, bringing you the latest developments, live. Shining a light on this tragedy, which has captured the heart of an entire nation. Back to you, Tom."

Disgusted, I stop the video.

People seem to think that shining a light on something is always a good thing. As if that means things can finally be seen for what they are. But the truth is that sometimes bright light distorts familiar shapes. Sometimes it casts wild shadows that bear no resemblance to an object's true form.

Standing here in the center of the spotlight, I can tell you that's exactly how this light they're shining on Clifford feels to me. As if my shadow on the sidewalk suddenly looks more like a monster than like a human being.

---

I park a block away from Jake's house, then I sneak down the gravelly alleyway between the Johnsons' and the Parkers' houses and into his unfenced yard. His dog—a mutt with German shepherd blood—is chained to a metal post, asleep in the center of a round patch of ground he's walked bare.

Brewster's eyes open and his nose twitches, but he knows me, so he just goes back to sleep as I pull my phone from my pocket.

come to the back door

A set of ellipses appears as Jake types a response. Then it disappears, but no message comes. Two minutes later, the door opens.

"What are you doing here?" He's whispering, and he keeps glancing over his shoulder into the dark, empty kitchen. "This place is on lockdown. My mom called Brother Bill."

Bill Ryan is the youth minister at First Baptist, Clifford, where the Mercers go every Sunday morning and Wednesday night. They have a guitar player during the Sunday services and video game tournaments during youth group all-nighters, but the sermons haven't yet veered into such contemporary territory.

"Why? What happened?"

"Mom heard about the Cryer. She signed up for Twitter just so she could keep up with it."

I groan. "She saw what they're saying about me."

And if Jake's mom thinks I'm the dead baby's mother, then she thinks he's the father. She'll probably flick holy water and brandish a cross at me the second she sees me.

He nods. "Why are you here, Beckett?"

"I told my mom about the bag. She's getting a warrant. But if you want to talk about that out here . . ." I shrug.

"Fine. But you have to be quiet," he whispers. As if I were planning to tap dance my way to his room until he talked some sense into me.

"Hey." I grab his arm before he can go inside, because I don't want to say this in his house. In his parents' territory. "I'm really sorry about the other day. About breaking into your car. About accusing you of cheating. Maybe you're right. Maybe we should just start over."

Jake blinks, and something I don't understand flickers in his eyes. "Beckett, your timing *sucks*."

# SIX

I've been at Jake's house a million times, and there are always dishes in the sink, because the dishwasher is broken—going on four years now—and Jake puts off hand-washing until the last possible minute. Until the Mercers run out of clean spoons and his dad tries to eat ice cream with a fork.

Tonight, the sink is empty. The dishes are haphazardly stacked in a white plastic-coated wire dish rack that is chipped and rusted in places. The trash can has obviously just been emptied, and the linoleum looks recently swept.

Jake's hoping to knock time off his sentence for good behavior. Even though he's being punished based on a rumor.

I follow him silently past the small dining room, which Mrs. Mercer uses as a work space for the ceramic Christmas houses she paints to sell at the flea market in Daley. The living room is dark and empty except for the multicolored glow of an old artificial Christmas tree. The angel on top sits slightly crooked, her halo brushing the popcorn texture on the ceiling.

Soft voices echo from Jake's parents' room on the far side of the living room. I can't tell what they're saying, yet I know exactly what they're talking about.

Me and my corrupting influence on the beacon of light and innocence that is their only son.

The other kitchen doorway leads into the hall, where Jake's sister's room is on the left and the bathroom is on the right. Emily's door is closed, but light leaks from beneath it. She's home from UT Knoxville for winter break, and I can't really blame her for hiding out in her room. For hanging her little brother out to dry.

Jake's room is at the end of the hall. His dresser is made of chipped pressboard, the mirror over it discolored from age. There's a path worn into the carpet between the bed and the door, and the wallpaper is yellowed in the corners.

I've always felt at home here.

He closes the door behind us, and I sit on the edge of his unmade bed, because there's nowhere else to sit.

This room is a catalog of every moment I've ever spent here, and I can't help flipping the pages. Living it all over again, in the two seconds it takes him to get from the door to the bed, where he sits next to me. Where the space between us forms a canyon carved by every word I've said in the past week. By every word he's held back.

"You think it'll be tonight? The warrant," he adds, when I'm not sure which conversation he's reviving.

"Probably. Everyone wants to close this case as quickly as possible." To put an end to the mortifying national media coverage. Not to mention the *social* media coverage. "I also told my mom you know the baby's gender. She's trying to figure out who the Crimson Cryer is, and that detail wasn't released to the public."

Jake exhales heavily. "I already told you—"

"I know. I told her you're not the Cryer. But they're going to ask you about it."

For a long moment, he only looks at me, and it suddenly feels strange to be sitting so close to him without touching him.

Over his head, my focus lands on a shelf that runs the length of the room. It's so full of baseball trophies that it's started to bow in the middle from the weight. Jake has been MVP, and All-Region, and Division II All-State Player of the Year. He set a school record for bases stolen.

Penn is a good baseball player, but Jake is *outstanding*. Last year, college scouts started coming to watch him play.

"Beck, are you okay?"

"I'm fine. Why?"

He frowns. "The threats. I've been reporting them to Twitter, when I see them, but—"

"What? I saw one before, but it was vague and stupid."

I pull my phone from my pocket and turn it on. I've been carrying it in case of an emergency, but I've kept it off, because of all the calls from reporters. When I open my Twitter app, several dozen new mentions scroll down the screen. I read through them quickly, and one catches my attention.

@BeckettBergen I hope you—

The tweet goes on, but my eyes refuse to read any more. Instead, individual words and phrases jump out at me from that tweet and several more, as chills crawl up my spine.

Kill yourself.

Rape.

Trash.

Die.

One of the posters is threatening to pull me out of this life limb by limb, like he claims I did to my baby.

"Oh my god," I whisper. "There were more of these, before you reported them?" This is different than that one from before. This is infinitely worse.

Jake leans closer to read from my screen. "Yeah, those are new. But they're basically the same as the ones that have already been taken down. I shouldn't have said anything. I didn't realize you hadn't seen them. Turn it back off."

He snatches my phone and holds down the power button until the screen goes black.

"You've been having them removed? For me?"

He hands my phone back, and his fingers brush mine. "Of course."

"But you're not even on Twitter."

"I am now. Logged into my mother's account." He shrugs. "She needed help setting hers up, so I know her password."

"Does she know you've been reporting tweets through her account?"

He actually laughs. "She doesn't even know that's a thing."

His leg is so close to mine that I can feel its warmth. I could take his hand and just . . . hold it. Like a thank-you—and an apology—that I don't have to verbalize. A gesture he'll understand, even without the words.

"Hey, why don't you let me pick you up tomorrow?" His fingers twitch, and I think he wants to hold my hand too. "I feel weird about you being alone, with assholes like that out there." He nods at my phone. At the threats I can still see every time I close my eyes.

"Thanks, but I'm fine." Not at all melting from the inside out, over his offer. "Anyway, I have to have my car, so I can pick Landry up."

"I could—"

Light flashes through the window, blinding me for a second, and I straighten my shirt out of an old habit, as if Jake's parents are about to walk in and catch us with his bedroom door closed. But the reality is even more serious than that.

"That's probably Brother Bill."

Jake stands and pulls down a couple of the slats in his dusty mini-blinds so he can peer into his front yard. But I know he's wrong even before he sucks in a sharp breath.

"It's your mom. And that cop who cleared everyone out of the gym on Friday."

"Robert Green." The same officer who escorted me to the library.

A car door slams out front, and a door squeals open at the other end of the house, a warning signal we're both well attuned to. I mentally track two sets of footsteps into the living room, then one of Jake's parents opens the front door just as a second flash of light arcs across Jake's room.

Brother Bill has pulled into the driveway.

I consider trying to sneak out the window, but since Jake's room is on the front side of the house, my chances of being caught are high, especially with two cops and a youth minister on the front porch. So I stay put, hoping my presence doesn't make things worse for Jake.

He opens his bedroom door, and my mother's voice floats toward us from across the house. "Grace. Nick," she says in greeting.

"Julie?" Jake's dad sounds wary. "What can we do for you?"

"We have a warrant, and we're going to need to see your son."

"Are you going to arrest him?" Grace's words seem to hang in the air, insubstantial as dandelion fuzz, and Jake turns to me with wide eyes. We hadn't considered that possibility.

I shake my head. *Surely not.*

"No, no. It's nothing like that. We're just here to ask him a few questions and take a DNA sample."

"A DNA sample." Jake's father's voice is the gruff rasp of a chain-smoker, even several years after he gave up the habit. "What the hell for?"

"I'm happy to tell you what I can, Nick, but the fact of the matter is that Jake's eighteen now, and that warrant's for him. So he's going to need to be present."

Mr. Mercer stammers an objection as a new set of footsteps approach the house.

"Evenin', Nick. Grace," Brother Bill says. "Why don't we take this inside?"

Jake heads down the hall without waiting to be called, but I stay back in the shadows, and when Mr. Mercer leads Officer Green and my mom into their kitchen, no one notices me. Grace follows them with her arm hooked through Brother Bill's. They don't look my way either.

I sneak past Emily's closed bedroom door and press my back against the wall outside the kitchen. From here, I can see a slim slice of the room including the refrigerator, the stove, and one corner of the table.

"Would anyone like some tea?" Grace's voice is unsteady, and I risk a peek around the door frame to see her holding a teakettle under the faucet. She twists the knob, and water runs into it.

"No, thank you," my mother says.

Nick Mercer waves one hand at the table. My mom takes one of the chairs, and Jake sits across from her while his dad settles in between them, which leaves Officer Green standing in the middle of the room as if he isn't sure what to do with himself.

"Okay, you've been offered a seat and a drink." Nick angles his chair toward my mother. "I think we've done what the Lord requires of us, in regards to hospitality, so why don't you tell us what this is about? Why do you need Jake's DNA?"

He's holding the folded warrant, but seems disinclined to read it.

My mother clears her throat. "I'm sure you're aware that last week Beckett found the remains of a newborn in a duffel bag at Clifford High."

"Horrible thing. Tragic." Grace turns off the water. "But what's that got to do with our son?"

"We have reason to believe that bag belongs to Jake."

"What reason?" Nick demands in his rasp of a voice.

Grace sets the kettle down on the stove, too hard. "He hasn't done anything." She turns the knob. The gas stove clicks, then the burner ignites with a soft *whoosh*. "It can't be his."

"It's mine," Jake says. "We all saw the picture online. It's my bag."

"How can you possibly know that?" his father snaps.

"I recognize the bleach stain. I dripped some on my bag last season, when I was trying to clean my uniform pants. The home game ones."

"Well, that doesn't mean anything," Grace insists. "You're not the only boy who bleaches his pants. Anyone could have a similar stain."

"That's true." My mother's chair squeals against the linoleum as she scoots it back a little, trying to see everyone in the room at once. "And Jake will get a chance to take a closer look at the bag and ID it, as soon as the lab is done—"

"Jake, go get your damn bag," his father orders. "Show her she's wrong."

"She isn't wrong," he insists quietly.

"This doesn't make any sense. How would your duffel bag get into the girls' locker room? That's where she found the poor thing, right?"

The kettle begins to shriek, and Grace jumps, startled, before she hurries to turn off the flame.

"I lost it," Jake says. "Or maybe someone stole it."

My mother turns to him, and for a second, her gaze catches on me. I duck back into the hall, my pulse racing. Waiting to be called out.

"Jake, when did you last see the bag?" she asks instead.

"I don't know. I'm sorry. I didn't even realize it was missing until—" He bites off the rest of the admission before he can drag me into it. "Until I saw that picture."

"Well, that's unfortunate," Officer Green says.

And he's right. The truth doesn't exactly cast Jake in an innocent light.

"So, how does this DNA test work?" Nick asks. "You need to draw blood?"

I hear a crinkling sound, and I peek again to see Officer Green holding up a clear cylinder and a sealed cotton swab.

"No, it's just a simple cheek swab."

"But whatever for?" Grace pours hot water into the first of two mugs, and a tea bag floats to the top. She sets the mug on the table, in front of the last chair, and she gestures for Brother Bill to take that seat.

"Thank you, Grace." Brother Bill sits, then he lifts his mug and blows over it.

Mrs. Mercer doesn't seem to have heard him. She's staring at my mother with her arms crossed over the front of her blouse.

"You can't assume that baby has anything to do with Jake, just because it was found in his bag."

"Actually, we kind of have to assume that," Officer Green tells her.

"We have to try to identify all the DNA found on that bag," my mother explains. "We expect to find some from the baby and some from its mother. And if the bag really belongs to Jake, there's a very good possibility that some of the DNA on it is his, just by virtue of the fact that he carried it regularly. We need to take a sample from Jake so we'll have something to compare it to."

"So, he's not a suspect?" Grace's relief feels brittle. Ready to be shattered.

"Ma'am, we don't even know that a crime has been commit-ted just yet," Officer Green says.

"How could there not have been a crime? That poor baby is dead!"

"Yes. But until we hear back from the coroner, we don't know that the baby didn't die of natural causes. It could very well have been stillborn." My mother's calm tone is a balm for the open wound that the Mercers' kitchen has become.

"So then, what are you investigating, if you don't even know whether there's been a crime?" Nick asks.

"Well, at the moment, our efforts are twofold. First, we're try-ing to identify the baby, so we can notify the next of kin. Other-wise, we have no one to release the . . . um . . . the remains to."

"*So* sad . . . ," Grace breathes.

"Yes, it is," my mother agrees. "We're also obligated to collect and preserve evidence in case we *do* have to start a criminal investigation."

She turns to Jake then, and I back up until I can see only the two of them and Officer Green.

"This warrant authorizes us to compare your DNA to what-ever we find on the bag. But with your permission, we'd also like to run a paternity test."

"Absolutely not!" Nick's objection thunders through the room.

"Again, Mr. Mercer, with all due respect, Jake is eighteen," my mother points out. "That warrant is for him to read, and this question is for him to answer. We're letting you and your wife join us as a courtesy, but that will end if you try to interfere. Or if Jake would rather do this in private."

I wish I could see Nick Mercer's face. I *really, really* wish . . .

My mother turns back to Jake. "I know you're in a difficult position," she says. "And I believe that you have no idea how your bag got into the girls' locker room. If that baby isn't yours, you have nothing to lose by letting us run a paternity test. And if that baby *is* yours, we'll find out anyway, when we're able to get another warrant."

"Why don't you have that warrant now?" Grace asks, cradling her own hot mug.

"Because a warrant for a paternity test is a more complicated case to make before a judge, and we didn't have time for that tonight. We *will* have time for that tomorrow, but Jake, you could save us all a lot of trouble by signing this form we've brought. By giving us permission."

"No," his father growls.

"We're just trying to identify that poor baby and find her next of kin." Wisely, my mother aims her appeal at Grace. "If there's even a *chance* that you had a granddaughter, even just for a few minutes, don't you want to know? If she's your family, wouldn't you want to know her real name and give her a proper burial? Wouldn't you want a place to visit her, in her eternal rest?"

"That's not—" Nick begins, and again, my mother cuts him off.

"And you have my word that if the paternity test is negative, the Clifford PD will release an official statement to that effect. If that's what Jake wants."

For one long moment, silence stretches from the kitchen. And finally, Brother Bill speaks up.

"Grace, that might be worth considering. This could clear his name."

I have no idea why he's talking to Jake's mom. It isn't her decision.

My mother's mouth opens, but then it snaps closed again, and I recognize that impulse. She started to disagree that a paternity test would clear Jake in any criminal investigation, but then she changed her mind.

I lean in a teeny bit more, just in time to see Grace take her son's hand.

"Jake, is there *any* chance . . . ?"

"Of course not," he says. "I'll sign the form."

"I don't think—" Nick begins, but Jake speaks over him.

"It's my choice. Give me the damn form."

My mother waves Officer Green forward, and he pulls a folded sheet of paper and a pen from his pocket. Jake signs the form without reading it—he hasn't read the warrant either—then he hands it back. And opens his mouth.

Officer Green unseals the swab and takes a DNA sample from the inside of his cheek. Then he slides the swab into the clear tube, which he drops into an evidence bag and seals and labels in front of everyone.

"How long will that take?" Grace asks.

"Less than a day, once they get started." My mother shrugs. "Robert will drive it down to the nearest state lab tomorrow, but I don't know how soon they'll get to it. It could be as little as a few days, as much as several weeks, if they're backed up. Okay." She turns back to Jake and pulls her phone from her pocket. "I only have one more question for you, since you've confirmed that the bag is yours. Do you recognize this shirt?"

I can't see the picture she's showing him, but that turns out not to matter, because—

"If it helps . . ." Officer Green pulls a notebook from his pocket and reads from it. "It's a navy Tennessee Titans licensed T-shirt, made from Dri-FIT cotton, with the Titans logo screen printed in a three-dimensional font. Size large. It's available for purchase in the NFL store online, and in several brick-and-mortar gift shops across the state."

"Yeah, I know the shirt." Jake shrugs. "A bunch of us bought one like that at the Titans game on the senior class trip."

"How many is 'a bunch'?" my mother asks.

Another shrug from Jake. "Half the guys in the senior class. It was the most affordable souvenir, other than key chains and postcards. And shot glasses. Which the teachers wouldn't let us buy."

"When was that trip?" Green asks.

My mother answers, still watching Jake. "October. So you own a shirt just like this?"

"Yeah."

"Why?" Nick asks. "What does the shirt have to do with anything?"

"Jake, is it possible that this is your shirt?" My mother taps the image on her phone with one blunt fingernail.

"No, mine's in the laundry. Hang on."

Jake pushes his chair back and crosses the kitchen into the tiny utility room, where I can hear him rummage around for a few seconds.

"Here." He returns to the table and hands my mother a familiar navy blue shirt. "This one's mine."

My mother lays it flat on the table and stares at it for a few seconds, comparing it to the image on her phone. "Okay, thank you," she says at last.

"What does the shirt have to do with anything?" Nick repeats.

"It's just another bit of evidence we're trying to identify." She stands and puts one hand on Jake's shoulder. "Thank you very much for your help."

She and Officer Green head toward the hallway, and I race silently back into the shadows, planning to slip into Jake's room. But then Emily's door opens, casting a rectangle of light on the hallway carpet, and I duck through the open bathroom door instead.

"What's going on?" Emily pulls her headphones off, obviously surprised to see police in her home.

"Nothing, honey," Nick Mercer says from well outside my field of vision. "Officer Bergen and Officer Green were just leaving."

*Detective Bergen*, I mentally correct him, because I know my mother won't.

Footsteps continue across the hall into the living room, and for just a second, I think I've gotten away with it. Then Emily steps into the bathroom and flips the wall switch.

Light floods the small room, and she screams, shocked to find me hiding there.

I flinch as footsteps pound down the hallway toward us. "What's wrong?" Mr. Mercer demands.

Emily blinks at me. I shake my head, silently begging her to claim she saw a spider or something. But then her father appears in the doorway.

"Beckett Bergen." He steps back and waves me into the hall with one hand.

My mother's eyes fall closed for a second, and she exhales slowly.

"Did she come with you?" Jake's dad demands, and my mom shakes her head. So he turns to his son. "Jake, what—?"

"It isn't his fault, Mr. Mercer. I just . . . I wanted to tell him that my mom would be—"

"Beckett!" My mother scowls at me, mortified.

"Young lady, you do not have permission to be in this house!" Grace snaps, and all eyes turn her way.

"I know Jake's grounded, but—"

"He isn't grounded." Grace looks puzzled. "He hasn't done anything wrong."

I frown at Jake, but he won't look at me, so I turn back to his mother. "Then why . . . ?" He said he was on lockdown. He snuck me in because— "It's me, isn't it? You told him to stay away from me."

"It isn't personal." Mr. Mercer is talking to my mom, as if Jake and I aren't even here. "I hate to say it, Julie, but we never had a moment of trouble out of our son before he started spending time at your house. And if we'd known about the issues Kyle was dealing with, we never would have—"

"Nick," Brother Bill says softly. "That isn't relevant."

But Mr. Mercer doesn't even look at the youth minister.

Hearing my dad's name on Jake's father's tongue feels like a slap in the face. He's wielding it like a weapon, and I am defenseless against this blow.

"You have *no* idea what you're talking about," I tell him.

But he doesn't look embarrassed or ashamed of what he's said. He looks . . . sympathetic.

I want to slap the sympathy off his face.

He turns back to my mother. "I'm as sorry as I can be about the loss you guys have suffered, Julie. I can't imagine what you're all going through. But we have to think about Jake's college—"

"*Dad*," Jake snaps.

His father holds out a hand, as if to reassure him. "The tire plant's been good to me, but Jake's the best high school pitcher in the state, and between baseball and his test scores, he's got bigger things on the horizon. But these days, it isn't only stats that recruiters look at. We just can't have him associated with the kind of ugliness that's going around on the internet right now. With this baby killer hashtag business." Nick Mercer waves one hand at me in a vague gesture of disapproval.

Anger burns beneath my skin. I try to catch my breath, but oxygen only feeds the flames until I am a human torch, alight with my own indignation.

"You can't be serious." My mom blinks at him, incredulous.

Brother Bill steps forward, his hands out, palms down in a placating gesture. "I think what Nick is trying to say is that there's a lot of mud being slung right now, and if any of that hits Jake, it could have a devastating effect on his scholarship potential. For instance, there was a football player out in Virginia last year who lost his scholarship over the language he used on his YouTube channel."

"And that girl volleyball player," Grace pipes up. "From somewhere out west. She lost her scholarship because of some swimsuit photos. If cursing and bikinis can do that kind of damage, what do you think is going to happen if a recruiter googles

Jake and hears that his girlfriend is the unwed mother of a dead, abandoned—possibly murdered—baby? What role will they think he played in that?"

I catch Jake's mother's gaze and make myself hold it. "Mrs. Mercer, what they're saying isn't true. It isn't my baby. I just found it."

Jake's father huffs. "These days, a rumor is enough to kill a career. A fact I'm sure your mother is well aware of."

My mom's eyes narrow. "Okay, I think we're done here."

Her voice is a blade glinting in moonlight—a razor-edged threat. I'm *dying* to see it draw blood, but she only blinks and puts her professional face back on.

"I'll let you know when the test results come in."

"Beckett," Jake says as my mom practically hauls me toward the front door.

I twist in her grip so I can see him, but he can only shrug an apology at me, with his parents right there.

I shiver on my way down the Mercers' driveway. My mother opens the back door of the police car and makes me ride behind the partition, like a criminal.

"Where did you park?" she asks as she slides into the front passenger's seat.

"Around the block, on Elm."

"What were you *thinking*, Beckett?" she demands as Officer Green backs the car onto the street.

"I just . . . I wanted to warn him. It's scary for cops to show up at your house, and I thought he should have some notice."

She glares at me in the rearview mirror. "That doesn't excuse—"

"And I was going to apologize for assuming he was cheating on me. Not that I got a chance."

My mother's sigh carries the weight of the world.

"What did Mr. Mercer mean?"

"About what?" She turns to look out the window, avoiding my gaze in the mirror as Officer Green takes a right-hand turn, driving us through a puddle of light from the streetlamp.

"About the rumor he said you were aware of. What rumor was he talking about?"

"That's not what he said. He said I was well aware that a rumor could kill a career, and he's right. But he was talking about Jake, not me."

Officer Green pulls to a stop next to my car, and my mom gets out to open my door.

"Why did you ask him about that shirt?" I ask as I crawl out of the back seat.

"Beckett, go home."

"It was found with the baby, wasn't it? Is that what she was wrapped in?"

"Straight home," my mother says.

"Fine. Are you coming?"

"Maybe. Someone has to drive Jake's DNA to the state lab in Memphis. Not sure yet who that's going to be, but I'll let you know if I draw the short straw."

Fact-Check Rating: False.

My mother *just told* Grace Mercer no one would be able to take that DNA kit to the lab until tomorrow.

I get in my car and start the engine, then I watch as Officer Green pulls away, carrying my mother back to the station. She's going back to work, and she's lying about why. But the truth is no big mystery.

She stays gone as much as possible, because there's nothing to do at home but remember. Because even with Penn, Landry, and me in it, our house feels empty to my mother.

I can only imagine how empty her heart must feel.

# $EVEN

My father came home from Afghanistan with a cast on one leg and a prescription for Oxycontin. The cast went away eight weeks later. The Oxy stuck around.

He never talked about what happened over there. All I know is what I heard my mom tell one of her friends over a third glass of wine one night after my father went into the "hospital."

Two years ago, my dad was a full-time firefighter and a part-time reservist in the local CE battalion—a unit of army civil engineers. He'd been to the desert six times before that last deployment to Afghanistan, twice with the reserve unit, and four times when he was on active duty before joining the reserves. Before separating from the army after ten years of service and moving us all to his hometown, when Penn and I were in elementary school and Landry was barely three years old. But this time was different.

This time, several weeks before he was due to come home, Mom got a call in the middle of the night. She tried to be quiet, but I heard her crying, so I woke up Penn, and we went into her room just as she was hanging up the phone. She said Dad had broken his leg in three places. She said they'd flown him to a base in Germany, and that he had just come out of surgery.

She said that he would still get to come home with his unit, and that he was going to be just fine.

I think she really believed that at the time.

A year later, I heard her tell her friend that my father's jeep had hit a roadside bomb. The other three men who were with him died right there in what was left of their vehicle, but my father was thrown clear. He landed in the middle of the road, where his left leg was basically pulverized. It was a miracle he'd survived.

My dad's unit came home during the second week of June. He was the third one off the bus, greeted by a crowd waving American flags in a parking lot decked out with tables full of food, strung with red, white, and blue streamers. He walked with crutches and wore a haunted smile.

He spent the next two months on the couch with Landry, watching one cooking show after the next. Planning all the elaborate meals they were going to make for us as soon as he got his cast off. As soon as he got back on his feet.

If you look closely, you can still see his imprint in the far-right couch cushion.

No one sits there anymore.

---

I wake up Tuesday morning to the horrible electronic bleating of the old-fashioned alarm clock my mother dug out of a box in the garage. I've had to use it for the past two days, since phone calls from journalists rendered my cell phone unusable. But I can't take another hostile wake-up—not to mention the unsettling feeling of being disconnected from the world—so I turn my phone on in the bathroom while I wait for the shower to warm up.

There are three missed calls from numbers I don't recognize. But even if they're all from reporters, rather than the usual spam callers, that's a significant improvement from the weekend.

My Twitter app shows more than three hundred notifications, but I resist the urge to open it. This will blow over soon. People have short attention spans, right?

After my shower, I put on a little makeup, and on the way to the kitchen, I stop when I hear my mother's voice.

"Those vegetables were delicious," she says. "Even cold. What did you say they were called?"

"Vegetable tian." Landry's sigh is accompanied by the clink of glass, then the slosh of liquid being poured. "You should have warmed it up. Fifteen minutes on three-fifty, and it would have been like new."

"I was too tired to cook when I got home."

"That isn't cooking, Mom. That's just applying heat to food."

"Speaking of which . . ." I step into the kitchen and grab the Pop-Tarts box on the counter, surprised to see that my mom's still in her bathrobe. She must have overslept.

"You're going to die of accumulated preservatives," Landry says as I drop a s'mores-flavored pastry into the toaster.

"Yeah, but at least I'll go out smiling."

My smile fades when I notice what she's wearing over her favorite pair of black leggings. "That's my sweater."

"Oh yeah, can I borrow it? You left it in the dryer, and . . ." She shrugs.

"Well, you're already wearing it. But ask next time."

"I promise." And with that, she sets her empty juice glass in the sink and disappears into the hall.

"Little thief," I mumble as my breakfast pops up from the toaster, and I realize that though it's too big on her, the deep red of my sweater looks pretty good with her dark hair. Just like it does with mine.

My mother refreshes her coffee and sips it, hot and black. "Those were my earrings too. I think that's her way of holding on to us, even if she doesn't realize that's what she's doing. She's had a rough year."

I bite into my Pop-Tart without commentary. We've all had a rough year. I think Landry just knows that the cheapest shopping is done in someone else's closet.

"I got a text from June McAlister last night." The sympathy in Mom's voice rubs me the wrong way, like a shoe that's a size too small. "She said she couldn't get through to your phone."

Because it's been off, due to reporters and psychos calling me almost nonstop.

"She canceled for Friday night?"

My mother sighs into her mug. "Actually, she said they won't be needing you anymore. I'm sorry, hon."

"Great." The McAlisters were my most consistent source of babysitting money, and they won't be the only ones to decide their children aren't safe with the #babykiller. "Tell me this will blow over, Mom."

She sets her mug down and gives me the I'm Afraid I Have Some Bad News, Ma'am look. Another Julie Bergen classic. "I'm not sure it will, Beck. Not anytime soon, anyway."

I hear some mothers lie to make their kids feel better. Mine only seems to lie to make herself feel better. Speaking of which . . .

"So, did you draw the short straw?" I ask around a bite of chocolate and marshmallow creme.

"What?"

"Do you have to take Jake's DNA kit to Memphis? That's a two-hour drive each way."

"No, Robert's going to take it."

I chew in silence for a minute as I listen to the shower running from down the hall. Penn is finally up. "So, about that Titans shirt . . ."

My mother dumps the last of her coffee into the sink and sets her mug on the counter. "Beckett, I can't trust you after last night. So don't even bother."

"That's not fair. I had nothing to do with the Crimson Cryer leaks. And as for last night, I felt like I owed Jake a heads-up after what I accused him of. Anyway, Officer Green said you don't even know yet that a crime has been committed, so—"

"Until we know that baby wasn't killed, we have to run this investigation on the assumption that she was, because by the time we get the results from the coroner, it'll be too late to go back and preserve evidence. But regardless of all of that, you can't go tip off a suspect that he's about to be served with a warrant!"

"You told Jake's parents that he isn't a suspect."

"No, I didn't. Of course he's a suspect, Beckett! The baby was found in his bag, and that's the best lead we have so far."

"But it isn't the only one. You also have the shirt and the Crimson Cryer Twitter account."

"That account is a nuisance, not a lead. We have no reason

to believe the account holder knows anything more than we do about that poor baby. In fact, all its information seems to be coming directly from our investigation."

"But the shirt?"

"I'm not going to discuss this with you." My mother heads for the arched doorway into the hall. "I'm going to be late."

"Wait, just one more question. Unrelated to the investigation."

She turns back to me with her arms crossed over her robe. "Quickly."

"What's going to happen to the baby if they can't find her next of kin? If no one claims her body?"

My mother sighs. "There's a lot of paperwork, a public notice, and a ninety-six-hour hold after the body is released by the coroner, while we wait for relatives to come forward. But eventually, because the expense lies with Daley County, unclaimed remains will be cremated, which is the most cost-effective way to handle the situation."

"What will happen to the ashes?"

"The state requires that they be buried. Daley County has a paupers' lot."

"That's a cemetery?"

"Of sorts. The plots are very small, because ashes don't take up much space. There are no headstones, and no real funerals. Just a legally mandated final resting place."

Ouch.

"So, they're just going to incinerate her and dump her in an unmarked hole in the ground? No one will be able to visit her, even if the mom eventually comes forward to identify her?"

My mother exhales slowly. "Some stories don't have happy endings, Beckett."

I know that. And I know she's not just talking about Lullaby Doe.

But I also know that sometimes if you want a happy ending, you have to pick up the pen and write it yourself.

———————————

Before she left for work, Mom gave Penn a twenty-dollar bill and three ones to reimburse him for the groceries, and she gave me a ten for gas. So on my way to school, I stop at the cheapest gas station in town and ask the clerk to put ten dollars on pump number two. I can tell from the creepy way his gaze stays glued to me that he knows who I am. It takes every bit of self-control I have to keep from shouting at him that I am not a baby killer while I spend the last of my babysitting money on two hot chocolates from the machine next to the hot dog rotisserie.

I hope he isn't one of the Twitter psychos.

I hope he doesn't keep a gun under the counter.

Ten minutes later, I carry both steaming cups of gas station cocoa into the math and science hall at school, where I find Amira at her locker.

"What's this for?" she asks as she accepts one of the hot chocolates.

"It's an outright bribe. If you drink it, you have to help," I add as she takes the first sip.

Amira laughs. "I feel like you should have mentioned that part first." She sets the cup on the floor of her locker and lifts a textbook over it. "What have I gotten myself into, exactly? Fair warning: I'm not breaking into anyone's car."

"You heard about that?" I take a sip from my own cup.

"*Everyone* heard about that."

"Great." At this point, setting the school on fire might actually improve my reputation. "But this is nothing illegal. I could just really use some moral support."

Amira reclaims her cup and closes her locker. "What's going on, Beckett?"

I turn toward our first class. In a school this size, there are only enough kids for one section of most AP classes, so all the "smart" juniors have most of our classes together, all day long. Starting with first period AP English Lang.

I'm relieved when she falls into step with me, because as hard as it is to walk through the school knowing that all the stares and whispers are about me, it's even harder to walk the gauntlet alone.

"I just found out that if no one claims Lullaby Doe's body, the county is going to have her cremated and buried in an unmarked hole in the ground."

"That's horrible!"

"Yeah. I think I know how we can do better than that for her, but I'll have to get the Key Club involved, and coming from me . . ." I shrug. "I mean, I'm pretty sure our school doesn't have a varsity firing squad, but I don't want to be the reason they start one."

Amira gestures for me to follow her into an alcove, out of traffic. "You think you'll be giving the haters another opportunity to throw stones?"

"My gut says I should avoid any further association of my name with the baby everyone thinks I killed. But I can't just let them drop her in a hole and forget about her. She deserves better than that."

Amira nods. "So, what can I do?"

"Just come with me while I pitch my idea to Sophia Nelson. I could use the moral support."

Sophia is the Key Club president, and I've seen them hanging out, a little, since Amira and I grew apart.

She smiles as she lifts her cup for another sip. "I would have done that without a bribe."

Everyone stares when we walk into English four minutes before the late bell. Mrs. Eagleton is writing on the whiteboard, and she doesn't seem to notice that all her students have suddenly been struck mute.

Sophia and one of her friends are leaning over Colin Trent's desk, helping him with the homework he clearly didn't do. She stands and starts fidgeting with the cowl neck of her pink cashmere sweater when she sees us coming. Then she suddenly breaks away from the pack and heads us off in the middle of the room.

Evidently we were less than subtle in our determined march straight toward her.

"Hey!" Sophia's smile looks genuine, but the dip between her eyebrows says she's well aware that everyone is watching us. This isn't the kind of attention she likes to draw. "What's up?"

I suck in a quick breath and swallow my nerves. "Have you decided yet on this year's fundraiser for Key Club?"

---

"What's this 'emergency meeting' about? Have we ever even had a meeting?"

Cameron Mitchell drops into a chair in the circle of desks Sophia is still arranging around Coach Killebrew's classroom.

"Once," she says as she shoves the last desk into place. "To elect officers. That's how you became my vice president. Remember?"

"Oh shit, that's right!" Cameron snorts, then he leans over for a conspiratorial fist bump with Payton Cruz.

Payton is wearing a navy Titans T-shirt just like the one Jake showed my mom last night.

"Maybe I shouldn't be here," I whisper to Amira, where we're huddled next to Coach Killebrew's Keurig. "You don't need me for this, and no one has to know that the idea's mine."

"How would it look if you were a no-show at the fundraiser for Lullaby Doe?" Amira whispers.

"Like I'm guilty."

"Well, you aren't. So stop letting them treat you like you are." With that, she tugs me toward a chair at the back of the circle.

"Hurry up, guys!" Sophia calls to the last few stragglers as they come through the door. "Coach Killebrew said we could have her classroom during tutorial, but that's only fifteen minutes, and she won't give us late passes. So we need to get started."

Chair legs squeal against the floor as a dozen Key Club members find seats, and I can feel their gazes land on me. The only truly friendly face in this room belongs to Amira, who takes the seat to my left.

The seat to my right stays empty.

"What's this about?" Payton calls out as Sophia makes her way to the center of the circle. "I've got shit to do."

"I'm sure you've all heard about Lullaby Doe, the baby found in the girls' locker room last Friday. It has come to my attention"—her focus finds me briefly in acknowledgment—"that if no one comes forward to claim her, she will be cremated and buried in an unmarked plot in the Daley County paupers' lot. Did you guys know we have a paupers' lot?"

"What's a pauper?" Alex Thompson asks.

"Your mom," Cameron fires back.

Cabrini Ellis clears her throat. "You guys shut up and let her finish. This is serious."

I'm starting to think I brought this to the wrong organization. I would have just started a crowdsourced fundraiser myself if I thought anyone would donate to something started by the #BabyKiller.

"Anyway . . . ," Sophia continues. "Since Key Club is a service and leadership organization, I think this is the perfect opportunity for us to get out into the community and do some good. And, for those of you who're in National Honor Society, any hours you spend on our project will also go toward your community service requirement for NHS, so keep good records of your time."

"What exactly are we talking about?" Payton asks.

"A fundraiser. We want to raise enough money to give Lullaby Doe a proper burial. A tombstone, a service, and a real plot, in Holly Grove Cemetery."

"So, what?" Cameron says, and when he stares across the circle at me, I know where this is going. "We have to step in because Beckett Bergen can't afford to bury her own kid?"

"Don't be an asshole," Cabrini snaps.

Amira huffs. "He only has one setting."

"It isn't my baby." My voice comes out so soft that I'm not sure I really said the words aloud. So I clear my throat and try again. "It isn't my baby. I just found it."

Cameron snorts. "That's not what I heard."

My head snaps up, and my focus narrows on him. "So, should we believe everything we hear about you?"

"Hell yeah, you should!" He spreads both arms in an arrogant challenge. "It's all true!"

"I saw a cop escort you to the library," Payton says, and all eyes turn my way again. "Why'd you get a police escort if you didn't do anything wrong?"

"Because I'm a witness." I sit straighter in my chair, glaring across the room at him. "I found a dead baby in a duffel bag, and the only thing more messed up than that would be letting that poor baby be buried in an unmarked grave. Forgotten and unacknowledged."

"I agree," Sophia says. "Which is why we're doing this. And I expect every one of you to spend at least an hour in town over the next week asking for donations."

I can't tell that she believes me, but she jumped at the chance to get the Key Club involved in something beyond the annual Angel Tree and the canned food drive. Charity work that will no doubt look great on her college applications.

Matt Umbridge sits straight in his chair. "Why can't we just launch a GoFundMe?"

Sophia turns in the middle of the circle to face him. "We already have. Amira, Beckett, and I set up the fundraiser during

English class, when we were supposed to be peer grading essays on *The Scarlet Letter*. It goes live this afternoon. But Key Club is a community organization, and most of the businesses in our local community, unfortunately, have a very minimal online presence. Which means they will never see our GoFundMe if we don't show it to them. Which is why we've printed up these flyers for you to distribute downtown."

Sophia gestures to Abby Winegarden, the Key Club secretary, who holds up a stack of half-page printouts. "These have simple instructions for how businesses can donate. I suggest you work in pairs."

"Wait a minute." Alex frowns at the flyers, then turns back to Sophia. "You want us to physically carry pieces of paper around town, telling people how to go online and donate? What kind of sense does that make?"

She lifts both brows in his direction. "If you were to ask your grandparents to donate to a GoFundMe, would they have any idea what you were talking about?"

Cameron snorts.

"Less than none," Alex admits.

"Well, half the business owners in Clifford are your grandparents' age. If we want their money, we're going to have to show them how to give it to us. They can give cash on the spot or donate online. Now, the minimum bid is five dollars, but we really just threw that one in there for individual contributions. We're hoping businesses will be closer to the one-hundred-dollar range."

"What's the goal?" Page Denver asks.

Sophia turns to Cabrini, the Key Club treasurer. Cabrini

stands, tossing straight blond hair over her shoulder. "So, I spoke with someone at Rayburn Funeral Home during second period, and he told me that the average cost of a funeral is upward of six thousand dollars. That's not including the coffin and the plot itself, which both cost less for infants than for adults. That's also not including the headstone. So, we're aiming for eight thousand dollars, over all. Just to be safe. Anything we raise above what's needed will go to a charity to be voted on later."

Cameron snorts. "I say we donate it to Planned Parenthood, in Beckett Bergen's name. So she can afford birth control."

"That doesn't even make sense," I snap as Cabrini smacks him in the shoulder.

The bell rings, and Sophia grabs the flyers and lurches toward the door. "Wait! Take a stack of flyers as you leave!"

I grab my bag and follow Amira around the circle of desks. Cameron brushes past us and pulls Cabrini into an embrace, his hands wandering over her hips.

"All this just because some bitch couldn't remember to take one pill a day?" he mutters, looking at me over his girlfriend's shoulder.

"It takes two, you know," Amira snaps at him.

"In the beginning, maybe. But what good is it going to do a guy to take the day-after pill? Ultimately, this is on the girl."

Cabrini pulls out of his grip and glares up at him. "What the hell is wrong with you?"

"Hey, I'm just shining a little daylight on this thing. A little reality. The truth is that no matter what precautions the guy takes, if a girl gets pregnant, the decisions from then on are hers. That's what you all wanted, right? A guy has no say in whether or not she keeps the baby, but if she does, he has to pay for it for the next eighteen years. That's taxation without representation. Wars get started over that shit."

"Is that what you're trying to do?" Cabrini grabs her bag and slings it over her shoulder. "Start a war?"

"No, baby, come on. I'm just sayin' . . . why should the guy have to pay for the girl's decisions?"

"That's a real winner you got there," I tell Cabrini as Amira tugs me toward the door.

"Mind your own business, baby killer," Cameron snaps, and the room goes silent. Everyone still in line for a stack of flyers turns to stare at me, waiting for my response, and I feel their focus like a load of stones on my chest. Pressing the air from my body.

Seeing it online is bad enough. Hearing it whispered behind my back is even worse. But no one's had the balls to say it to my face so far, and now that Cameron has, it's obvious that the rest of them have just been waiting for that inevitability. Waiting for my reaction.

"It isn't my baby," I tell him again, and I can feel disappointment all around me. They want a more dramatic denial. Something explosive.

They want a confession.

How am I supposed to make people believe the truth, when the rumors are so much more interesting?

"You always wear baggy sweaters," Cameron says with a glance at the gray one I'm wearing right now.

Amira rolls her eyes. "It's December."

"You were absent all day, then you show up just in time to find a dead baby," Page says. "Why were you even in the locker room?" She sounds more curious than accusatory, but her question rubs me the wrong way. Why should I have to defend myself to these assholes?

"Because I have the worst luck in the world, evidently." I tug my backpack higher on my shoulder. "I came to school for a last-period French test, and I found a dead baby. I can't get her out of my head, and I think it's horrible that if we don't do something to help, the county will have no choice but to dump her in an unmarked grave. So, think whatever you want about me. What's important is that we do what we can for *her*."

Cameron snorts. "Whatever. Give me a damn flyer." He snatches a single sheet of paper from Abby on his way into the hall.

Amira gives me a hug.

"They're going to believe whatever they want," I mumble into her shoulder.

She doesn't bother to argue.

"Don't forget your flyers." Sophia shoves a stack at Page as she heads into the hall. "Sorry about that," she says as I take a stack for myself. I can't tell whether she believes that I only found Lullaby Doe or she just feels sorry for me.

I unzip my bag and slide the flyers inside.

"Hey, sorry I missed the meeting." My brother appears in the doorway. "I had to see the counselor about my transcript. What'd I miss?"

"Fundraiser." Sophia shoves the last of the flyers at him. "They can explain. I'm going to be late for class."

Penn frowns at the papers in his hand. "We're raising money for a funeral?"

"For the baby." Amira stares at the flyer on top of her stack, but she doesn't seem to be reading. "West Point will love it." She turns to me as she backs toward the hallway. "Beck, you wanna pair up and go downtown this afternoon? We could hit that stretch of Main Street down from the police station. You know, where that antique store is on the corner?"

"Sure. Penn, you wanna come?"

"Can't." He glances at Amira, then his gaze slides back to me. "My CFA's this afternoon with Coach Williams. I'll go this weekend with Daniela, if she's over the flu by then."

I hadn't even noticed that Penn's girlfriend missed the emergency Key Club meeting.

"Just you and me, then?" Amira looks a little relieved.

"Yeah."

Jake isn't in Key Club. Not that his parents would let him work with me even if he were. But I'm not thinking about the fundraiser as I head to my next class. I'm thinking about how Penn's girlfriend has missed the past three days of school. About how my brother was on that senior trip.

And how Penn has a navy blue Titans T-shirt.

**CRIMSON CRYER**

@crimsoncryer · 3h

Everyone, let's back off @BeckettBergen. No matter who her mother is, #LullabyDoe was obviously loved.

#RIP

 147    76    234

# EIGHT

"Thanks again, ma'am!" I call over my shoulder to the elderly clerk as we step out of YesterYear onto the sidewalk. She smiles and nods, short silver curls bobbing.

"Clifford's not big enough for a Walmart, but we have *three* antique shops," Amira says. "How is that possible?"

"No idea. I'm just glad she didn't recognize me."

That was not the case at the only real estate office in town, or at the office of the lawyer who handles probate . . . stuff. And my semi-infamous face has not been our only problem this afternoon.

So far, not one single business owner or employee has been willing to go online and donate. The frozen yogurt shop on the corner came the closest, when the twenty-year-old behind the counter agreed to give the flyer to his boss.

Amira slides the twenty-dollar bill from the owner of Yester-Year into the thin white envelope with the three other cash donations we've managed to obtain. "I think this gives us enough to have, like, one letter carved on her tombstone, so far."

Her voice fades into silence as she follows my focus to the police department, across the street and down one block, where my mother stands in front of the steps, giving a statement to another reporter and her cameraman. Which she would not be doing unless Chief Stoddard made her.

"Does she tell you much about the investigation?" Amira asks.

"Does your mom tell you much about physics and chemistry?"

Amira rolls her eyes. "Yes. And about what a pain in the butt all her Chem I students are. But I bet your mother's shoptalk is much more interesting."

"That's one way to put it." I pull my phone from my pocket and text Landry, to make sure she was able to get a ride home with Norah Weston and her sister.

A minute later, the reply comes. Landry and Norah are making copycat Moose Munch to snack on when Fletcher Anderson shows up to work on their science project.

"Okay. Cross the street and hit the flower shop, or stay on this side and brave the salon?" Amira turns to look through the glass front window of To Dye For.

Nothing on earth could make me go into the flower shop after the owner and her daughter called me out on the national news. "Definitely the salon."

Amira looks doubtful, so I tug her toward the door. The second I pull it open, a wave of familiar sounds and scents washes over me, immersing me in the upbeat chaos of the salon where my mother started bringing Landry and me for haircuts the year we moved to Clifford. Because when she'd tried to give my sister a trim on her own, three-year-old Landry had tilted her head at the last second, giving herself a lopsided bob that made my mother's eyes widen in guilt and horror.

To Dye For has six salon chairs—three on each side of a single aisle running down the middle of the room. At the back are the shampoo basins and the staff room. Today, only four of those six chairs are occupied: the last two on the left and the first two on the right.

Heads turn as we walk in, flat irons and round brushes going temporarily still. But then everyone goes back to what they were doing, and the uncomfortable weight of attention—a burden I've grown to dread over the past few days—fades.

"Hey, girls! Just have a seat, and someone will be with you in a minute," Renee, the owner, calls from the last salon station on the left, where she's darkening the roots of a stern-looking woman in her fifties.

She doesn't seem to recognize me, and I'm grateful for the anonymity.

I look at Amira, and when she shrugs, we find seats on the worn faux-leather couch. She sets her backpack on the floor at her feet and reaches for one of the outdated hairstyle magazines on a coffee table made of two repurposed chicken crates, painted black and topped with a rectangle of glass.

Around here, "vintage" and "reclaimed" are just fancy words for "affordable."

I lean back and watch as a hair dryer, two pairs of scissors, and a dye brush dance in complicated patterns.

The whine of the hair dryer finally dies, shocking us all with an abrupt moment of quiet. Which the woman in Renee's chair promptly shatters, obviously unaware, at first, that she's shouting.

"—believe something like that could happen in a town like Clifford!"

I know exactly what she's talking about, of course. The glance Amira shoots me says that she knows too. We should leave.

We should just get up and sneak out, so we can solicit donations from a business that isn't a hotbed of small-town gossip.

I don't know why I thought this was a good idea.

But I'm glued to my seat, both in fear of drawing attention to myself and because I want to hear what people are saying when they don't know I'm listening.

I shake my head at Amira and pick up a magazine, watching the salon over the top edge while I pretend to read. Steeling myself for the inevitable.

"It's a tragedy, to be sure," the woman in the chair next to Renee's client says, her focus glued to the mirror as her stylist trims her short gray curls.

Renee's fifty-something client nods dramatically, earning a scowl from poor Renee, who's holding a brush full of dark hair dye at the ready. "Karen, unless you want me to color your nose hairs by mistake, you're gonna have to hold still."

"Sorry, hon." Then Karen shifts her focus, without moving her head, to the silver-haired woman getting a trim in the next chair. "It's worse than a tragedy, Dana. It's a *crime*. Even if that baby died from natural causes, it probably wouldn't have if it had been born in a hospital. If the mother had gotten proper prenatal care."

"How do you know she didn't?" another woman asks from across the aisle, spinning her chair around. The timer on her station counts down the minutes until someone will have to check her color to see if it's ready to rinse.

Karen shrugs into her mirror. "If the mother had been in the care of an obstetrician, the police would know who she was by now. I'm sure they've asked every doctor in town about any pregnant teenage patients."

"Pshht." The woman across the aisle rolls her eyes. "They know who the mother is. It's the girl who 'found' the baby."

She uses honest-to-god air quotes, and even though I haven't done anything wrong, I find myself trying to melt into the couch cushions.

Amira gives me a pleading look, which I ignore.

"You know what they say," the woman waiting out her dye timer says. "The guilty dog barks first. Or loudest. Or whatever."

"Well, if they know who she is, why haven't they arrested her?" another of the stylists asks, and Amira nudges me with her foot. She nods toward the door, silently begging me to leave with her, but I shake my head. I need to hear this.

This isn't a bunch of anonymous assholes online. This isn't a few idiot boys at school. These are adults. Tax-paying, mortgage-holding, grocery-buying adults who're supposed to believe in concepts like "innocent until proven guilty."

"They're not going to arrest her," the woman with the timer says. "Her mother is that lady cop who got her husband off on all those drug charges last year."

Blood drains from my face, leaving me cold. My hands clench around the magazine I'm holding, and it trembles in my grip. I can feel Amira watching me, and suddenly it feels like a miracle that none of the other women have recognized me yet.

"We don't know that that's true," Renee pipes up, using the end of her long dye brush to separate another part of Karen's hair to be colored. "Julie Bergen is one of my clients, and I can't imagine her—"

"You're such a sweet, trusting soul." Karen smiles at her in the mirror. "But the truth is that we never know who anyone is

112

until they show us their true colors. I remember that mess last year. It was right before he killed himself, wasn't it?"

My dad didn't kill himself.

"What a waste," the woman with the timer says.

"Why? What happened?" the stylist closest to me asks. She must be new in town. "I don't know this story."

The woman with the timer leans back in her chair and crosses her legs. "Kyle Bergen was a couple of years ahead of me in school. Everyone knew his family. Lived in a single-wide, out on the edge of town. Uncle in prison. Mother cleaning houses, off the books. Dad drawing disability. Kyle got in trouble his senior year—no surprise—and the judge gave him two options. Jail, or the army. Kyle chose the army."

She shrugs, as if these words spilling from her mouth don't carry any more weight than the breath used to speak them. As if they aren't bullets fired straight into my soul.

"Kyle showed up again ten years later with a bunch of medals, a pretty wife, and three little kids. Army suited him, I guess. He looked good. Used his VA loan to buy a house in town and went to work for the fire department. For a while, it looked like he really had his shit together. Like he might pull the Bergen name out of the mud." Another casual shrug. "But blood will out."

I squint at her over the edge of a magazine at the mercy of my rage-filled grip. Trying to decide if I know her. If she's telling the truth. The parts of her story that I recognize are true. Ten years in the army. Pretty wife. Three kids. A chest full of medals. And yes, my grandmother lives in a trailer on the edge of town, which, these days, is falling apart around her. My grandfather died of liver failure when I was a kid, though, and that great-uncle died in prison.

But I've never heard about any trouble my father had in high school. I never heard that he was basically forced into the army. The father I remember *loved* the army. The CE battalion. And every single star and bar on the American flag.

"Blood will out," Karen echoes solemnly. "Which explains the pregnant teenage daughter, even if she didn't kill that poor baby."

My skin prickles, the hairs on my arms standing up like soldiers ready to march.

"The one I feel sorry for is the mother," the stylist waiting on the timer says as she sinks into one of the empty client chairs. "The wife, I mean. The cop. She's not from around here, and she probably didn't know what she'd married into until Kyle dragged her back to Clifford. Unless she really is a crooked cop."

Renee sighs, her dye brush hovering over the part in Karen's hair. "Ladies, I know Julie Bergen, and—"

The back door opens, letting in a gust of frigid air, and the woman who steps inside carrying a cardboard drink carrier full of Styrofoam Sonic cups beams at me across the entire length of the salon. Which is when I realize, too late, that the magazine I've been holding up as part shield, part disguise has slowly lowered until my face is visible.

I can feel disaster coming. I can see it, in the form of Mindy Carter, weaving toward me from the rear of the long, narrow salon, dodging purses like land mines on the floor, twisting her generous hips this way and that to avoid footrests and elbows jutting into the aisle.

"Beckett Bergen!" Mindy calls as she sets the drink carrier on the front counter, blessing me with a friendly, red-lipped smile.

The salon stills into a riotous silence. Heads turn my way. A couple of the women look away immediately, obviously embarrassed. Like Renee. Others stare at me boldly, and the weight of their judgment pins me to the couch cushion.

I don't know what to do. But Mindy, bless her heart, is oblivious to the new tension.

"Tell me you're here for a trim. I have someone scheduled for twenty minutes from now, but I could push that back a little and work you in."

She leans on the leather-bound appointment book with her dimpled elbows. Mindy's thick, shoulder-length ringlets are dark green today, which sets off the green flecks in her blue eyes. Those ringlets bounce with every move of her head. I've always been jealous of her curls, and their tendency to change color.

The employees at To Dye For are supposed to wear all black, so that hair color accidents don't ruin their work wardrobe. But Mindy's smock-like black top is dotted with bright red pairs of stemmed cherries, and that colorful rebellion is what I love most about her.

That, and her hair.

"I wish I could." I haven't had a haircut in ages, and my ends are definitely split. But even if I had the time and money for a haircut, at the moment, I wouldn't spend it here. Not ever again.

"Oh come on, darlin'! I haven't seen you since . . ."

Her smile dies when she remembers the last time we saw each other. At my father's funeral.

"How's your mom?"

"She's fine," I say into the tense silence.

Fact-Check Rating: Unclear.

My mother wouldn't complain about being warm if she were drenched in gasoline and set on fire.

"We're actually here for the Key Club today." I set my magazine on the coffee table and stand, aware that every gaze in this place is trained on me as Amira and I approach the counter. "This is Amira Bhatt."

"Hi!" Mindy reaches across the counter to touch a strand of Amira's glossy black hair, letting the silken strands trail through her fingers. "I'd love to get ahold of your hair, hon."

"Definitely," Amira tells her. "Next time. Today we're soliciting donations from local businesses for a fund to provide a proper burial for Lullaby Doe. The baby—"

"Oh, I know!" Mindy temples her hands over her mouth, her eyes suddenly wide and sad. "It's all over the news. Hell, it's all anyone's talked about in here for days now."

As if her own words have finally clued her in, Mindy turns to find the other women staring at us, curling irons and dye brushes frozen in action, as if someone's pressed the pause button on the entire salon.

Mindy spins back to me, sympathy swimming in her gaze. "A week ago, I was the only one here on Twitter, but now all the stylists have accounts, so they can follow the Crimson Cryer," Mindy whispers as she leans toward me over the counter. "But I know it's bullshit, what they're saying about you."

"Yeah, there's a lot of bullshit being shoveled around town lately." I speak at full volume.

"It's true that you found her, though? In the locker room?"

Mindy arches her dark, dramatically plucked brows at me, and I can practically feel ears perking up all over the room.

"Yes. But I'm not supposed to talk about it, because the police are still investigating."

Someone heaves a skeptical huff from down the single aisle of salon chairs, but I can't tell who it was.

Mindy shakes her head, green ringlets bobbing. "So sad, about that poor baby. And its mother," she adds. "Whoever she is, I don't believe she would have left the poor thing there all alone if she had any other choice. My thoughts are with her."

They're kind words, but they sting upon impact, for the simple fact that they were aimed at me. Turns out that as supportive as she is, Mindy *does* believe some of the bullshit she's been reading about me.

"Yes. It's sad," Amira agrees, when I can't seem to find words. "And if we can't raise eight thousand dollars, the county is going to cremate Lullaby Doe and bury her in an unmarked grave in the paupers' lot."

"Well, that's just *wrong.*" Mindy frowns. "Poor baby ought to at least have a headstone."

"Exactly. We're really trying to rally the community. So, do you think the salon would be willing to donate?" Amira pulls another flyer from her backpack and sets it on the counter in front of Mindy.

"Well, that's up to Renee." Mindy turns to the bleached-blond owner of the salon, who's staring hard at Karen's freshly dyed roots. "Renee! These girls have come to ask for a donation."

"What for?" Renee darts a quick glance at me before she turns back to her customer.

Coward.

"We're here representing the Key Club." Amira holds up one of her flyers for the entire room to see. "To give Lullaby Doe a proper burial. You can donate as an individual, or on behalf of any business you own. I'll leave some flyers here on the counter. They have instructions for how to go online and—"

"The nerve," someone mumbles, and even at a whisper, the words slice right through Amira's prepared pitch.

"Dana . . . ," someone else scolds.

The gray-haired woman in the chair next to Karen shrugs. "I'm sorry, but we were all thinking it. Most online fundraisers are scams, and this one's exploiting a dead child and preying on the generous hearts of the people of Clifford."

By the girl who may or may not have killed the child in question. She doesn't have to say that part out loud for everyone to hear it.

"It's not a scam," I say through clenched teeth. "It's a GoFundMe. There are guarantees in place to make sure the money goes where we say it will."

"And we're just supposed to take your word for that?" Dana waves her stylist back and spins in her chair to face me.

"Dana . . ." Renee drops her dye brush into the bowl on her tray.

"This is still America," Dana snaps at her. "And I'm free to say my piece."

She turns back to me, and my entire existence narrows into the tunnel centering this hateful old woman in my sight. I should leave. I should just turn around and march out the door. Yet I am paralyzed.

"You killed that baby," she snaps, sparks of her hatred flying like spittle to sizzle on the floor. "If you didn't kill her outright, then you killed her through neglect in the womb. Then you just abandoned her like garbage, and now you expect the good citizens of Clifford to pay for your mistake. To provide for a child you didn't care enough about to take to the damn hospital. To keep alive. Assuming that's really what the money's even for."

My skin buzzes, flies crawling over the rotting corpse of my dignity.

I can't make my voice work. This is . . . This is . . .

"Utter crap," Amira snaps. "Not a word of that is true." She slams the flyers down on the countertop. "If any of you have a conscience, you can get instructions for how to donate to give an *innocent baby* a decent funeral right here. The rest of you can—"

Her mouth snaps shut, holding back profanity at the last second, as a bell hanging over the front door rings behind me.

"Fuck off," I finish for her. "The rest of you can *fuck off.*"

"Well!" Dana gasps, glancing around at the other ladies as if to drive home her point that *I've* insulted *her.* That I am Trashy McTrasherson, from a long line of Trashersons.

That blood will out.

Then her gaze focuses on a point over my shoulder, and I get the prickly feeling that whoever's just come in is staring at me.

"Beckett Bergen?" a new voice says, and I spin around to find a camera in my face held by a heavyset man in sagging jeans, with a massive headset over his ears.

"Are you Beckett Bergen?" the woman beside him repeats, holding a microphone inches from my face. She's wearing a pale blouse and a bright red skirt, with some kind of laminated badge hanging around her neck. "Could we get a word on camera for WBBJ in Jackson?"

But it's clear, since they came in right before I finished Amira's sentence, that they've already gotten several words from me. Naturally, 27 percent of those words were expletives.

"She's a minor," Mindy snaps, rounding the counter with her hands waving in front of her. "Get out of here. And turn that camera off!"

She shoos the reporter and her cameraman out onto the sidewalk. Then Mindy turns to me, and I can see that her lips are moving. I can hear syllables coming from her mouth, but I can't process them because they sound . . . stretched. Warped. As if she's saying them in slow motion.

Distantly, I'm aware that everyone in the salon is staring at me again, and that a timer is going off. Someone's color is ready to be rinsed.

"Beckett!"

Amira has her hands on my shoulders, and she's talking right into my face, trying to tell me something about a door. But I can't focus on her either. All I can think about is how the walls seem to be closing in on me, the faces zooming in until they look like reflections in a carnival mirror.

"I have to go," I mumble. Then I turn and shove my way through the door and onto the sidewalk.

Outside, cold air hits me like a slap to the face, shocking me back to reality—just in time for the cameraman to aim his lens at me again. I've run right into the reporter. Which is when I realize that Amira was telling me to go out the *back* door.

"Beckett, is it true that you gave birth to the Clifford baby, known online as Lullaby Doe?" The reporter goes straight for the big questions this time.

I push past her and take off down the sidewalk as fast as I can run, and for several steps, she keeps up.

"Beckett! Did you kill your baby? Are you aware that the Crimson Cryer account tweeted in defense of you? Do you know who the Cryer is?"

But the reporter's wearing heels and her cameraman is out of shape. They can't follow me for long.

I lose them when I turn the corner, and I've gone two more blocks before I realize I'm crying. That tears are starting to freeze on my eyelashes, even as they scald my cheeks.

I swipe them away and keep running.

Three blocks later, downtown turns into narrow residential streets full of one-story houses built in the sixties. Some of them have been kept up, but most have missing shingles and paint peeling from wooden siding. Most of the low, shallowly pitched roofs are outlined by a single string of Christmas lights, already lit up, though it won't be dark for another hour.

Drifts of dead oak leaves gather in the shadows of cracked concrete porches, most of which sit just a few inches above the ground. There are no basements. No attics. Life happens right here on the ground.

This neighborhood isn't mine, but it might as well be. In Clifford, there's one "good" neighborhood: Briarwood, where the local dentists and doctors live. Those houses are two stories tall, and they have attached, two-car garages. A few of them have in-ground pools.

There are also several trailer parks, where single-wides are lined up at an angle from a central gravel through-way. None of those trailers are new. In fact, in my entire life, I've never seen a new single-wide. I'm not even sure they're still making them. But I know where all the old ones have wound up.

Clifford also has an assortment of larger trailers—double-wides with bricked-up foundations, permanently installed on individual lots around the edges of town, or out in the country.

But everything that isn't Briarwood or a trailer is basically my neighborhood, cloned all over town. One-story houses shaded by old-growth oak trees, connected by cracked sidewalks. Some of the yards are neatly mowed. Some of the backyards have trampolines or above-ground pools. Some of the front doors have screens. Just like my neighborhood.

But this is not my neighborhood.

A fissure in the sidewalk catches the toe of my right shoe as I run, and I go down hard, skinning the heels of both hands.

"*Damn* it," I curse as I sit up, inspecting the new tear in my jeans, over my right knee. Blowing on the raw, red skin to ease the burn.

At least the camera didn't catch my wipeout.

A car rounds the corner behind me, and I turn to find Amira rolling slowly down the street in her mother's sedan. She's clearly looking for me, but she doesn't see me until I push myself to my feet.

She stops at the curb, and I get in.

"Hey," she says as I buckle my seat belt. "You okay?"

"Yeah. Sorry for bolting."

She shrugs. "You're lucky I found you. I might not have, if that reporter hadn't told me which way you turned."

"So the devil does have a heart?"

Amira gives me a sad smile. "She's just doing her job."

I blink at her as she pulls away from the curb.

"You're too nice. Clearly I don't have that problem. Neither do those gossiping bitches at the salon. They don't know a damn thing about me or my family. My father's never been arrested. My mother would *never* break the law."

I stare out the window, watching houses slide past in a kaleidoscope of color from the Christmas lights. Amira puts her blinker on and turns right, heading toward the high school, where I left my car, and when I look at her, I find her staring straight through the windshield, both hands clutching the wheel.

"What's wrong?"

"Nothing."

"Amira. What?"

"Nothing." She drums her fingers on the steering wheel, refusing to look at me.

"Just spit it out." She's always been terrible at keeping secrets.

"Fine." Amira glances at me, then she quickly turns back to the road. "But don't get mad at me."

"I'm not going to get mad at you."

She sucks in a deep breath. Then she steals another brief glance at me. "Your dad *has* been arrested. Back when he was in high school. I know that much is true, because my mom went to school with him too."

# NINE

As we turn down Elm Street, plastic candy canes blow in the wind where they're suspended from light posts.

"Your mom went to high school with my dad?"

Maybe I knew that, once upon a time. Maybe my dad told me that, back when Amira and I first became friends in the third grade. Maybe that fact got buried beneath the avalanche of more important things on my mind when I found my father's body on the living room floor, in a puddle of vomit.

But I don't think so. I don't think my dad ever talked about high school. About friends he had as a teenager.

And for the first time, I wonder why.

"They were in the same graduating class. Only . . . your dad didn't graduate. He got arrested and joined the army." She shrugs again. "I guess he got his GED."

"Are you sure?"

Why don't I know this? How can I know how he liked his eggs and how he made his coffee, but not know he was arrested as a teenager? How can I know the nuance of every smile he ever shined on me, but not know that he didn't graduate high school?

Amira shrugs as she takes a left-hand turn. "Well, I believe my mom."

"What was he arrested for?"

I'm not sure I believe her. Yes, my father had problems, but it doesn't seem fair to his memory to apply one more black mark on his permanent record, when he isn't here to defend himself. Yet I need to know.

"I don't know, Beckett. I'm sorry. I didn't ask for details. At the time, that felt . . . invasive." Amira pulls into the school parking lot and heads for my car, which stands all alone now in a sea of cracked concrete. "This was right after your dad died. I was trying . . . I was trying to understand what you were going through. My mom was trying to help."

Mrs. Bhatt was three degrees removed from the tragedy of my father's death, but she had the time and energy to help Amira figure out how to help me. When my mother was burying herself in work to avoid having to exist in rooms haunted by my father's memory.

Not that it worked. One day, Amira just stopped coming over. She stopped snapping and texting me. She basically ghosted me, and I let her go, because what was the point of trying to keep someone around when that someone didn't want to be around?

My father taught me that lesson.

"What else did she say?"

"Not much." Amira pulls into the spot one over from my car and shifts into park. She twists in the driver's seat to face me. "I didn't ask much. But, honestly, what she *did* tell me about your dad was pretty much in line with what that lady in the salon said."

"What about the rest of what that lady said?"

My voice sounds as hollow as I feel, as I silently beg her to say something warm. Something validating about my father, or the rest of my family. Something to fill this void inside me so it will stop sucking at the world around me.

"The rest of it?"

"I know my dad had issues when he got back from Afghanistan that last time. But my mom's not a crooked cop. Even if my dad had gotten into some legal trouble—and he didn't, as far as I know—she would never have broken the law to get him out of it. I don't think she even *could*." I shrug. "I mean, that's not really how it works. Cops don't decide who gets prosecuted."

"I only know what I've heard, Beckett." Amira looks worried now. There's something she doesn't want to tell me.

"Which is what?"

With a sigh, she pulls her keys from the ignition and drops them on her lap. "Last year there were all kinds of rumors about your dad."

"Because he went into rehab?" And because I called the fire chief? I know he tried to fill *his* void with pills and alcohol. And I know that that killed him.

Amira shrugs. "Cabrini's mom works at the hospital. She said your dad came in through the ER all the time, and that he kept asking the doctor for a prescription. She called him a 'frequent flyer.'"

"Because he was in the ER a lot? He broke his leg in three places, Amira. He was in constant pain, even after the cast came off."

"I know!" She nods, eager to agree. To sympathize. "But that's not what her mother meant. Cabrini said frequent flyers are the people who come in complaining of pain just to get a script. They're . . . notorious. Because they're there so often. Some of them even hurt themselves on purpose just to get pills."

"My father *never* did that." My jaw aches from clenching my teeth. "He would *never*."

"I know. But Cabrini said . . ." She takes another breath, and I can see her steeling herself to forge ahead. "I mean, Cabrini wasn't the only one saying it. But she said he stole a prescription pad and tried to forge a script. That he might have sold some of them. That's why he was arrested last year. That's what I heard, anyway."

There's a sound building in the back of my head. It's a roar, like an oncoming train. Or, like a tsunami about to crash over land. Whatever it is, it's coming. Fast and hard.

I can't be in this car when it hits. I can't be with Amira when this thing demolishes me. But I have to know.

"And my mother? What did they say about her?"

Amira shrugs, as if it's a casual thing for her to talk about my family like this. To string our shames out in a neat row, like laundry pinned to the clothesline behind my grandmother's trailer.

"They say she fixed his problems. I'm not sure what that means. Maybe that she buried evidence?" Another shrug. "She made it so that he was never officially charged."

"And everyone thinks that? They all think my mother is crooked? That my father was a criminal?"

I knew there were rumors. I could feel the stares and hear the whispers for months on end. But I thought it was about my dad being in rehab. Losing his job.

Beckett Bergen, daughter of an opioid addict. Until I wasn't.

Beckett Bergen, daughter of a dead opioid addict.

But I had no idea it went beyond that. No idea they were talking about my mother too. Or that they thought my father was a criminal.

Amira lays her hand on mine, and I *swear* her fingers burn. "*I* don't think that."

When I can't figure out what to say, she frowns. "Doesn't that matter, Beckett?"

Does it?

---

When I get home, Landry is in the kitchen, and the whole house smells amazing. Like garlic and cheese. It's almost enough to make me smile.

Almost.

"Hey! What's for dinner?" I set my backpack on a bar stool and steal a pinch of shredded parmesan from the bowl on the counter.

"Don't!" Landry scowls at me as if I just threw the whole thing on the floor. "That's the good stuff. Eight dollars a pound. It is *not* to be scarfed with abandon before dinner's even done."

"Mom let you spend eight dollars for a pound of parmesan?"

"No, our food budget would only cover the green canister full of the powdered crap. I bought this myself. But this was only an eight ounce block, so . . ." She shrugs, as if her purchase were no big deal.

Penn and I do dishes and clean the bathroom, but Landry's only household chore is to make dinner five nights a week. In part because no one else wants to do it. She gets an allowance of ten dollars every week, just like we do. Which means she spent

nearly half her allowance—her own money, outside of the grocery budget—on this cheese.

"What's wrong with the stuff in the green canister?"

Again, disdain bleeds from her eyes. "*That* stuff is crap. *This*
stuff is good."

"It sure is." I steal another pinch, and she moves the bowl out
of my reach. "What'cha makin'?"

She turns back to the skillet sizzling on the stove, to stir
whatever she's sautéing. "Garlic lemon chicken, with zucchini
noodles."

I groan. "What is it with you and vegetables?"

"They're good for you. And they taste good. You'll see."

"You know what tastes good?" I don't wait for her to ask,
because she clearly isn't going to. "Spaghetti. Actual noodles."

"Well, when *you* cook dinner, you can boil as much starchy
pasta as you want. But tonight, you're having zucchini noodles,"
she says, pointing to a big bowl where the fake noodles in question sit next to a canister of salt. "We eat in twenty minutes."

"Great. Need any help?"

She props her hands on her hips, over the ties of a worn,
stained kitchen apron. It was dad's, so it's big on her. "Do you
know how to juice a lemon?"

"Um . . . Ask it nicely to release its tart nectar?"

Landry rolls her eyes. "No, I don't need any help. Thanks,
though."

I steal one more pinch of parmesan on my way out of the
kitchen, then I text Jake.

call?

His reply comes as I close myself into my bedroom.

just a sec

My phone rings a minute later.

"Hey," I say into it as I sink onto my bed and lean back on my pillow.

"Hey," Jake says. "What's up?"

We haven't spoken since his parents basically kicked me out of his house last night.

"Did you hear rumors about my parents last year?"

He huffs into my ear. "You have a strange way of starting conversations."

"That's not an answer."

Over the line, I hear the familiar creak of his bedsprings. "I don't know what you want me to say. I mean, yeah, I heard things."

"What things? About my dad?"

"Yeah." I can practically hear him shrug one shoulder, the way he does when he doesn't really want to tell me something.

"What did you hear? Was it more than just the rehab thing?"

"I feel like you're fishing for something specific, Beck."

"I'm trying to figure something out. What did you hear?"

Jake sighs. "I heard your dad got arrested for stealing drugs from the hospital."

"Drugs?"

"Prescription painkillers. Oxy. Vicodin. Stuff like that."

"Hmmm . . ."

"What? Is that not what you thought I'd say?"

"Amira heard he was arrested for stealing a prescription pad and forging signatures."

I'm not sure if this means that neither version is true or that both of them are. Or that life is like that game of Telephone from when we were kids. The one where you'd whisper something from ear to ear around a circle, then laugh over how the final product hardly resembled the original statement.

"When did you hear that? About the pills?"

"I don't know, Beck. I've slept since then. Several hundred times."

"Guess."

Jake exhales again. "I think it was around the time your dad lost his job with the fire department. That's the only reason I listened. It kinda . . . It kind of seemed to make sense. At the time."

"So you believed it?"

"I mean . . . ," Jake says, and I can almost hear that silent shrug again. "I gave it about an eighty percent credibility rating."

"And you didn't think you should tell me?"

"Beckett, I don't know what you want me to say. Why would I want to tell my girlfriend that her father may or may not have been arrested for stealing prescription pain pills? Besides, I figured your mom could handle it."

"*Handle* it?" I sit up straight, fire sparking in my veins. "You think she got the charges dropped? Did you hear that at school too? That my mother's a dirty cop?"

"No!" Jake groans. "I mean yes, I heard that she fixed things for your dad, when he was arrested. And that maybe that wasn't the first time. But that's not what I meant by 'handle it.' I meant I figured it was up to her to decide what to tell you. Her, and your dad."

"Why? Why would you think that? Parents try to protect their kids. That's their job, even if that means lying. Or omitting. I expected the truth from you. I *needed* the truth from you."

A bitter feeling of déjà vu overwhelms me, and my eyes close. I can feel the echo of this plea to him reverberating backward through our relationship. Me begging for the truth. Him withholding it. Or trying to explain why he can't give me what I need.

Just like with the texts he didn't want me to see.

"That's not fair. *No one* wants to get in the middle of someone else's family drama. Besides, I liked your dad, and I didn't know for sure that any of it was true. I *still* don't. And back then, you and I had just gotten together. If I'd started accusing your dad of criminal shit with no proof, you'd have dumped me. After you kicked in my teeth."

Fact-Check Rating: One hundred percent true.

"What about later? When we'd been together awhile? Why didn't you tell me then?"

"Because after the rumors died down, I didn't think it mattered. People seemed to forget. Until your dad died, and they started talking again. But then, there was *no way* I was going to ask you if he'd been arrested. I wasn't raised to speak ill of the dead, Beck."

That's fair. Jake didn't do anything wrong. So why am I so mad at him?

This feels like the cosmic version of having spinach stuck in your teeth. Wherein spinach is a father who may or may not have been arrested for stealing a prescription pad and forging prescriptions. Or stealing actual drugs. But who was definitely in rehab at least once, and who definitely died of an overdose of alcohol and painkillers.

Why would no one tell me I had cosmic spinach in my teeth? Why would no one give me a chance to find out for myself whether or not my father was the man I believed him to be?

"It doesn't matter, Beck."

Jake's voice is soft in my ear. So soft that he could be here with me. Curled up around me, with my back resting against his chest, while he leans against my headboard. And suddenly I want that *so* badly.

"It doesn't matter whether any of the rest of that shit is true. Even if it is, that isn't who he was to you. He was the man who taught you to tie your shoes and sing the alphabet song. The man who came back from Afghanistan with a tiny hourglass filled with sand on a silver chain, so that the next time he was in the desert, you would have a little bit of that same desert to keep near your heart."

I'd forgotten I told him about that.

"He was your dad, even if he was someone else's criminal. Don't take that away from him when he isn't here to defend himself."

I don't know where the sob comes from. One minute, I'm remembering that I had a very similar thought half an hour ago, in Amira's car. The next, I'm crying. And I don't know why.

God, I wish Jake were here right now. Almost as badly as I wish my father were here.

"Hey! You okay?" His bedsprings creak again, and I know he's sitting up. "Beckett?"

I sniffle and wipe my eyes. "I'm fine. Sorry."

When is this going to get easier? When will it not hurt to think about him?

"Can I come over?"

Yes. *God*, yes, come over and hold me.

"No." The word burns my tongue, but I say it anyway.

"You're upset. I just . . . I want to help you. I want to be there with you." He sucks in a deep breath, and the rest comes out like a confession. "I miss you, Beck."

I shove my face into my pillow and scream into it for a second. Then I pick up my phone again. "I can't. I'm so sorry, Jake, but I just can't."

"Why not?"

Because everything is *so* complicated right now. Because I love him, but I don't know how to move forward if I can't count on him to tell me the truth, about what he heard about my parents or about whatever he doesn't want me to see in his texts.

Because I can't be sure I won't throw myself at him the minute I see him, despite all of that.

"Because you were right," I tell him. "My timing sucks."

Silence echoes between us, and I think he's going to hang up. That he may never call back. "Okay," he says at last. "Um . . . At the risk of making everything worse . . . I think I remember where I left my duffel bag."

The abrupt switch of gears throws me off balance for a moment. But then I swipe my cheeks dry with one hand and sit straighter. If I come to my mother with more information about the case, she might be more inclined to reciprocate.

"Where?"

"*There*," Jake says. "I think I left it at your house, about a month ago. The last time I remember having it was when I took you home after the last football game. I brought it in with me so I could change my shirt. It rained that night, remember?"

I do remember. And he definitely had his bag with him that night. I don't remember him leaving it here, but knowing that I might have had access to that bag would make me look even worse to everyone harassing me with the babykiller hashtag.

"I don't . . . Jake, I don't think it would help the police to know that."

"So, you're asking me not to tell your mother?"

I exhale slowly, well aware of the hypocrisy I'm about to commit. "I can't tell you what to do. All I'm saying is that I don't think that'll help the police, and it definitely won't help me."

Silence stretches over the phone again while he considers.

"Okay," he says at last. "I'm not going to lie if they ask me, but I won't volunteer the information either."

"Thank you. I—" I close my eyes and exhale slowly. "I'm sorry. I can't seem to get my shit together, and I feel like I'm running around in circles in my own head. But I miss you too." Admitting that feels like letting go of a breath I've been holding for years. "Maybe . . . Maybe we could talk more tomorrow? At school?"

"Dinner!" Landry shouts from the kitchen.

"That would be good."

Jake's voice echoes in my ear, and a smile sneaks up on me. "I gotta go. Say hi to your mom for me. Tell her she raised a real peach."

He laughs. "I'm sure she'll be thrilled to hear your opinion on the subject."

He thinks I'm joking, because his parents were on the "Beckett Bergen is going to hell" bandwagon long before the rest of the world got on board. But there's one thing his mom and my mom have in common, both with each other and with every other mother on the face of the planet. They love to hear how great their kids are.

In this case, it happens to be true.

On my way out of the room, I stop and grab the tiny vial of sand on a chain from where it hangs over the corner of the old wooden jewelry box my grandmother gave me years ago. I drop it over my head and tuck the vial into my shirt, where I can feel it against my skin.

My dad may have fallen for the last time here in Tennessee. On the living room floor. But we all know that he really died two years ago in Afghanistan. With the other three men in that jeep.

**CRIMSON CRYER**

@crimsoncryer · 3h

You guys! The students at @CliffordHSOfficial are raising funds to give little #LullabyDoe a proper funeral! Click here to donate: bit.ly/2HPrzTu

#RIP
#GiveALittle

 399         1004         1267

# TEN

"I can't help noticing that you ate all your zucchini noodles," Landry says as I stand from my bar stool and take her empty plate.

It's my night to do the dishes. I think. We've kind of stopped keeping track.

"I have to admit, they were not bad. Firmer than I expected. Al dente." I arch one brow at her. "Can vegetables be cooked al dente, or is that term reserved for real pasta?"

"I have no idea." She slides from her bar stool and pulls her apron over her head. "Don't dump the leftovers. Mom thinks she hates zucchini too, so I want her to try this."

She opens the pantry door and hangs the apron on its hook.

"I'll save them for her," I promise as I reach for Penn's plate.

"Wait!" He stabs at the last of his zucchini noodles, and his fork scrapes the plate with a horrible screech as I pull it away from him.

"You've had three helpings! How can you still be hungry?"

"It takes a lot of energy to run five miles a day," he insists, making a grab for his plate.

And the truth is that with his level of physical activity, he probably needed *actual* pasta. But he won't complain in front of the chef. He'll just carbo-load on his own later.

"I'm going next door," Landry calls from the living room, and I lean over the narrow island to see her stepping into her shoes as she shoves both arms into her coat.

"It's a school night!" I remind her.

"I'll be back in an hour. Norah and I are working on our science project."

"Without Fletcher?" Penn calls after her, but the only answer he gets is the click of the front door closing. "They're not working," he mumbles, already headed to the pantry for something else to eat.

But I'm not really listening.

"Hey. What's up with you?" Penn pokes me with the corner of a box of Pop-Tarts, and I realize I've been staring into the sink, without seeing the dishes stacked in it.

I open my mouth to tell him about what I heard in the salon. About the reporter. About Amira and Jake's confirmation that pretty much all of Clifford thinks our dad was a redneck criminal and our mom is a dirty cop. But I can't do it. Not while he's wearing the cap the West Point recruiter gave him at the college fair, thinking about how great his life is going to be once he's out of this shithole town.

Unfortunately, what comes out of my mouth instead isn't much better.

"Hey, where's your Titans shirt? The one you got on the senior trip to Nashville."

"What?"

He sinks onto the middle bar stool and opens my last box of

Pop-Tarts. They're chocolate peanut butter. My favorite. He better not eat them all.

"Your Titans shirt," I repeat as I start loading the dishwasher, as if my question is no big deal. "I haven't seen you wear it in a while."

"What the hell are you talking about?" The wrapper crinkles as he rips open one of my Pop-Tarts. "Why do you care about my shirt?"

I pull the sprayer out of its hole next to the faucet and rinse off the skillet Landry used to sauté the chicken. Or maybe the zucchini noodles. I'm a little fuzzy on how this whole meal came together.

"Beckett. You have the subtlety of Godzilla on a rampage. What's going on?"

I turn, leaning against the sink with my arms crossed over my chest. "Mom's trying to find the owner of a Titans shirt just like yours."

"And by Mom, you mean the cops?" Penn drops his half-eaten Pop-Tart onto the open wrapper still containing its twin. "This is about that baby? Do you *seriously* think I have anything to do with that?"

"No." Maybe? I feel like a bitch for even asking, but . . . "Basically any of the senior guys who bought that shirt are going to be questioned. I just thought you should have a heads-up."

"Then why didn't you just tell me that, instead of trying to interrogate me on the sly?"

"Okay. Look." I push off from the sink and lean against the island across from him, pointedly ignoring a few drips of lemon garlic sauce. "Jake thinks he left his duffel bag here. And you came back from the senior trip with one of those shirts. And your girlfriend has missed nearly a week of school. So . . ." I shrug, feeling like an ass.

"You should jump to conclusions in the Olympics, Beckett. Do you *really* think Daniela and I are the parents of a dead baby abandoned on the floor of the locker room?"

"I'm not saying that. I'm just . . ." Another shrug. "Is there any chance you mistook Jake's bag for yours? Did you maybe carry it by accident? Leave your shirt in it? Would Daniela have had access to it?"

Penn blinks at me, stunned. "I can't believe you! No, I didn't use Jake's bag. Not that I know of, anyway. And I don't know where my shirt is. I ripped it beneath the armpit a couple of weeks ago, and I haven't exactly been looking for it since then, because until I learn how to sew, I can't wear it anymore."

"Okay. I'm—"

"And Daniela has the flu. Like I told you this morning. She's never been pregnant. She's on the pill, and we're *very fucking careful*, Beck. Because West Point won't even consider applicants with children, and I am *not* going to get stuck here slinging tires for the rest of my life. I have *plans*. Big ones. People who go to West Point become federal judges. Four-star generals. President. So there's no way in hell that's my baby. It's not Daniela's either. Fuck you, if you don't believe me."

With that, Penn storms out of the kitchen with my entire last box of Pop-Tarts, flipping me off with his free hand, just for good measure.

I kick the dishwasher shut.

———————

When my mother hasn't come home by midnight, I sneak into the kitchen and eat her leftovers, standing over the sink. She probably grabbed cheap tacos at work anyway.

As I swirl zucchini noodles onto my fork—they warm up surprisingly well—my phone beeps with an alert that the Crimson Cryer account has posted something new.

Yes, I've set up alerts.

Though I'm just now getting the notice, when I tap to open it, I discover that the tweet was posted several hours ago. It's a link to the GoFundMe that the Key Club started, along with an appeal to the public to donate. It already has more than twelve hundred likes, a thousand retweets, and nearly four hundred comments.

And the Crimson Cryer account itself has several thousand new followers since I last checked. Including half a dozen reporters from national news networks, according to their two-line bios.

If that keeps up, much bigger sharks than WBBJ will be swimming in our little pond again, trying to take a bite out of me.

I click the link to the GoFundMe and nearly choke on my zucchini.

We've already received more than twice our donation goal. Seventeen thousand four hundred dollars, and some change. There's *no way* all of that came from the good people of Clifford.

It appears, whether I like it or not, that the Crimson Cryer is a bona fide celebrity.

On the bright side, we have plenty of money for Lullaby Doe's funeral. And I don't even care that Sophia Nelson will get credit for the fundraiser.

Wait, yes I do. No one's accusing *her* of being a baby killer. A little good press could go a long way for me. But I know better than to push my luck with karma. Or the media.

The front door opens as I'm setting the empty leftover dish in the sink, and my mother comes in dragging her feet.

"Hey!" I call, leaning over the kitchen island so she can see me.

"Hey." She drops her keys in the bowl on the coffee table, then she comes into the kitchen. "What are you doing up?"

There are bags under her eyes, and those little baby hairs around her face have long since won the battle against whatever product keeps them in place for the first half of her workday.

"Couldn't sleep. So I thought I'd eat."

"Oh, to be sixteen again."

"Careful what you wish for," I warn her.

When she was sixteen, there was no social media "justice" and no viral death threats.

She sinks onto the right-hand bar stool and scrapes at a dried bit of sauce on the island. "What was this?"

"Lemon garlic chicken with zucchini noodles."

My mother's grimace looks eerily familiar. Why is it that I see the resemblance between us only when something unpleasant crosses her mind?

"It was surprisingly good. I just had the last of it. But I'm fine with letting Landry think you ate it."

"Agreed." She folds her arms on the island, heedless of the dried sauce, and leans over to lay her forehead on them. "I'm too tired to go to bed."

"Why were you out so late? Was there a break in the case?"

I don't expect her to answer. And maybe she's not planning to. But then I pull out the left-hand bar stool and she looks up, surprised, when I sink onto it.

"Actually, as it turns out, there *is* no case."

"What does that mean?"

Her brows dip and she presses her lips together. I can practically see her internal debate as she tries to decide whether or not she can trust me.

"The coroner's report came back," she finally says, twisting on her bar stool to face me. "The baby died without ever taking a breath."

"So, what does that mean, exactly?"

"It means there was no murder. The baby was stillborn, which means she died either in utero or during labor."

"Okay, but *why* did she die?"

"The coroner wasn't able to tell us that. Science doesn't have an answer for everything, Beckett. And this case is more frustrating than most, because this baby doesn't appear to fall into many of the high-risk categories for stillbirth. There's no sign the mother smoked or took drugs. There's every likelihood that she is young, whoever she is, and most stillbirths occur to older mothers. The only likely risk factor is a low socioeconomic status, which the coroner said can lead to poor prenatal care. But it seems just as likely to me that in this case, the lack of prenatal care was in an effort to keep the pregnancy secret."

"So then, would she have lived if her mother had gone to the doctor? Or called an ambulance when she went into labor?"

Was there any truth to what that woman at the salon said, even if she was wrong about me being the mother?

"Possibly. But there's no way to know that for sure." My mother sighs, hunched beneath the weight of her job. "Sometimes there are just no answers."

"So, what happens now?"

"Now, I try to get a little sleep, so that I don't look like a zombie when I hold another press conference tomorrow to tell the world that the role of the Clifford PD is now limited to identifying and notifying the next of kin of the baby now officially known as Lullaby Doe. Speaking of which, Jake's test results came back today too. He's not the father, Beckett."

My relieved exhalation practically blows her hair back. I didn't really believe it was Jake's baby. At least, I didn't *think* I believed that. But having it confirmed is such a huge relief.

"Oh, thank goodness. I didn't think you'd get the results back so quickly."

"Me neither. It seems the press coverage has made the Lullaby Doe case the lab's top priority." My mother clears her throat. "Normally this isn't information I could give out, without permission from the subject of the test. But I'm sure Jake is planning to tell you himself anyway. And when he does, I suggest looking a *little* less relieved. As if you were never in doubt."

"Wait, he already knows?"

"We called him out of class this afternoon to tell him. I figured he deserved to know as soon as possible. I mean, he *already* knew, presumably. But I thought he deserved to know that he was no longer a person of interest in the case. Which no longer exists, anyway, as of about three hours ago."

Jake's known for half the day, and he didn't tell me. Not even when I spoke to him on the phone this afternoon. Why wouldn't he want to clear his name, after I practically accused him of being Lullaby Doe's father?

Unfortunately, Jake isn't the only person I hurled that particular accusation at.

"What's wrong?" my mother asks. "I thought you'd be happy about all of this."

"I am. But I kind of . . . also accused Penn of being the baby's father."

"Beckett!"

"I know! I'm sorry! It's just that at the time, it seemed like a legitimate possibility."

She stands and rounds the island, where she runs water into a glass at the sink. "You're going to have to walk me through that one."

"Daniela's been absent from school for several days. And Penn can't find his Titans shirt."

"What?" My mother turns away from the sink holding her glass. "What's wrong with Daniela?"

"He says she has the flu. And to be fair, her Insta has been full of artfully focused pictures of cold medicine and tissue boxes for days now." I lean over the island and pull open the junk drawer, so I can hand her a packet of antacid tablets. She definitely grabbed tacos at work. "Would it be paranoid of me to point out that anyone can take pictures of cold medicine and tissue boxes and claim to have the flu?"

Am I out of my mind to suspect my brother's girlfriend?

Mom tears open the packet and drops two white tablets into her water glass, where they fizz vigorously. "Beckett, I think it's time to consider the possibility that a career in law enforcement may not be in your future."

"Mom, I have no intention of becoming a cop."

She gives me a surprised look as she lifts her glass. "So, what's the deal with Penn's shirt?"

"He says he hasn't seen it since he ripped one of the armpits. But that he hasn't really been looking for it, because he can't wear it now anyway."

Mom sets her glass down without taking a drink. For a second, she only stares at it, her eyes half-focused. "I'm sure Daniela really just has the flu, hon."

"I know. And Penn's shirt is probably buried at the bottom of his hamper."

We both know he prioritizes gym clothes when he does his laundry.

My mother nods. Then she takes a long gulp from her fizzing water. "And the duffel bag you found wasn't Penn's."

"I know. But this afternoon, Jake told me he thinks he left his bag here." Me telling my mother that isn't the same thing as Jake telling the police in an official interview. "Which means Penn could easily have grabbed it thinking it was his at any time in the past month. Like I said, at the time, it all seemed to make sense. But now . . ." I shrug. "Penn's really pissed at me, and he has every right to be. Still . . ."

She takes another drink. "Still what?"

"I need to know, Mom. People are out there accusing me of hiding a pregnancy and killing a baby. Demanding my arrest. I can't answer my own phone. Reporters are following me down the street. I'm getting death threats on Twitter."

"I told you not to look—"

"That's a lot easier said than done. I'm wrapped up in this, and it feels like that's not going to change until we figure out who that baby's parents really are. Until I can show the world that it's not me."

My mother sets her glass down and captures my gaze from across the countertop. It's a mom-gaze, not a cop-gaze. "Beckett, there will always be someone out there willing—even eager—to believe the worst of you. That's true for all of us. Admittedly, what you're getting is more baptism by fire than the gentle sprinkling of unfounded hatred most people will experience over the course of a lifetime. But the principle remains the same. You're never going to be able to completely clear your name. Even if you had ironclad proof, someone would refuse to believe it. There are people out there who still don't believe we ever landed on the moon, Beck. If you spend your life trying to prove yourself worthy of someone else's respect, you'll run yourself into an early grave."

"I just don't want some wack job to think the Clifford baby killer got off too easily and decide to take matters into his own hands. Chances are that those dogs are all bark and no bite. But it only takes one psycho to—"

"That's fair," my mom says. "And I'd be lying if I said that wasn't something I'd thought of. But so far, none of the threats against you have proven credible."

"You've looked into them?"

My mother blinks at me. "Of course I have. Every last one. I've already had nearly two dozen accounts suspended from Twitter for policy violation—threatening physical harm—and I'm reporting every single one of them to the FBI."

"Holy shit." I stare at her, stunned. "Why haven't you told me any of that?"

"I assumed you knew. I'd do that for *anyone* in Clifford who was being threatened. That's my job. And you're not just anyone, Beck."

"So, I've been going around accusing people, basically at random, of the very thing the internet is accusing me of, and you've been out there tracking down test results and reporting threats against me to the FBI. Mom, that is badass."

My timing is bad. My mother chokes on the sip she's just taken. But then she smiles.

"Thanks. I guess." She coughs again, then she takes another drink. "You need to get some sleep, hon."

"I know." I slide off my bar stool as she grabs the empty antacid packet to throw it away. "Tell Landry you liked the zucchini noodles. Use words like 'al dente' and 'filling.'"

"You want me to lie to her?"

"It's not a lie. The words are true; you just didn't experience them. So just think of yourself as a speaker broadcasting words that I recorded."

My mother frowns as I walk backward out of the kitchen. "I'm a little worried about your definition of a lie, Beckett."

# *ELEVEN*

"Hey."

My brother's foot appears in the bathroom, pushing the door open slowly. He's dressed and ready, though he doesn't have to leave for school for another twenty minutes, even if he's dropping Landry off first.

"Hey. I'll be out in a sec."

I lean toward the mirror again and apply a second coat of mascara. The tube is practically empty, and I have neither the time nor the money for a run to the store. But I saw a video on Instagram the other day—back before I had to disable comments on all my posts—promising to show me how to make use of every bit of mascara from a tube I'd assumed was empty. Maybe I can find that video again without uncovering too many more death threats.

"I don't need the bathroom." He digs his phone from his pocket. "I just wanted to say, after last night—"

"Penn, I'm sorry. I had no right—"

"Just let me finish. You did enough talking yesterday."

"Okay." I shove the wand back into my mascara tube and twist it closed. "Sorry. Go ahead."

"You're a hypocrite."

I blink at him in the mirror. That's not the opening line I was expecting.

"All these people online—and in school—are saying Lullaby Doe is yours, just because you found the body. It isn't right for you to jump to the same conclusion about me."

"I know. I'm—"

"You're doing the same thing to me that they're doing to you."

"I'm sorry! Okay?" I spin away from the mirror to face him. "You're right. I'm an asshole."

"Sometimes," he agrees. "And just to rub that in . . ." He unlocks his phone and shoves a picture of his girlfriend, Daniela Montes, at me. "She sent me that on Wednesday night. One week ago. Two days before Lullaby Doe was born. Do you see any way she could have been pregnant in this picture?"

The short version? No.

My brother's girlfriend is crazy-hot. And in this selfie, she's about to combust. She's posing on her bed in nothing but a matched set of lacy red underwear and a Santa hat, the phone angled to show her entire body from above. Including part of a butt sculpted from years of soccer and a tiny, tiny little waist.

I know that sometimes a pregnancy isn't noticeable through clothing until late-term. I've done the same googling everyone else has over the past week. But there's no way on earth that Daniela is thirty weeks pregnant in that picture.

There's also no way the picture is from last year, because last Christmas she and my brother weren't together yet.

Also, last year her hair was down to her waist, and in this

picture, it's just below her shoulders. She cut it in October, so she could fit it into an updo for the Fall Ball, which the school settled on last year as a way to cut spending by replacing the homecoming dance and the winter formal with one event.

Yes, they canceled the homecoming dance. Permanently.

"I believe you." I hand his phone back to him. "I believed you even without the picture. I'm sorry, Penn. I guess I've just been a little preoccupied with clearing my name."

"By dragging mine—and Daniela's—through the mud?"

"All I can say in my defense is that last night the pieces really seemed to fit. And I *really* need the truth. Sorry I got carried away. This whole thing just really sucks."

Penn exhales slowly. Then he comes in to sit on the closed toilet. "It's getting pretty bad, isn't it?"

I turn back to the mirror and select a lipstick I don't hate. "Yesterday I got chased down the street by a reporter from WBBJ."

"I saw."

"What?" I spin again, and Penn pulls his phone from his pocket. "They used the footage? I didn't even answer any of their questions!"

"Evidently you're news either way. I don't know whether it was on TV, but they posted the clip to their website and to Twitter, and the Crimson Cryer retweeted it half an hour ago. It already has five hundred retweets."

He hands me his phone, and I tap the play triangle superimposed over an image of my face frozen in midshout, with the local flower shop visible over my shoulder.

It is not a flattering shot.

The video starts, and instead of the footage I expect to see of myself running down the sidewalk, ignoring the reporter and her cameraman, the clip begins in To Dye For, with me shouting expletives at a room full of stylists and customers.

"Great." I stop the clip and hand Penn back his phone. I can't watch anymore. "How am I supposed to convince the world that I'm not evil when I'm online cursing at a bunch of senior citizens? Believe it or not, that horrible old lady started it."

Penn shrugs. "I believe you. And I thought you were kind of awesome."

Somehow, I don't think Jake's parents will agree. Even if they no longer believe I'm Lullaby Doe's mother.

He stands. "I can pick Landry up, if you'll drop her off this morning."

"You're not working?"

Penn cleans out kennels at the animal shelter in Daley three afternoons a week, for minimum wage.

"Nah. Mr. Mattson said maybe I should stop coming in until all this dies down."

"Why? What happened?"

He shrugs. "That salon wasn't WBBJ's only stop yesterday."

"Crap. I'm sorry."

"It's only temporary," he insists.

But he can't possibly be sure of that. Mr. Mattson will have to replace him and there may not be any job for Penn to go back to, by the time all this blows over. But I decide to look on the bright side. For once.

"Maybe that'll be sooner than we think. Mom said the coroner's report came in last night. Lullaby Doe was stillborn. Which means no crime was committed. Surely once everyone knows that, this'll all just go away."

"I hope so." Penn's jaw clenches. "If I'm associated with this, I'll never get into West Point. The admissions board scours social media for anything that might reflect poorly on the army or the academy."

"I know. Jake's parents are worried about his scholarship potential for the same reason."

I'm glad I have nearly another year before I have to worry about that. Not that I'll be applying to West Point or expecting athletic scholarships . . .

The truth is that I have no idea what I want to do after high school. But every day that someone online calls me a baby killer and threatens to shoot me in the street, my options seem fewer and fewer.

"Speaking of West Point, how did the CFA go? Did you pass?"

His smile lights up the whole planet. "I kinda killed it. Not that it matters. All the top candidates will have strong CFA scores."

"I'm not worried," I assure him. "You'll stand out." And with any luck, that will have *nothing* to do with Lullaby Doe.

––––––––––––––

There are three news vans parked in front of the school when I get there. Either they don't know what my car looks like yet or the principal has banned them from the grounds, because they don't follow me into the parking lot.

I park as close to the building as possible, but before I can get out of the car, I see Jake walking toward me from across the lot.

He looks great, as always, in his crimson and white letter jacket, his backpack slung over one shoulder.

His grin sets my insides on fire.

He opens my passenger's side door, letting in a gust of frigid air as he slides onto the seat. "Hey."

"Hey. Were you waiting for me?"

Jake shrugs. "You said we could talk today."

"Yeah." And I'm even more grateful now that the student parking lot is behind the school, where the reporters can't see us.

"Does that mean you're thinking about what I said the other day?" He reaches across the center console and traces the length of my index finger with his own. "About us starting over?"

"Actually, I'm still thinking about the things you *haven't* said."

He blinks at me. "Okay, I'm sorry I didn't tell you what I heard about your dad. I didn't want to—"

"Not that. You're right. There would have been no good way for you to even start that conversation with me. I'm talking about the paternity test results. My mom said she called you out of class yesterday. Why didn't you say anything while we were on the phone?"

"Because I wanted you to believe me without proof. Just this once." His crooked smile feels like a dagger straight to my heart. "And if you weren't going to do that, then I wanted to tell you in person. That's part of why I wanted to come over."

"I did believe you."

Fact-Check Rating: Inconclusive. I really *wanted* to believe him. But I couldn't quite let go of the possibility that he was lying.

"But I'm glad you got proof, for your sake," I add.

"I didn't need it. I've never been with anyone but you, Beckett." He takes my hand, and suddenly I'm clinging to him, grasping for balance as my head and my heart pull me in two different directions.

"Then why were you hiding texts from me? And don't say you weren't, because—"

"I was," he says. I try to pull my hand free, but he tightens his grip. "But those texts weren't about some other girl. There's no one else. There never has been."

The sudden intensity of his focus makes me feel like the world no long exists outside this car. "Beckett, I fell for you the first day of your sophomore year. Do you remember that morning? Penn gave me a ride to school, and you were in the back seat, looking at me in the rearview mirror with those big blue eyes. I couldn't look away. But your brother thought it'd be weird to see a teammate with his sister, and it took me a while to change his mind. Then even longer to change *your* mind. I *worked* for this. For us."

He squeezes my hand again, yet somehow I feel the pressure in my chest.

"I wouldn't mess that up for anything. I don't want anyone else. I want *you*."

My heart explodes into a thousand shards of white-hot regret, and I lean across the center console. My mouth finds his, and suddenly we're kissing, like the past week never happened. His hand slides behind my neck, his fingers diving into my hair, and I am *gone*.

Game over.

This is the best of us. This is what I've missed *so much*, and I'm so hungry for him that I don't pull away until my lungs demand a deep breath.

He groans as he leans back in the passenger's seat, and I wonder if his pulse is racing like mine is. "Well, that went better than I expected. So, a do-over, then? Clean slate?"

My heart is a mess of shredded tissue, still trying to beat. "I want that. I do. But I can't deal with secrets, and—"

"And I need you to trust me." His thumb strokes over the back of my knuckles. "Just believe in me, Beckett. I would never hurt you. Will you let us start over?"

I exhale. "Jake, I'm so messed up right now. Everything is in chaos. I can't think straight, and I just need to . . . I need to take it slow."

"Fine. I can do slow. Just stop pushing me away."

"Okay."

"Okay?" His smile is the sun breaking over the horizon, lighting up the whole world.

"Yeah," I say, and he leans over the console to kiss me again.

"I have to get to the weight room, but I'll see you at lunch?"

"Yeah." Another kiss, and I'm starting to doubt that slow is a thing that really exists.

Tingling all over, I watch him get out of the car and head into the building. Then I take a minute to get my head back in the game before I go inside.

On my way down the main hall, I hear Coach Killebrew complaining to Amira's mother that reporters were hounding her on her way into the building. Shouting questions about the circumstances under which Lullaby Doe was found.

I know exactly how she feels. Frustrated and mystified that this has managed to stay in the headlines for five days, when, according to Penn, school shootings only seem to hang around for three or four, and corrupt politicians are hardly a blip on the radar.

But, as Mrs. Bhatt laments to Coach Killebrew as I pass them in the hall, everyone loves a dead baby.

---

At lunch, I glance out one of the tall, skinny cafeteria windows to see that the reporters have all left, but I don't understand why until Amira plops down across from me holding her phone. She offers me one of her earbuds without explanation, and I accept it when I see my mother on her screen.

The press conference has started.

I've missed the first few minutes of it, but I get to hear my mom reiterate that the Clifford PD is no longer involved with the Lullaby Doe case, except in the search for a next of kin to notify, which is standard procedure in every case involving an unidentified decedent. Evidently I missed the part where she told them the baby was stillborn, so there would be no murder investigation.

The press room—really it's just the multipurpose room where they set out cake when someone has a birthday—erupts as reporters start shouting questions.

"Is it a crime in the state of Tennessee to fail to report a death? If so, wouldn't that mean the mother should still face criminal charges?"

"That is not something the Daley County district attorney general is interested in pursuing at this time."

"Why might that be?" another reporter shouts, and I recognize her voice. That's the WBBJ reporter who chased me down the sidewalk outside To Dye For.

My mother turns to her right, and a man in a suit steps up to the microphone. Evidently he's the county's district attorney general.

"At most, failing to report a death would be a misdemeanor, punishable by probation and a fine, on the outside. Pursuing such charges would cost the county money and produce little result, yet would likely keep the next of kin from coming forward to claim the remains. The county court system and the Clifford Police Department have no wish to add to the suffering of that family, whoever they are. Our interests are in helping reunite this poor baby with her family and seeing her properly laid to rest."

"We would also like to offer to connect her mother with counseling services, at no charge, should she come forward and claim the remains," my mom adds as the attorney steps back again.

"Detective, isn't it possible that the mother's prenatal neglect directly led to the death of that baby?"

I can't see which reporter shouts this, but the question gives me chills.

"Couldn't she be charged with criminal neglect?"

"Again, we have no reason to suspect, based on the coroner's report, that—"

I pull the earbud from my ear when Jake walks into the cafeteria. I can't listen to any more of that anyway.

He looks around for a minute, then he takes the chair next

to me without going through the line for a tray. I guess none of us are really very hungry today.

"Is that the press conference?" He glances at Amira's phone.

She nods and offers him an earbud.

"No thanks." Jake takes my hand, and Amira arches one brow at me with a tiny grin. "My mom just texted to say that your mother exonerated me on live TV. Right at the beginning." He glances at the phone again. "She said that the only paternity test the police had run so far had come back negative."

Which means she cleared Jake without naming him as a potential suspect. Because unlike the Crimson Cryer, my mother is a professional.

Amira gives him a half-hearted smile. "Congratulations, I guess?"

Maybe I should see if the police department will run a DNA test on me, to prove my innocence.

Then again, when it comes back negative, they'll probably accuse my mother of wasting taxpayer dollars and using her position to help her daughter. Or even of falsifying the results.

I swear, I'm not even capable of optimism anymore. Over the past week, the internet has taught me that most people *aren't* good at heart, and that mob mentality never leads people to do something positive for the world, like adopt puppies and kittens en masse.

Why must mobs always carry pitchforks and burn people in effigy? Why can't a mob, just this one time, carry cotton candy and throw out air kisses? Or candy, like at a parade?

People are always more pleasant when they've had a little sugar.

---

If I'd thought that having Jake's name cleared would clear mine as well, I would have been sorely disappointed. Fortunately, based on my new embrace of pessimism as a life choice—nay, a religion—I was expecting no such thing.

The only conclusion I can draw from the fact that people seem to believe he's not the father, yet rumors still claim that I'm Lullaby Doe's mother, is that they must think I cheated on him. The irony of that burns deep into my soul.

I'm still fuming about it when I walk through my front door to find my mother standing in the kitchen, leaning over the island with her back to me. She turns when I close the door, and the startled look on her face tells me I'm not who she was expecting.

"Beckett." She's still wearing her badge.

There's a uniformed cop behind her, and when he turns from the sink holding a glass of water, I realize it's Doug Chalmers.

"I thought you were picking up Landry this afternoon."

"Penn said he'd do it, since they asked him not to come in to work anymore."

My mother frowns. "He didn't tell me that."

"A reporter showed up, and I guess the animal shelter doesn't agree that all publicity is good publicity." I glance past her at Doug. "Any chance this is a social visit?"

The fact that he's still wearing his uniform doesn't necessarily mean it can't be, considering that he only lives across the street.

"Um . . . ," Doug says, articulate as usual.

Then I notice the still-sealed cotton swab lying on the kitchen island.

Uh-oh.

"That's not for me, is it?"

"No." My mother pulls out one of the bar stools. "Sit down, Beckett. Please."

"You're giving Penn a paternity test?" I squeak, knowing this is my fault. My wild conclusion jumping has infected my mother. "Daniela was never pregnant. This morning Penn showed me a selfie she took two days before I found the baby. There's no way she was thirty weeks pregnant in that picture, Mom."

"Please sit down."

I sink onto the bar stool and let my backpack slide down my arm to thunk on the floor. "Don't you need a warrant?" I demand, pinning Doug with an angry glare.

"Seriously?" He glances from me to my mother.

"No, we don't need a warrant." My mom sinks onto the center bar stool and twists to face me. "Penn's still underage, and I've given my permission for the test."

"Why?"

She exhales slowly.

"Because we *have* to identify that baby," Doug says. "The whole department is under enormous pressure right now."

"Reporters have been calling all week," my mom adds. "Several of them want to do features on our 'small-town tragedy.'"

"The *governor* called this morning," Doug continues. "I never thought I'd get to talk to the governor, but I answered the phone, and he just started yelling. He's pissed about the negative news coverage, and he said, and I quote, 'I want a happy ending for this shit storm in one week, goddamn it.'"

Doug turns to my mother, who suddenly resembles a punctured balloon, the air rushing out all at once.

"What kind of happy ending does he expect to get at the end of a story about a dead baby?"

"Doug, will you give us a minute?" My mom stares at her hands as she picks at a hangnail.

"Sure. I'll just wait outside."

Because there's no other way to give us privacy without going into one of the bedrooms. But instead of heading for the front porch, he goes out the kitchen door into the backyard.

"Mom? *Why* are you doing this?"

She finally looks up from her hands, and the pain staring out at me from her eyes feels eerily familiar. It's not the look she got when my screams woke her up, and we waited for an ambulance we already knew that my dad wasn't going to need. It isn't the clenched-jaw, hold-it-in pain she breathed through for three straight days while we planned, then endured, the funeral. And it isn't the weary, almost impatient ache that flickers behind her eyes when someone we haven't seen in a while hears about my dad and cracks her heart open all over again by offering belated sympathy.

This is my mother's middle-of-the-night pain. Her two a.m.-glass-of-wine pain. Her ugly-crying-because-she-thinks-no-one-else-is-awake pain. The kind that wrings her out like a wet rag and leaves her limp in her bed, clutching my father's pillow.

This is the kind of pain that will kill her if she can't figure out how to let it go.

I don't understand what's happening right now, and I'm not sure I want to.

"I have to know, Beck," she says at last. "Not for Chief Stoddard. Not for the press. And not for the goddamn governor. If that baby was my granddaughter, I *have* to know."

Now I understand. She wasn't just grasping at straws when she convinced Jake's mother to let him take the paternity test by playing the granddaughter card. My mother was asking Grace Mercer to imagine a possibility that she has obviously been steeling herself for from the moment she asked me if Lullaby Doe was my baby. Only this time, Penn's on the hot seat.

But he shouldn't be.

"She isn't, Mom." I take her hands, because she's picked that hangnail until it's bleeding. "She wasn't Penn's baby, and she wasn't your granddaughter. I'll get him to send me that picture. You'll see. There's no way Daniela was—"

"Beckett." She reclaims her hands. "This isn't about Daniela. The baby could be Penn's even if it wasn't hers."

I frown, trying to figure out what dots she's connecting. "I don't . . . ?"

"You found that baby in Jake's duffel bag. But she was wrapped up in Penn's shirt. It's ripped in the armpit, just like you said. On the left side."

"Wait. You think I was *right*? That Jake left his bag here, and Penn used it? Like . . . he left that torn shirt in it?" I've never wanted to be wrong so badly in my life.

"*Maybe.* I think there's a *possibility* that your brother used that bag, and that he left it at her house, whoever she is. But we won't know for sure until we get the paternity test results."

"This is crazy. Last night you basically told me to hang up my magnifying glass and step away from the Sherlock Holmes novels because I was a horrible detective."

"I didn't want it to be true, Beckett. I still don't. And I certainly didn't want you jumping to unfounded conclusions. But then I checked the shirt out of evidence today and I saw that rip again. Right after that, the governor scared the crap out of Doug, and Chief Stoddard basically told us to test every kid who bought one of those shirts until we find a familial match. Since there was no crime, we can't get a warrant, so we'd need voluntary samples or parental permission. And if I'm going to put all those other parents through this, I kind of have to start here at home. Especially if it's really Penn's shirt."

"Okay, but that doesn't mean you have to spring a DNA test on him. You could just show him the shirt. Or ask him if he got some other girl pregnant."

My mother gives me an odd look.

"You think he'll lie."

"No," she insists. "But I feel obligated to verify whatever he tells me. With the test."

I have no idea what to say to that. And it turns out I don't need to say anything, because I can hear Penn's truck—my dad's truck—pulling into the driveway. I can see the blur of motion through the thin front curtains that tells me he's opening his door. That he's about to walk into the shock of his life.

At least, I hope it comes as a shock.

Both truck doors slam, and my mother flinches. "I was hoping you and Landry wouldn't be home for this." She rubs her palms on her slacks, then she stands, and Detective Bergen is back with us. My mother has left the building.

And for the first time in my life, I realize that she isn't just putting on her professional face when she does that. She's putting on a costume. Like maybe it's easier, in moments like these, to pretend the mother half of her doesn't exist.

I wonder what would happen if she were forced to be both at once, the same way I used to wonder what would happen if you pressed both the brake and the gas pedal at once. Because those are opposites, right? A car can't go faster and stop in the same instant. Just like Julie Bergen can't be both police detective and mother at the same time.

I think I'm about to witness the implosion of the entire planet.

Landry comes in first, and she looks *so damn excited* to see Mom standing in the kitchen. Her joy hits me like a rock slamming into my windshield on the highway. I feel the initial blow with enough force to make me flinch. Then come the cracks splintering outward, webbing across my poor shattered heart from an impact my sister hasn't even felt yet.

Penn comes in right behind her, and Mom doesn't even look at Landry. I don't think she can, in this moment. I don't think she's capable of thinking about anything else in the world until she's performed this dreadful duty.

"Hey, Mom! You're home early," Landry says with a frown, glancing from Mom to me. She knows something's wrong.

She looks scared.

Penn elbows Landry out of the way when she lingers in the doorway.

The back door creaks open behind me just as the front door swings shut behind Penn, and Doug's boots thunk on the kitchen linoleum.

Finally, Penn interjects. "What's going on?"

"Landry, why don't you go next door and—" In that moment, I can't think of a single reasonable excuse for my sister to go see her best friend, when on any other day, she would much rather have been at Norah's house than at ours. "Maybe you and Norah could—"

"I'm staying." Landry drops her backpack on the coffee table and sinks onto the couch.

"Mom?" Penn looks past her, and I turn to see that Doug's holding the sealed cheek swab.

"Sorry, man," he says.

My brother's jaw tightens as his bag slides to the ground. Ironically, it's his Clifford Cougars duffel.

"It's just a swab," my mother assures him.

"Fine. But you have to say it," he spits. I've never seen Penn like this. He's mad. Really mad. He's punishing her. And she's going to let him. "You have to tell us all what's about to happen, Detective Bergen."

My mother exhales. "Penn, I've given permission for Officer Chalmers to take a DNA sample from the inside of your cheek." I can see her fall into the familiar words, into the official process, as if it's part of her costume. As if it makes sense, in a way none of the rest of this possibly could. "This sample will be used to check for a familial match to the remains found last week in the locker room of Clifford High School. To test for paternity."

Landry sucks in a breath. Her gaze flicks from face to face in sharp, shocked little motions.

"Let's do this, then." Penn glares at me while he stomps across the living room carpet toward the kitchen.

"I'm sorry!" I mouth as he passes me, but his glare only hardens.

This is all my fault.

# TWELVE

"Hey, what kind of pizza do you want?" I ask as I lean around the doorway into Landry's room. She's on her stomach on her bed, propped on both elbows with an algebra textbook in front of her. But she hasn't even opened it yet. She's on her phone.

"Caramelized pears, gorgonzola cheese, and prosciutto."

I roll my eyes at her. "Little Caesars pretty much has pepperoni and sausage. Bacon, if you call ahead."

"Well, you weren't very specific about where you were going."

I step into her room and lean against the wall, which puts me close enough to reach out and touch her. Landry's room used to be the laundry room, which means there's just enough space for a twin bed, a nightstand made of repurposed wooden crates, and her narrow chest of drawers. No closet.

She and I shared a room until three years ago, when my mom decided every thirteen-year-old—me, at the time—should have a little space of her own. So my dad converted the laundry room into a bedroom for Landry and moved her into it. She was thrilled, even though her bed sits too close to the floor, because it used to be the top half of our set of bunk beds.

Dad was so pleased with his own work, and with how much she loved it, that he bought a metal sign that said "Laundry

Room" and painted an artful slash through the letter *U*, then he added an apostrophe-*S*. Turning "Laundry Room" into "Landry's Room." He strung a pink ribbon through holes punched in the top corners and hung it from a nail on her door.

That sign still hangs there today, and it rattles against the wood anytime she opens or closes her door.

Our washer and dryer now stand in one corner of the kitchen.

"You know there's no place near here that serves gor . . . gouda cheese—"

"Gorgonzola."

"—on pizza, Lan."

In fact, the only place to get *any* pizza in Clifford is the Pizza Hut satellite location, inside the gas station on the highway access road. I'm going to have to drive to Daley just to get Little Caesars, which I volunteered to do because after watching Penn get his cheek swabbed by a cop, our little sister retreated to her room and declared tonight one of her two "nights off." Not that I can blame her.

"So again . . . Pepperoni or sausage?"

"Like it matters." She rolls onto her back, scrolling through something on her phone, using her algebra book as the world's least comfortable pillow.

"Landry. What's wrong with you? Pick a damn protein." When she doesn't answer, I lean forward and snatch her phone.

"Hey!"

"You can have it back when you—" I glance at the screen, and a sick feeling churns in my stomach. She's on a third-party app that lets people who don't have Twitter accounts read through someone's feed.

Landry's reading my @ replies. Post after post calling me everything from a #babykiller to a hell-bound whore. No wonder she looks like she's ready to hide from the entire world.

"Why are you looking at this?" I swipe the screen closed. I wish I knew how to block it.

"Some of those assholes are threatening to kill you, Beckett."

"Don't curse."

"You do."

"I'm sixteen."

"I'm not a little kid. And anyway, age is just a number."

My long, slow exhalation reminds me way too much of our mother. "Yes. It's a number that quantifies an accumulation of experience and wisdom. Besides, as you pointed out, people online are threatening to kill me, and that comes with a 'get out of jail free' card, for profanity."

Mom seems to agree. She hasn't told me to watch my mouth even once since the Crimson Cryer accused me of abandoning my dead baby on the locker room floor.

"*You* are still living the life of a normal eighth grader. So lay off the language."

Landry rolls her eyes. "Fine. Some of those *jerks* are threatening to kill you."

"Yes, but they're all bark and no bite."

"How do you know?"

"Mom's monitoring the threats and reporting them to the FBI. There's been nothing credible so far."

"So far?"

"Nothing at all. And there won't be."

"Again, how do you know?"

"I know because it's a lot easier to say something anonymously online than it is to follow through with it. That's true for everything from pledging to call your congressman to threatening to kill innocent sixteen-year-olds you've never even met." I give her a casual shrug and hope she's buying it. "Fortunately, the American public is *really* lazy."

She spins around to lean on her pillow, which is propped against the wall at the head of her bed. "Why does Mom think Penn is that baby's father?"

Her swift subject change leaves me reeling for a second. "It's not that she actually thinks that." I sink onto the edge of Landry's narrow bed and hand her phone back. "She's trying to officially rule him out."

"But why would she need to do that?"

Sometimes I forget how smart my sister is. When she's in the kitchen, I swear she's thirteen going on thirty. Large and in charge, and inspiringly confident. But now . . .

Thirteen has never looked so young.

"That wasn't his bag," she says. "The one in the picture. It can't be, because he was carrying his bag today."

"You saw the picture?"

She shrugs. "It's all over the internet. That's all anyone's talking about at school."

Of course it is. "Okay, you can't tell anyone this, but no, the bag was actually Jake's. Which is why he took a paternity test a couple of days ago."

Her eyes widen, and I hold up one "shhh" finger before she can start firing questions at me.

"It was negative. So now they're testing Penn, because they found one of his shirts in that bag."

No need for her to know that Penn's Titans shirt was little Lullaby Doe's first and only outfit. The entire extent of the poor thing's wardrobe.

"Penn's *really* mad," Landry says.

"Yeah. I can't blame him. He wants Mom to believe him without needing a test for proof." The fact that I'm echoing what Jake told me has not escaped my attention. "But it's not that simple. The police are not in the business of just believing people."

"Is there something they can do about the threats?" Landry holds up her phone, which helps me follow the derailment in her train of thought. "Something other than just monitoring and reporting them?"

"I'm sure Mom's doing everything she can. And I don't want you to worry about any of that. The police have it under control, and now that they know the baby died of natural causes—"

"As opposed to being killed by her own mother?" Her big brown eyes look wide and haunted. Which is exactly why people try to shield kids from stuff like this.

"Well, I don't think they actually *thought* that. But again, they had to rule it out. Which they've done now. So I really think things are about to calm down and go back to normal. Speaking of which . . ." I stand and back toward her door, careful to keep an easy smile on my face. Battling horror and sadness with a fanatically casual affectation. "What do you want on your pizza?"

Finally Landry gives me a small smile. "I'll take pepperoni."

———

Down the hall, I start to knock on Penn's door, to ask if he wants to drive to Daley with me, but my hand freezes with my knuckles an inch from the wood when I hear my mother's voice.

"I'm sorry, Penn," she says, and I spin away from the door to flatten my back against the wall. I shouldn't listen. But I'm going to. "I didn't intend to spring it on you in front of everyone. I thought Beckett was picking up Landry, and we could have the test done before they got home."

"Doesn't matter." Penn's probably sitting with his back to her. Shutting her out. He does that when he's mad. Or upset. "Secrets have never served this family well anyway."

"So, Beckett seems pretty sure the baby couldn't have been Daniela's."

"You want to see the picture too?" Penn demands, and there's an edge in his voice now. Not sharp like a knife, but rough like a rock. An edge that will grind you into nothing. "You want to see the picture of my girlfriend in her underwear? Because I'm sure she'd be fine with me showing that to my whole damn family."

"No, I don't want to see it. But I do have to ask . . . is there any chance that you could have fathered a baby with someone other than Daniela?"

I expect Penn to hit the roof. To start shouting at Mom for doubting his honor. For accusing him of cheating on his girlfriend.

Instead, silence echoes from beyond the door to my brother's room. Then his bedsprings creak, and I lean closer to the door so I can hear better. Because I think he's just whispered the word "yes."

"Right before Daniela and I got together, there was one other girl. It was just once. It was stupid, and you can't tell Beckett." He lowers his voice even further as I press myself against the door, palms flattened on either side of my face, my cheek flush against the wood.

I have no idea what his confession has to do with me, but I need to hear it.

"Amira?" my mother guesses, and Penn makes this shocked sound.

*No.*

"How did you know?"

My mother's laugh sounds like the pop of a cork from a champagne bottle. A sudden release of pressure. "Have you forgotten what I do for a living?"

But Penn isn't laughing. "Like I said, it was just once. She was here, trying to be helpful right after Dad died, and Beckett was ignoring her. I offered her a ride home, and she started bawling on the way. She was upset because she thought Beck was freezing her out, and she didn't know how to help.

"I was trying to make her feel better." Penn huffs. "My dad had just died, and I was trying to make *her* feel better. But then, maybe that's what she was trying to do for me too. I honestly have no idea. All I know is that I pulled over behind the Dairy Queen so she could calm down before we got to her house. And I gave her a hug.

"The next thing I know, we're in the back seat of the car."

The car. *My* car. Because Penn hadn't taken over Dad's truck yet.

"It was a mistake. I wasn't thinking straight, and I messed up.

Daniela and I got together about a week later, and things have been weird between Amira and me ever since."

"I bet they have," my mom says. "Were you careful?"

"Kind of?" Penn's voice is closed off again. "Like I said, I wasn't thinking straight. But she would have told me . . . I mean, Amira would have said something, if . . ."

My mother's sigh carries a world of doubt.

My brother slept with my best friend in *my* car.

I'm not sure why that matters. But it does. It matters that I've been driving around for seven months in that car, with no idea that it could be where—

Oh my god. Lullaby Doe could have been conceived in my car.

I back away from my brother's door as quietly as I can. In the living room, I grab my keys and the twenty-dollar bill Mom set out for dinner, and I shout, "I'm going for pizza!" But in the driveway, after I start the engine, I can only stare at the dashboard while my brain pelts thoughts at me like a mental hailstorm.

I pull out my phone and open the calendar, then I count back to my father's death. Thirty-two weeks.

Lullaby Doe was born one week ago, at around thirty weeks' gestation.

Amira could very well have stopped coming over—stopped trying to pull me out of my grief—because of things getting weird with Penn. Or because she was secretly pregnant with my niece.

Numb, I drop my phone in the tray between the seats and shift into reverse to back out of the driveway. And though I make it to the Little Caesars twenty-five minutes later, I have no memory of actually driving to Daley.

---

Mom doesn't go back to work after dinner. She just shoves the leftover pizza into the fridge and puts a load of towels in the washer. Then she helps Landry with her algebra.

I try to catch Penn alone, unsure whether I intend to interrogate him about Amira or apologize—again—for telling Mom about his Titans shirt. But as soon as he's done eating, though he hardly touched his pizza, he changes into running clothes and leaves the house on foot.

When he gets home, just after nine, his eyes are red and his nose is running, and I'm not sure all of that is from the cold. He goes straight into the bathroom to shower, then he locks himself in his room. Mom sees me eyeing his door and tells me to give him some space. So I close myself into my own room and try to focus on my homework.

A few minutes later, the rattle of the sign against Landry's door tells me she's doing the same thing. Which leaves Mom all alone in the kitchen.

Though the truth is that she'd pretty much be alone even if we were all three in there with her.

---

My eyes open in the dark, and at first, I'm not sure why I'm awake. I pick up my phone from the nightstand, and the clock tells me it's 1:18 a.m. I start to roll over and go back to sleep, but then I hear the clink of glass, and I notice that there's weak light shining from under my door.

I get up and pad barefoot into the hall, my feet whispering on the worn-thin carpet, to see that my mother's bedroom door is open across from mine, and her light is on. She's sitting on the floor at the end of the bed with her back to me, still fully dressed, surrounded by cardboard boxes. A nearly empty wine bottle and a nearly full stemmed glass stand on her windowsill, in front of vinyl shades that are missing a couple of slats.

Dad always meant to replace them.

If our house is an inventory of my father's unfinished projects, including his three kids, then my parents' room is a record of everything he ever did right. Everything he left behind. And right now, it's all scattered around my mother. A sea of memories.

Her shoulders shake as she sobs softly. I think she may be drowning.

"Mom?" I whisper.

She twists, startled, and wipes her damp cheeks with both hands, leaving a smear of dust beneath her left eye. "Beckett."

She sits straighter, and I get the distinct impression she wishes she were wearing her badge, because at least then, she'd know how she's supposed to act.

The police department has guidelines for what to do in any situation. But to my knowledge, there's no such manual for parenting.

She sniffles. "Did I wake you?"

"Nah. I had to pee," I lie as I pick my way across the room, stepping over the remnants of my father's life. Piles of clothes. Books. Shoeboxes full of photographs. His acoustic guitar is propped against the wall next to the window, the fretboard worn free of the finish from years of contact with his fingers.

When I was little, he used to play me a song before bed every night. One he'd made up just for me.

"You can't throw out his guitar." I push aside a shoebox of army challenge coins—one from every platoon he was ever in—and pull the guitar into my lap as I sit.

"I'm not throwing anything out, Beck. But I have to do something with all of this." She shrugs, then she reaches for her glass. "Donate it. Store it. I'm open to ideas."

I strum my fingers across the strings of the guitar, wincing when the twang sounds out of tune. I have no idea how to fix that. Or how to play. I always meant to learn.

Dad always meant to teach me.

Mom stares at the guitar as she sips her wine. There's *maybe* enough for one more glass in the bottle, even though she didn't open it until after dinner. But she doesn't seem drunk. She just seems . . . sad.

"He hadn't played in several months."

*When he died.*

We both know that's what she means.

I pick up the box of army coins and run my fingers through them. There are at least a dozen, all of them big, heavy, and shiny.

"Penn will want one of these."

Maybe he'll want all of them.

If he gets into West Point, he'll have one of his own soon. But Dad will never see it.

"I only have half as many." Mom leans toward me to peek into the box. "But we both used to drink for free all the time with these."

"How?"

"When you're out with guys from your platoon, someone

179

inevitably throws one onto the table. Everyone else has to follow suit, and anyone who's forgotten theirs has to pay."

Mom only served one six-year enlistment in the army. During that time, she did two deployments to the desert, married my father, finished college on the GI Bill, and had Penn. She was pregnant with me when she got out.

The pictures blow my mind. Sometimes I forget that I'm basically being raised by superwoman. Penn forgets that too, but my sister never has.

"Landry was upset tonight." I set the box down and pick up a stack of letter-size envelopes wrapped in a big rubber band. It's at least four inches thick.

"I know. But she wouldn't talk about anything but algebra. She's closing me out."

"She's trying to keep you from worrying. Before dinner, I caught her reading a list of my Twitter hate comments."

My mother groans. "Great."

"I told her you have it under control." I snap the rubber band on the envelopes. "You do, don't you?"

"Yes. I promise you, Beckett. I may be a shit mother, but I'm a good cop."

For a second, I can only stare at her. "You're not a shit mother."

My response seems underwhelming, but I don't know what else to say. I'm not prepared to rate my mother's parenting skills while we're surrounded by my dead father's things.

She snorts. Then she takes a long drink from her glass and sets it on the windowsill. "I didn't know Landry was on Twitter. I told her she was too young."

"She doesn't have an account. She was reading the replies to my account on a third-party app."

"I didn't know Penn was sleeping with Daniela, much less—" Her mouth snaps shut hard enough to clack her teeth together.

"Amira?"

She blinks at me. "You knew?"

"Not until tonight." My laugh sounds harsh. "Turns out I'm not such a bad amateur sleuth after all."

My mother suddenly looks bitterly, tragically sad. "Don't become a cop, Beckett. This job will break your heart over and over, until there's nothing left."

But I don't think her job is the only thing that's broken my mother's heart.

"Are you going to ask for a DNA sample from Amira?"

She sighs as she lifts her glass again. "I don't think there's any need for that unless Penn's test comes back positive. Maybe not even then. If we have proof that he's the father, I can't imagine Amira will deny that she's the mother." My mom's shrug feels a little hysterical. "Unless you think there's a *third* girl your brother could have gotten pregnant."

"I don't think he got anyone pregnant. It's not his baby, Mom. We don't even know for sure that it's his shirt, do we? Has he identified it?"

"No, it's still in evidence. But it's ripped in the left armpit, just like he says his was. And it was found in Jake's bag. Which Jake says he left here, right?" She drains her glass. "I mean, that's still all circumstantial. As a cop, I know that. But as a mother . . ." Another shrug, as she sets her empty glass down. "It's hard not to fear the worst."

"What are these, anyway?" I hold up the bundle of letters, hoping to change the subject.

"Oh my god, I haven't seen those in years." My mother grabs the bundle from me and flips through them without taking the rubber band off. "These are the letters your dad and I wrote to each other during his first deployment, after I got out of the army. You were just a baby."

"What was wrong with email?"

She shrugs as she stares at the top envelope. "Our connection was dial-up back then. Super slow. I hardly ever went online. Besides, you can't carry an email around in your pocket and reread it." I laugh, and she rolls her eyes. "Okay, you can now that we all have smartphones. But back then, we had these. Your dad said he always carried my latest one with him."

"You two were literally too cute for words." Though the envelopes in her lap seem to argue otherwise.

While she pulls one of the letters out of its envelope, I pick up a box of pictures and thumb through shots of my father and a bunch of other men in uniform. I recognize some of them. Others, I don't think I've ever met. But in all the pictures, my father is smiling. He looks strong. Healthy. He looks like the father I want to remember.

Behind the pictures from deployments and platoon picnics, I find several shots of my dad with Penn, Landry, and me when we were little. He's in uniform, holding Landry on one hip, while Penn stands on his left and I clutch his right hand. In the background is a parking lot full of folding tables decorated in red, white, and blue, where other men and women in uniform wait in line with their families for food, drinks, and keepsakes like little American flags.

I hold the picture up. "Homecoming?"

My mother squints at it for a second. "Yeah. I think that was his first deployment with the reserve battalion."

She must have been the one taking the picture, because she's not in it.

"This is the newest one in the box."

"Yeah. That's around the time we quit getting them printed." She wraps the rubber band around her stack of letters again. "I always meant to start that up again. Walmart will do it pretty cheaply. But there never seemed to be enough time."

"Can I have this one?" I hold the picture up again.

She nods. "Yeah. I think you should. Remember him like that, Beckett. That's who he really was. That last year . . . he was sick. You know that, right?"

I stand, and she grabs my hand. Her grip is warmer and tighter than I would have expected. She squeezes even tighter. As if she can press the words right into my skin.

"Yeah, Mom. I know."

I want to ask her about the rumors. About who he became when he was sick. When he wasn't himself. But those questions feel blasphemous, with his guitar and his army coins sitting right there. With his clothes all over the place, filling the room with the scent of his cologne and his deodorant, as if he might walk in from the bathroom any moment and pull my mother up into an embrace.

But that isn't going to happen, because thirty weeks ago, on a warm night in May, I woke up in the middle of the night and found my father facedown in a puddle of his own vomit, on the living room floor. There was a fifth of whiskey on the end table with the cap still off and an empty pill bottle wedged between two of the couch cushions.

I tried to shake him awake, and when I realized he wasn't breathing, I started screaming.

Penn cleared his airway and started CPR while Mom called for an ambulance. I held Landry while she sobbed, trying over and over again to turn her so that she couldn't see him, but she's nearly as big as I am. So in the end, I just held her as tight as I could until we heard the sirens. Until red lights began to strobe into our living room through the window in the front door.

Penn thinks he did it on purpose. I *know* he thinks that, even if he's never said it out loud. He thinks Dad got tired of fighting an enemy he couldn't see. An enemy he couldn't shake free of or hide from. He thinks Dad was grasping for peace, the only way he knew how.

But I don't believe that. I *can't* believe it. My father would never have left us on purpose. He would never have left us *like that*, knowing that one of us would find him, if he could possibly help it.

Because no matter how hard I try to remember him in uniform or playing his guitar, I'm never going to be able to forget the way I found him. The way he died.

None of us will.

And he would never have done that to us on purpose.

**CNN**

@CNN · 3h

Students at Clifford High School are raising money for a funeral for little #LullabyDoe. Find out how you can help give the #CliffordBaby a proper burial. cnn.#it/3957e20

 462        3008        20646

# THIRTEEN

Amira finds me at my locker eight minutes before the first bell, and my mouth opens to ask why she never told me that she slept with my brother. To ask if she's Lullaby Doe's mother.

To ask if she's the reason I'm getting death threats.

But after accusing both my brother and my ex of the same thing—after risking irreparable damage to both relationships—I've learned to be more circumspect in the conclusions I draw. In the accusations I throw out.

So I just smile at her as I dig a textbook from my backpack, then I shove the bag, books and all, into my locker. Because they haven't let us carry purses or bags around campus unless they're transparent since the second semester of my freshman year. In case someone brings a gun to school.

"You okay?" she asks as we turn toward first period English.

Today, we only have half the normal number of classes, but they will each last twice as long. Because it's the first day of midterms.

"Yeah. I mean, things are pretty weird at my house right now, but that's basically always the case."

"Did you ask your mom about . . . what we talked about the other day?"

I shake my head. Amira has no way of knowing that something even bigger came up before I could work up the nerve to ask my mother if she's ever abused her position as a police officer to benefit our family.

"You guys!" Sophia Nelson races to a breathless stop on my right, her eyes lit up like they could guide ships to shore. "We crossed fifty thousand."

"Fifty thousand what?" Amira steps to the left, closing in our little circle, and we have officially turned our backs on the rest of the semicrowded main hall, five minutes before the first bell.

I heartily approve of this maneuver.

"Dollars. People have donated *fifty thousand dollars* to Lullaby Doe's funeral fund. And the number keeps going up by the minute." Sophia shows us her phone, and sure enough, that number on the right changes as I watch, jumping up by twenty dollars.

Amira grabs Sophia's phone and starts scrolling through the list of donors. It comes as no surprise to me that I don't recognize a single one of the names. They're strangers. From all over the country. No, from all over the *world*.

"Wow. But you know we can't keep all that extra, right? We said we'd give anything over the funeral costs to a charity to be determined—"

"I know. But I didn't think we'd really get to do that. I didn't think we'd actually get to eight thousand! And now we have so many options!"

Sophia takes her phone back and starts walking, and Amira and I fall in next to her, listening to words spewing from her mouth like water from the crack in a dam.

"We have to hold another Key Club meeting and vote on some charities. And with this much money, I'm thinking we should hire someone to manage it. I mean, if it keeps coming in, this could be way more than a single donation. It could be an endowment."

"What's an endowment?" I ask. And immediately I wish I'd just kept my mouth shut and googled it later, to avoid looking like an idiot.

"It's, like, instead of giving all the money to a single charity, you put the money in the bank and draw interest from it, so you can donate to that charity for a long time without ever touching the principal." Sophia shrugs. "My uncle sets things like that up, at his job."

"How did this happen?" Amira's still staring at Sophia's phone. The number's gone up by another one hundred thirty dollars since we've been watching it. In small donations from people in California. And Georgia. And Wisconsin. And New Mexico. "This is crazy."

"It's the news. CNN ran a feel-good story about our GoFundMe last night, and donations *skyrocketed*."

"Holy crap," I breathe, still watching the numbers change on her screen.

"Yeah. So I'm calling another emergency meeting of the Key Club during tutorial, and it'd be great if you could each come up with a charity or two to suggest. For us to vote on. Oh!"

Sophia stops walking again, and I really hope she's done consuming caffeine for the day.

"Beckett, can you find out how soon we can have the funeral? When they're going to, um . . . release the body?"

"The coroner released his report two days ago, and there's a ninety-six-hour hold, unless a relative comes forward to claim her before that. But I'm not sure when that hold began. Or if it even has. I'll ask my mom."

"Okay. That's four days. Since we have the money now, maybe we should hold a vigil, while we wait for the ninety-six hours to run out."

"Why?" In retrospect, I realize that sounds a little harsh.

"Because people are invested in this!" Sophia looks shocked by my reluctance. "Our town has lost a citizen we didn't even know we had! We're in mourning, and this will bring the community together!"

"This will bring weirdos from all over the place," I tell her.

She scolds me with her disappointment in my community spirit. "It will bring well-meaning people in support of our town."

But that's easy for her to say. None of those "well-meaning people" are currently threatening her online with a "retroactive abortion" or chasing her down the street with a camera.

"You're right," I say, because I'm already the #babykiller and the girl who cursed at an old woman on camera. Standing in the way of a vigil will not improve my standing in the community. "Just tell me how I can help."

Kill 'em with kindness. That's what my dad advised in nearly any situation.

Sophia smiles again and darts ahead of us to spread the word on her way to English.

Twenty minutes into our English midterm, a red light begins to blink on the landline on Mrs. Eagleton's desk. Mrs. Eagleton hurries toward the front of the classroom—she's been wandering around during the test—and picks up the receiver.

"Hello?" She listens for a moment, and her face pales as most of my classmates look up from their test packets. "Okay. Yes, thank you." Then she hangs up.

"Guys, I need you to listen carefully and follow my instructions exactly and immediately."

Suddenly she has everyone's attention. There's something in her voice. A slight tremor, maybe. Or perhaps it's the fact that her desk phone hasn't lit up once since school started in August.

"What's going on?" There's a line pressed into Colin Trent's cheek at an angle from where he fell asleep on his desk, right on top of his test packet. "Is something wrong?"

"School is being dismissed immediately. Leave your testing materials on your desks. Drivers are to go straight out to the parking lot. Everyone else is to head out front, where you'll be loaded onto buses and taken to a safe location."

"What's wrong with *this* location?"

"Should we call our parents? Where can they pick us up?"

"What's going on?"

Mrs. Eagleton holds one hand up for silence. "There's been a bomb threat against the school. These things are almost always just stupid pranks, but we have to proceed as if the threat is real, for obvious reasons. So, again, you'll either be heading straight to the parking lot, where the officers from the Clifford PD are on hand to direct traffic out both the entrance and the exit, or you'll go straight out the front doors of the school. Do not stop at your lockers or the restroom. Do you understand?"

Twenty-eight heads nod. For a moment, this feels like elementary school, which was the last time I remember all of us ever cooperating fully, without complaint.

"On your way out of the classroom, you're to tell me whether or not you're a driver. I'll be turning in both lists of names, so you can be checked off whether you leave from the student lots or on a bus out front. Got it?"

Another series of nods.

"Good. Let's go!"

We all stand and grab our things. Sophia scoots into the line behind Amira, who's behind me, and she leans forward to whisper, as we shuffle quickly toward the door, where Mrs. Eagleton has her class roster clipped to a clipboard.

"Since this is definitely just a prank"—Sophia's wide eyes say she's much less sure of that than she's trying to sound—"and we're basically getting a free day off, want to meet at my house and start planning the vigil?"

"Sure," Amira says. "Otherwise, I'd just be home alone."

"Um . . . let me make sure no one called in a threat at the middle school," I tell them. In which case, I'll probably have to pick up Landry.

"Beckett?" Mrs. Eagleton says as I step to the front of the line.

Beyond her, I can see people hurrying in a surprisingly orderly fashion, either toward the parking lot exit at the back of the main building or toward the three sets of double doors up front, by the office.

"Driver," I say, and she writes a cursive $D$ next to my name.

"Amira?"

"Driver," she says, and I guess that's close enough to the truth; she comes to school with her mother.

"I'll text you both my address," Sophia says. Then she heads quickly toward the exit.

"Let me check in with my mom; then can I ride with you?" Amira asks.

"Yeah. I'll be in the parking lot."

We split at the next hallway, where she heads toward her mother's class in the math and science hall, and I keep going straight, toward the main rear exit into the student lot.

I'm sure the bomb threat is no more credible than the online threats to my life have been. And I'm equally sure that this bomb threat is about me. Or at least that it's coming from some psycho who read about our school, thanks to Lullaby Doe. But even if there's no real danger here, it feels oddly unnerving to be evacuating the school during first period, everyone filing quickly and quietly through the exits.

What if this *is* real?

There are cop cars parked at both the entrance and the exit of the main parking lot, and Doug Chalmers is one of the officers waving cars out onto the street. A third cop stands in the middle of the road, stopping traffic to let all the student cars out onto the street.

Organized chaos. It's actually kind of impressive.

"Hey." Jake falls into step with me, even though he parks in the band and athlete lot. "This is nuts. Think it has something to do with the baby?"

Considering that in my two and a half years at Clifford High, we've never had a bomb threat before? Yeah.

"I think that for the past week, *everything* has had to do with the baby. She's really brought the wackos out of the woodwork. And I'm afraid that's only going to get worse. Sophia wants to hold a vigil."

He follows me down one aisle, then between a rusted Taurus and a ten-year-old Altima. "Do you think that's a good idea?"

"No. But it's not like I can say, 'Wait, let's not rally around this poor dead baby.' I'm the *last* person who can say that."

But the truth is that a vigil won't help Lullaby Doe. The only thing we can still do for her is find out who she is. Give her a headstone with her real name on it.

"That doesn't seem fair." Jake leans against my hood while I unlock my car. "You're still getting threats."

"I know. Landry saw them, and I think it really freaked her out." I unlock my car with the key fob and open the driver's door. "I told her those threats aren't credible. And I'm sure this one isn't either," I say with a glance at the school, where kids are still pouring out the back door.

"I don't think we can really be sure of that anymore."

"Beckett. Jake," my mother calls, and I look up to see her crossing the parking lot toward us, the badge on her hip half-concealed by her blazer. Her focus slides from him to me, and her brows rise in silent question. Because I haven't actually told her that we're kind of sorting things out. "You two need to go home."

"Amira's riding with me to Sophia Nelson's. She wants to plan a vigil for Lullaby Doe," I say, and for the second it takes my mother to shield her thoughts, I can see that she feels the same way I do about the idea of a vigil. "Unless there was a threat at the middle school? Do I need to pick up Landry?"

"Nothing reported against the middle school so far." My mother props her hands on her hips beneath her blazer. "You can go to Sophia's, but send me the address, so I know where to find you. Just in case."

She's never told me to do that before. She must be a lot more worried about this than she's letting on.

"So, what's going on? Is this threat legit?"

"We have to assume it is, until the bomb squad has cleared the building for occupancy."

"What bomb squad?" Jake asks.

"Jackson PD is sending one. Now, I need you two to clear out of here. Penn's already left to check on Daniela. She's still out with the flu."

Jake gives me a quick kiss. "'Bye, Mrs. Bergen," he says, walking backward away from us.

"*Detective* Bergen," I mumble, unable to feel as irritated as I sound, when I can still feel the ghost of his lips against mine.

"Hey, Detective Bergen," Amira says as she comes to a stop in front of my car, with no idea she's just read my mind. "Is it okay if we—"

"Yes, yes, it's fine. Just clear the parking lot, please."

"See you tonight," I say to my mom as I slide behind the wheel. "I'll pick up Landry, unless I hear otherwise."

"Thanks." My mother closes my door, and as I start the car, she waves me toward the exit, where Doug is still directing traffic.

---

Sophia Nelson lives in Briarwood. Naturally. Her mother is Clifford's only divorce attorney, and her father is an orthodontist with an office in Daley.

Small-town police detectives don't make a ton of money. Neither do small-town firefighters. But we were doing pretty well when both my parents had full-time jobs and my dad was a part-time reservist. "Pretty well" in Clifford, Tennessee, means that my parents had a mortgage instead of paying rent. It means that they each drove a vehicle that was less than a decade old.

When my dad deployed with his reserve unit, he collected full-time military pay, and when he got back, he would always do something big for us with that extra money.

Once, that something big was a trip to Disneyland. I wish Landry had been old enough to remember it.

When my dad lost his job at the fire station, our lives changed. Our income was cut nearly in half. And rehab wasn't cheap.

We're doing a lot less "pretty well" now, even with one fewer mouth to feed. But even when we were a two-income household, our idea of "pretty well" looked nothing like Sophia Nelson's.

Her parents aren't home enough to have time to clean, so they use a cleaning service from Daley. Which I know because there are still two ladies in khakis and blue polos vacuuming her living room and scrubbing her guest toilet when Amira and I arrive.

Sophia hands out cold sodas and ushers us up to her room, where she plops down on a fuzzy pink rug and leans back against the padded white footboard of her full-size bed. Then she pulls a shiny laptop from her backpack and starts typing, while Amira and I stare around in awe.

Her bedroom looks like a TV set. Or a picture in a magazine, about how teenage girls' rooms are supposed to look. Maybe her bed is only made up today because the cleaning service made it up. Maybe that's the only reason her windows are free of grime and her rug is spotless.

But somehow, I think her room probably always looks just like this.

In a million years, I would never have figured out, on my own, how to organize a vigil, but Sophia is in her element, and Amira is a quick study. By lunchtime, we've gone through several more sodas and applied for a permit to assemble in the park tomorrow night. We had to have an adult's signature, so her dad agreed to stop by city hall on his way to lunch so he could sign and submit the form she emailed him.

We pile into Sophia's car to pick up burgers—her treat—and by the time we get back with our lunch, her dad has already texted to tell her the permit has been approved.

While we eat, Amira and I use her desktop computer to design posters, while Sophia calls every Walmart within a fifty-mile radius and solicits donations of white candles. All three of them promise us free candles once they hear what we're doing.

Thanks to Amira's graphics skills, the posters look amazing. Classy and respectful. Sophia emails them to a print shop in Daley, then we drive out to get them—the print shop donated them—and while we're out, we grab as many of the candle donations as will fit in her car.

That afternoon, I pick up Landry from the middle school, and she insists on coming with me to Sophia's house to help. When we get there, I discover that our three-woman operation has become a large group effort; Sophia has recruited the rest of the Key Club. And somehow, that reporter from WBBJ in Jackson has come to watch and film our efforts.

"Okay, everybody make sure you tweet the link to the event site!" Sophia calls as she ushers us into her huge kitchen, which has become an assembly line for candle drip protectors made from plain white paper plates. "We only have twenty-six hours until the vigil, so we want to give people as much time as possible to plan to come! Cameron, can you take a group to staple up the posters in town?"

Sophia finds Landry a seat at the end of her long kitchen bar and sets her up with a pair of scissors and a stack of paper plates. My sister digs into her task, sneaking the occasional wide-eyed glance around the room at all the high schoolers, and to my relief, most of them return her shy smile.

Even if they still think I'm the #babykiller, they evidently aren't going to take that out on my little sister. Not while there's a television camera in the room, anyway.

"Hey!" Sophia tugs me aside before I can grab a paper plate and get started. "So, I met this reporter while we were distributing some of the posters downtown, and she said she could help us get the word out if I let her film the prep work for the vigil. And she asked if you were going to be here, so . . ."

I look over her shoulder to see that the reporter currently directing her cameraman to pan around the open kitchen/dining/living area *is* in fact the same one who chased me down the sidewalk two days ago.

"So you told her I would be?"

Sophia shrugs. "Well, I wasn't gonna *lie*. Anyway, she's hoping to get an interview with you. You know, since you're the one who found poor Lullaby Doe."

"I'm not supposed to talk to the press," I tell her, but Sophia is already waving the reporter over.

"Well, you don't have to agree to an interview. But you should at least hear her out. Since she's already agreed to do a story about the vigil."

"Sophia, there will probably be lots of reporters there. She's not doing us a favor. She's doing her *job*."

But by then, the reporter is just feet away.

"Sorry," Sophia tells her. "Beckett is camera shy."

"No problem. And she's right. This is my job." The reporter sticks her hand out for me to shake, and I only take it because her cameraman is still aiming his lens in the other direction. "I'm Audrey Taylor, WBBJ on-scene reporter."

"Yes. We've met."

Fact-Check Rating: Half-true. Really, she just came into the salon and started shouting questions at me last time.

"You aired footage of me cursing at an old woman. Yet you didn't manage to capture what she'd said to deserve it."

In retrospect, that was probably a good thing. The last thing my family needs is to have our name dragged through the mud on television.

"Yes, I'm sorry about that," Audrey says. "Airing that wasn't my call."

"But it was your call to submit the footage?"

"That's WBBJ policy. Producers have the final say on what airs." Yet she does look like she feels a little guilty. "But this is your chance to control the narrative. To put your best foot forward."

"I'm not supposed to be speaking to the press."

I turn to make sure Sophia has heard that too, but she's already snuck off to open a box of cookies and set more cold sodas on the counter.

"But the criminal case is over, right?" Audrey pulls my focus back to her. "No crime, no case. So what's the harm in speaking to me now?"

I gape at her. "I'm getting death threats!" I hiss, lowering my voice to keep from causing a scene. "My school got a bomb threat today! The footage you aired of me hasn't made any of that better, and more publicity will only bring even more psychos out of the woods."

"You're getting death threats?" She pulls her phone from her pocket and begins typing one handed. "When did that—"

"Stop! You can't report that. It's off the record."

"You have to tell a reporter that something is off the record *before* you say it."

I roll my eyes. "I'm underage. My mom's a cop. You don't have permission to interview me. So put your phone away."

Audrey's eyes narrow, and I get the distinct impression that she's finally taking me seriously. "Go on camera, and I won't mention the death threats."

"Most of the threats are being posted in public. Anyone who wants to know about them already knows. And I've already told you I can't talk about the baby. There may not be a criminal case, but they're still trying to ID her, and—"

"You don't have to talk about any of that. Just tell us about the vigil. Give me something to air, other than this background footage. Let the world see your face."

"Why would the world want to see my face?"

"Because you found a dead baby. Your mother's the detective in charge. Until we find out who the baby's family is, *your* family is the story." She shrugs. "If you go on camera, the story about the vigil will get more airtime. The station will post it online."

Sophia waves her arms over her head at me from behind Audrey's back. *Do it!* she mouths. And suddenly I realize everyone's looking at me. Including Landry. Waiting to see whether I'm *truly* willing to help the cause.

Because surely if I were really a #babykiller—even through prenatal neglect—the last thing I'd do is go on television and talk about my victim's candlelight vigil. Right?

"Fine," I say at last. "Five minutes. And I'll only talk about the vigil."

just the two of us, before I went looking for help. Before I
~~~ht this notoriety down upon Clifford like a plague of locusts.
That's why I'm here.

Or maybe I'm drawn to the spectacle just like everyone else.

"It's your interview," Amira insists. And she may actually be
~~~ght. WBBJ licensed it to one of the national networks—or
~~~owever that works—and according to Sophia, several million
~~~people saw me on the news last night.

The very thought makes my chest feel like it's being com-
pressed in some kind of vise.

I didn't watch. I couldn't. Audrey Taylor didn't stick to my
conditions. After I talked about the vigil, she asked me what it
was like to find Lullaby Doe lying there on the locker room floor,
and despite having no intention at all of talking about that on
television, with the camera's red light blinking at me—with the
entire Key Club and my little sister staring at me from behind
the lights aimed at me—I didn't know how to gracefully decline
to answer.

So I told the truth. That it was a shock. And very sad. And
the whole time she was making me remember that, I kept glancing at Amira. I could hardly see her through the bright lights,
but all I could think about was that I might be talking about my
best friend's baby. My brother's baby. I was thinking about how I
didn't really have any right to do that, no matter what Audrey
Taylor asked me.

*Then* she asked if I'd like to address the rumors that I'm actually the baby's mother. At which point I realized there was nothing stopping me from reminding her that I hadn't agreed to talk
about any of that.

# FOURTEEN

"Holy crap," Amira whispers as we step onto the stone

The park is *packed*.

These little white stone paths form the spokes of a whe hub of which is a beautiful gazebo at the center of the park basically the prettiest thing in Clifford. But I can't even see tonight. All I see is an ocean of people milling in the light from several streetlamps, because Sophia and her Key Club army are still handing out the donated candles.

Amira and I had to park behind the yogurt shop four blocks away, because every single lot anywhere near the park is packed. Both sides of the street are lined in cars.

At the intersection a block down, I can see Doug Chalmers's familiar silhouette, dancing with blue light from the strobe on top of his cop car while he directs traffic.

"You did this," Amira whispers.

"No way. I'm not taking the blame for this. This is you and Sophia. The vigil was her idea. You two did most of the work organizing it."

I'm not even sure why I came. My presence does nothing for Lullaby Doe. But unlike all these people, I feel like I actually met her. Like I owe her something, because of that one moment when

According to Amira, they didn't air that part. But evidently what they did show was enough to bring at least a thousand people to the vigil. And there's no way all these people are from Clifford.

Of course, the fact that the Crimson Cryer also tweeted about the vigil—and retweeted my stupid interview—probably didn't hurt the turnout either.

"Hey! There you are!" Sophia Nelson appears out of the crowd, carrying a canvas bag over her shoulder. "Here you go!" She digs into the bag and pulls out a candle for each of us, complete with our homemade paper plate drip shields. "We're not giving out matches, obviously. We're just going to light our own candles, then spread through the crowd and let everyone else light their wicks from ours."

"That seems wise," Amira says over the buzz of dozens of low-pitched conversations.

But I'm hardly listening. I've just realized that not all this light is from the streetlamps. There are journalists here, from several different stations. They have lights of their own, aimed at on-air reporters who're shooting intro pieces with their backs to the crowd.

"Reporters." I *told* Sophia this would happen. But she's mistaken my dread for the triumph this moment has evidently brought her.

"This is because of your interview!" She grabs my hand, her eyes wide, and continues to speak in high-pitched exclamations. Like the yip of a small dog. "Thank you for helping us shine the light on Clifford! You made such a difference!"

Is that what I did?

"Sophia." I squeeze her hand until I see the excitement in her eyes die. Until she's back on earth with me, hopefully able to really hear what I'm saying. "Don't forget that this is for that baby."

She cocks her head to the side, long, straight brown hair shining in the light as it falls over her shoulder. "It isn't, though. Not really. We're doing everything we can for Lullaby Doe with the fundraiser. With the funeral and the headstone. But she's already gone, Beckett. This is for the people of Clifford. To heal our wounds. To bring the community together in the face of an unspeakable tragedy."

I can tell from the way she says it, with that polished conviction, that she's practiced those words. That she's going to say them just like that into a microphone in a few minutes, probably when she introduces Brother Bill, the youth minister from First Baptist, who's agreed to lead everyone in a prayer.

"Is that what you think this community deserves? You think Clifford has earned this big spectacle of a Band-Aid for its 'wounds'?"

Sophia blinks at me, insulted and confused. "Don't you watch the news, Beckett? Don't you know what they're saying about us? Claire Tillman and her mother went on TV and made us sound like a bunch of ignorant rednecks. That reporter said this is our fault. That Lullaby Doe died because we let her down. Because we refused to see the problem or were just too damn lazy to notice. They're *lying* about us on national television. Crucifying us for things we didn't do. That's why I invited the reporter to film us organizing the vigil. Someone has to stand up for Clifford. Someone has to show the world who we really are." She lowers her voice even further as her eyes shine with conviction bordering on fanaticism. "Someone has to *defend our honor!*"

I don't understand why she feels personally victimized by the news coverage. No one's calling her a #babykiller. No one's threatening to shoot or dismember her.

I also don't understand why she seems so convinced that the Clifford community is blameless in all of this. "Sophia . . . can't the truth be somewhere in the middle?"

She frowns. "What does that mean?"

"I mean, isn't it possible that we're not as bad as they're making us out to be on TV, but we're not as good as you think we are either?"

Her cheeks flush as if I just slapped her. "Why would you say that?"

"Because no one cared about Lullaby Doe before she died!" I whisper fiercely, near the end of my patience for her rose-colored delusion. "No one even cared enough to notice that she existed. That there was another pregnant teenager who probably needed help."

"How were we supposed to know, if—"

"*Someone* should have noticed," I insist. "Someone should have seen that a student or a daughter—or a friend—was acting strange. Pulling away."

I glance at Amira, and she's staring at me with wide eyes. Her entire body is tense.

"But no one gave a damn until it was too late, and now there's a dead baby, and you think we should defend this 'community' for not caring enough to notice there was a problem. That we should reward Clifford with good press. That we should heal

205

wounds I *guarantee* you no one but the baby's mother is feeling right now."

"Well . . ." Sophia looks like a spring under too much pressure. Like she's going to break if I make her think about this for one more second. "Well, this is for Lullaby Doe's mother too. She's a part of this community."

"Is she?" I hold Sophia's gaze, because I can't wring her neck. "Do you think she feels like she's a part of this?" I spread my arms to take in the whole circus.

"I really, really hope so," Sophia says. And the truly stupid thing—the truly miraculous thing—is that she actually seems to mean that. "I gotta go make sure the microphones are set up."

She gives her head a shake to fluff out her hair, then she plucks a fresh smile from the endless supply that evidently blooms deep in her soul, nourished by her relentless optimism.

"Find me in about five minutes, and I'll light your candles."

Then she practically runs from me, headfirst into the crowd. Accepting greetings and praise for her work, which probably chase away every unpleasant thought I tried to baptize her with.

"You okay?" Amira whispers.

"Peachy."

"Beckett," my mother calls, and I turn to see her headed toward me with Landry at her side, my sister's eyes wide as she stares at the huge crowd. My mom's wearing her badge; it's all hands on deck tonight for the Clifford PD.

"Hey."

"I want you to take Landry home, and both of you stay there. You can watch the vigil on TV, if you want. It looks like several stations will be covering it live."

"What? Why?"

My sister wanted to come because all her friends were coming, and because she'd helped with the candles. Why would my mother bring her, only to tell me to take her home?

"Chief Stoddard just called. He said internet chatter says there'll be protests tonight, and I'm worried it could get out of hand."

"Who would protest a vigil for a dead baby?" Amira asks.

My mother gives me a look, and suddenly I understand. "That's not what they're protesting," I say. "Don't they need permits?"

"In a public park? Not as long as the demonstrators number fewer than fifty per group and they don't use a sound system."

"I don't understand. What are they protesting?" Landry asks.

My mother sighs. "It appears that a couple of different groups have latched onto Lullaby Doe as a symbol for causes they were already championing."

Amira frowns. "They're using a dead baby to further their own political agendas?"

I shrug. "That's what Sophia Nelson's doing. Only without the political angle."

"No it isn't!" Landry insists. "She's just trying to help. Because she cares."

I exhale slowly. "I agree. But Lan, I think she's also gotten a little caught up in the attention this is bringing her."

Landry frowns, but I can't think of any gentler way to phrase the truth. "I want to stay," she says.

"No. Go—"

"We'll stay on the edge of things," I promise my mother as

the squeal of microphone feedback makes the entire crowd flinch and grumble. Sophia's about to start speaking. "And I promise we'll bug out if this gets weird. We're parked behind the yogurt shop."

My mother hesitates, glancing from Landry to Amira, then to me. "Fine. But I want your word, Beckett. You'll all three leave if this gets bad." I can't help noticing that she's including Amira in her warning.

"I promise."

Hands on her hips, which keeps her blazer open to expose her badge, she gives me an official-looking cop-nod. Then she heads into the crowd to Assess The Situation—another Detective Julie Bergen specialty.

"I'm going to go find a candle," Landry says, and when she starts to push into the crowd, I grab her arm.

"Here. You can have mine."

"You don't want it?"

"Not really."

All the news stations—there are three of them—have set up at the perimeter of the gathering. None of the reporters have noticed me yet. Maybe they won't, with this many people.

I scan what I can see of the crowd, hoping to spot the protesters before they begin chanting, or waving signs, or whatever protesters do. So I can steer us away from them. But if the protesters are here, they're blending seamlessly with everyone else so far. I see no sign of matching hats or shirts. No sign of . . . well, signs.

But I do see my brother.

"There's Penn. Come on."

I tug Landry with me, but she resists until Daniela steps out of the crowd with a lit candle, which she holds wick to wick with my brother's to light it.

"Hey," I say as I stop next to them.

Penn scowls at me, but he can't ignore me in front of our sister or his girlfriend unless he's willing to explain why he's mad at me. And he's definitely not willing to tell Daniela that the police gave him a paternity test.

"Hey!" Daniela looks amazing, as usual, and she's obviously finally recovered from the flu. But instead of the knee-length gray wool coat and black leggings she's actually wearing, all I can see is the tiny red bikini underwear and Santa hat from the selfie Penn showed me. Which, ironically, makes me think of Amira.

But when I turn, I realize Amira's still standing at the edge of the crowd, holding an unlit candle, pretending she doesn't see my brother.

Or me. Not that I can blame her. I don't think she and Penn have said four words to each other in my presence in . . . well, around thirty weeks, give or take. Which was easy for me to miss, because she'd basically quit coming around.

"Hi," I say, returning Daniela's greeting. "Glad you're feeling better."

"Thanks. The flu sucks. Hey, let's get you a candle!"

"No, that's okay. I'm holding one in spirit."

"Yeah, I guess you are." Her smile fades. "I heard that you found her. That must have been so traumatic."

I feel like that statement is going to follow me for the rest of my life. Maybe I should have it printed on some business cards.

"Yeah." I turn to Penn. "Can you watch Landry? Get her out of here if this goes downhill?"

"I don't need to be watched," my sister grumbles.

Penn cocks his head to the side. "Downhill, meaning . . . ?"

"Mom said they're expecting protesters. Looks like a couple of groups are trying to commandeer the Clifford baby as their own personal political symbol."

"How awful!" Daniela flips long, straight black hair over her shoulder. "I don't see any, though. Maybe they changed their—"

"Hello! What an amazing turnout! Thank you all so much for coming out tonight, in spite of the cold!" Sophia Nelson's voice echoes over an unseen speaker, and I look up to discover that I can actually see her. They've erected a podium in front of the gazebo, and she's standing on it with a lit candle in one hand and a microphone in the other.

"What is this, a pep rally?" Penn mumbles.

"Hey, keep an eye on Landry, okay?"

"Why?" He turns to me with a frown. "Where are you going?"

"Nowhere. I just don't want her with me in case any of the reporters"—or protesters—"recognize me."

Penn nods with a glance around at the reporters, who're now all filming Sophia.

"Thanks." I head back to Amira, and Landry doesn't even seem to realize I've gone. She's holding her lit candle, staring, rapt, at Sophia and Brother Bill on the podium.

I'm not supposed to know that Amira slept with my brother, so it would make sense to ask her why she hung back. And I'm tempted, considering she may be the reason I'm getting death threats.

Is that why she's suddenly back in my life? I thought she felt bad for what I've been going through, with the rumors, and the reporters, and the online vitriol. But is this actually just an attempt to ease her conscience? Does she feel guilty because I'm being blamed for what she did? For abandoning her stillborn daughter on the floor of the locker room?

Is that why she's been so involved with the fundraiser and the vigil? So that she'll have a place to visit her secret daughter?

"Hey," I say, while unspoken questions tumble around in my head like shoes clunking in the dryer.

"Hey." Amira's gaze stays locked on Sophia. Her unlit candle hangs at her side, clutched in a white-knuckled fist.

I wonder what she's thinking.

Suddenly she turns to look at Penn, but my brother doesn't notice. He truly doesn't believe the baby was his. Could he be wrong and not know it? If so, don't I have a right to know that, considering how deeply snared I am in this whole thing?

In a moment of bold indignation, I step closer to Amira so she can hear me over the speakers. So that no one else will. "So, why didn't you tell me—"

"When are we going to talk about the real problem?" a voice shouts, echoed by the staticky reverb of a bullhorn. The question bashes through Sophia's hopeful tribute to community spirit, and her voice falters.

"What was that?" she asks, and even from back here—from over the heads of all these people—I can see the dread and disappointment wash over her. She looks like someone just crashed her third-grade sleepover.

"Lullaby Doe is the victim of an epidemic sweeping the world!" that same voice yells, followed by that same staticky echo. "The criminal devaluation of human life! The moral decay of—"

"Shut up, you fanatic nutjob!" another voice shouts before I can spot the woman with the bullhorn. I can't tell who this new voice belongs to either, but as I stare into the crowd—as people turn, looking for the source of the disruption—I notice an orderly pattern of movement within the emerging chaos.

Pink shirts. People wearing short-sleeved pink tees over their normal, season-appropriate long-sleeved shirts are moving quietly through the crowd, converging on a point I haven't identified yet. And they're all carrying signs.

A flurry of movement to my left draws my attention. One of the reporters is frantically directing her cameraman to zoom in on something. She's found the bullhorn. But she's only a few seconds ahead of the rest of us, because suddenly the crowd starts moving. It *splits*, people bouncing off one another in the chaos like bumper cars, trying to figure out where they belong, until finally a group of around twenty men and women wearing pink shirts stand on the left. Holding up signs.

Their signs have drawings of a dead baby. And calls for the #babykiller to be arrested, or otherwise—and ominously—"held responsible."

Across from the pink shirt wearers, facing them down from the other side of the divide that has split the crowd in half, is another group of protesters. They don't have matching shirts, but they do have signs of their own, and I don't recognize a single one of their faces.

None of these protesters are from Clifford.

I catch Penn's eye and toss my head toward the street, telling him to take Landry home. He nods and starts ushering our sister and his girlfriend away from the crowd.

"Go protest a clinic!" the woman in front of the right-hand protesters yells at the people in pink shirts. "This is a memorial. You don't belong here."

"We're here for Lullaby Doe!" a man in a pink shirt shouts. "She didn't have to die. The baby killer should pay!"

"The baby was stillborn!" someone from the other side shouts.

"She didn't have to be!" that same man yells back.

The woman behind him shoves her sign into the air. "Fetal neglect is child abuse!"

"The only thing criminal going on around here is the *criminal* lack of quality sex education classes and the availability of birth control," a woman from the other side returns. "Ignorance is a disease—"

"Moral decay is an epidemic!"

And suddenly everyone's shouting.

My mother appears out of nowhere, with Doug Chalmers and John Trent, the patrol supervisor, at her side. "Okay, everybody, let's just—"

"We have a right to peaceably assemble!" one of the ladies in pink shouts.

"Yes. With emphasis on the word 'peaceably,'" my mother tells her. "So I want to make sure everyone understands—"

"Do your job!" one of the pink-clad men yells. "Arrest the mother for child neglect."

"For manslaughter!" another voice calls. "Where is she? Where's the baby killer? Is she here?"

"Come on." Amira tugs on my arm, pulling me out of the shock that has frozen me in place. "Beckett, *come on*," she whispers. "They're looking for you. It's going to turn into a mob."

I lurch after her, numb. As I stumble away from the crowd, the light from the streetlamps streaks across my vision, and on my left, one of the television cameras swings my way.

"There she is!" someone calls out. Behind me, the gates of hell give way, and the crowd surges forth. I swear, torchlight casts shadows in the shapes of pitchforks on the ground ahead of me.

Amira and I race from the park into the street, and I can't tell if people are actually following us, or if those footsteps are the sound of my demons chasing me. In the end, it doesn't matter.

"Through here!" Amira pulls me into an alley, and we keep running, my shoes pounding the cracked pavement, my lungs burning with every breath.

I'm crying, and I don't even know when that started.

In the parking lot behind the yogurt shop, we stumble to a halt next to my car, bent over to catch our breath. There's no one else here, but I can hear the roar of chaos still echoing from the park.

I hope my mom's okay.

I hope Penn got Landry out before she saw any of that.

"Are you all right?" Amira asks, one hand on my shoulder, and even through a film of my own tears, I recognize the guilt on her face.

"No." I stand up straight and swipe tears from my cheeks. "No, I am *not* okay. Threats from strangers online are one thing, but this has gone *way*, *way* too far."

"I know. That was crazy."

"I can't take any more of this. You *have* to tell me the truth, Amira."

"I . . ." She frowns. "What truth?"

"*All* of it! Did you sleep with my brother? Are you Lullaby Doe's mother? Did I find your baby—my own niece—on the locker room floor?"

"What? *No!*" Amira looks around the parking lot, obviously worried, suddenly, that we aren't really alone.

And that's a valid fear, considering how many strangers with cameras are in town. How many of them have called my phone or chased me down the sidewalk.

"Then why do you suddenly want to be my friend again? Why did you get so involved with the funeral fundraising and planning the vigil? Why did you disappear from my life in the first place?"

"Because—" She bites off whatever she was going to say, and light from the only pole in this parking lot reflects on the tears standing in her eyes. "It's complicated, Beckett."

"How complicated can it possibly be?" I'm shouting now, and this wasn't my plan. I was going to try to get to the truth without driving someone else from my life. But suddenly I *have* to know. "Is this because of you?" I throw one arm out in the direction of the park. Of the potentially violent mob we've just run from. "Are you the reason reporters keep calling my phone? The reason people are demanding my arrest and strangers are threatening to kill me?"

"No! It's not my baby, Beckett!"

"No one believes me when I say that. Why should I believe *you?* The pieces all fit."

A tear rolls down her cheek. "I'm telling you the truth. I've never been pregnant."

"They took Penn's DNA. For a paternity test," I tell her. "We'll know the truth soon, so you might as well just tell me."

"Oh my god, Beck!" She looks pale, even in what little light is shining on us both. "Even if the baby is Penn's, that doesn't make it mine! Why aren't you accusing Daniela?"

"I already tried that. She sent him a selfie two days before the baby was born, and she definitely wasn't pregnant. She also may not have eaten anything in the past . . . ever."

"Well, that doesn't make the baby mine!"

"Lullaby Doe was wrapped in Penn's shirt, Amira."

I tick the points off on my fingers as I shout them at her, beyond fed up with not knowing. With being unable to defend myself. And—I'll just say it—with being unable to deflect the blame.

"The baby was at thirty weeks' gestation, and you slept with my brother approximately thirty weeks ago. After which you basically disappeared from my life. Then, as soon as I found the baby, you came back, like you wanted to help me. And the worse everything got, the guiltier you looked. Like you wanted to apologize for everything that was happening to me. As if it were all your fault.

"And then you got super involved with the fundraiser and planning the vigil. I thought you were being nice at first, but aren't those all exactly the things the baby's mother would do if she wanted to be there for her child, but she couldn't tell anyone about it?"

"Well, probably!" Amira admits. "And I can see why you

might think that. But you're wrong. I thought *you* were the mother!"

I blink at her, surprised for a second. Is that the truth, or is she just trying to shock me away from what I've uncovered? "Why would you think that? Just because everyone else does?"

"No! I *didn't* think that before. Not really. Not until tonight, when you started talking about the community failing Lullaby Doe's mother. About how someone should have noticed that a friend was pregnant. I thought you were talking to me. About what a crappy friend I've been, because I didn't notice you were pregnant." She exhales. "Because I wasn't paying attention. Because I was being selfish."

"I was talking about *me*," I tell her. "*I* was the crappy friend who didn't notice that *you* were pregnant. With Penn's child."

"But that's not true! I've never been pregnant. I've only ever . . . I mean, it was just that one time, with Penn—that one time ever, actually—and it shouldn't have happened. He gave me a ride home, and we were both upset, and I'd always kind of had a crush on him, so . . ." She shrugs. "And afterward, it was *so* awkward. I thought you knew, and you were mad at me. Or, if you didn't know, I didn't know how to tell you. And then the next week he got together with Daniela, and he basically never spoke to me again, and I was so embarrassed. So I just kind of . . ."

"You disappeared."

She nods. "I didn't know how much you knew. Or what to say to you. Or how to be around him. Then you found that poor baby, and all this happened, and I thought . . . I thought maybe everybody was right. Maybe she was yours, and I disappeared from your life right when you needed me most, and this whole thing was my fault, because if you'd been able to tell someone . . ." She shrugs. *"That's* why I feel guilty. Because I abandoned you to deal with all this on your own." Another shrug. "That's what I thought, anyway. I mean, I *did* disappear when you needed me most, even if you weren't pregnant. Right after your dad—"

"Don't. Just . . ." I dig my keys from my pocket and click the fob. "Just get in the car."

As I slide behind the wheel, something occurs to me. "Were you in school last Friday?" If she was in class all day—in front of witnesses—then there's no way she could have been giving birth in the locker room.

Amira groans. "I went home in the middle of first hour. I was having a really bad period."

I blink at her as I start the car. So much for her alibi.

"You don't believe me, do you?" she asks as I pull out of the parking lot through the narrow rear exit. Away from Main Street. Away from the park and the protesters.

"I don't know what to believe anymore."

My father may have been a thief.

My mother may be a dirty cop.

My brother and my best friend may be the parents of a dead baby.

"I just . . . I need to think." And based on the way she stares out her window on the drive to her house, I think she knows what I really mean by that.

This time, I need to disappear from *her* life. At least until I know for sure what's going on.

# FIFTEEN

"Hey. It's two in the morning. What are you still doing up?" My mother drops her keys into the bowl on the coffee table and sinks onto the couch next to me. She looks half-dead.

"Waiting for you. How bad did it get?" I saw part of it on television, but they didn't allow any filming inside the police department.

"Twelve arrests. Four people sent to the hospital, but no one admitted. Just bumps and bruises. One idiot got pepper-sprayed. Chief Stoddard's pretty pleased, considering." She shrugs. "If we'd known about the protesters in enough time, we would have called in assistance from the Daley PD, or from Jackson. As it was, we had to handle it all ourselves. But we managed."

Despite the Clifford PD's solid demonstration of competency, Jake's parents are feeling pretty smug about their decision to keep him as far away from the vigil—from anything concerning Lullaby Doe—as possible. Which I know from his frantic texts, once he saw footage of the protests.

If he weren't on lockdown—for real, this time—he'd have come over hours ago.

Mom glances at the darkened hallway. "Penn and Landry are asleep?"

"Probably not." Today was the last school day of the semester. We get to stay up late and sleep in for two straight weeks.

"Did your sister see any of it?"

"Penn took her home when the protest started. By the time I got here, they were watching recaps on the news. I think she missed the worst of it."

"Good. The last thing she needs is to worry about me getting hurt in the line of duty, after . . ." She shrugs.

After Dad's injury basically ruined all our lives.

"She's fine," I tell my mother. And I hope it's true. I hope at least one member of this family is mostly untouched by all this. "She was FaceTimeing Norah when I checked on her. Talking about the 'riot.' A characterization she clearly got from reading the Crimson Cryer's tweets."

"Well, I guess that could have been worse."

"I don't understand what they wanted. The people in the pink shirts. Why protest a vigil for a stillborn baby? Don't they usually target clinics and—"

"This wasn't about Lullaby Doe," my mother says. "Those people were fanatics who saw an opportunity to twist a tragedy for their own purposes."

"Yeah." I exhale. "Hey, any idea when they're going to release Lullaby Doe's remains? We've raised more than enough money in Key Club to pay for a funeral, so . . ."

"The coroner will release her tomorrow. Just let him know which funeral home to send her to."

There are only five thousand people in Clifford, but we manage to support two funeral homes.

"Thanks. I'll let Sophia know."

Sophia, who messaged me an apology three hours ago,

admitting I was right about a vigil bringing out the crazies. I left her on read, because I'm feeling pretty bitter about being chased from the park by an angry mob, but I'll reply tomorrow.

The funeral is still a good idea, even if the vigil wasn't.

The funeral was *my* idea.

My mother heaves herself off the couch and double-checks the lock on the front door. "I'm gonna crash. I have to go in early to help process all the arrests. Don't stay up too late, okay?"

"I won't."

Fact-Check Rating: Abjectly false.

I will stay up until nearly four a.m. watching footage online and reading the Crimson Cryer's account of the disastrous Lullaby Doe candlelight vigil.

---

The only upside to a bomb threat during midterms is that the school board decided to cancel all the tests. Or, more accurately, to make them optional. They didn't think it was fair to force students to perform under such stressful conditions. Also, I don't think the teachers wanted to grade tests any more than we wanted to take them.

Those who *want* to take midterms for a chance of raising their grades will be allowed to when school's back in session after the holiday. (Of course, that small group includes my brother.) The rest of us just got lucky.

That midterm exemption may be the only stroke of luck I've had in two weeks, and I have to say, it's a hell of a way to kick off the winter break. Violent protests and negative news coverage of Clifford notwithstanding.

Mom has already left for work by the time I get up around

eleven a.m., so I wake Landry by caressing her cheek with a bag of chocolate chips. She blinks up at me, squinting while she waits for my face to come into focus. "What's going on?"

"Mom's at work. Penn's out, probably trying to deadlift single-wides at Dogwood Village to impress the West Point admissions committee. You and I are going to make cookies."

She sits up, a grin splitting her face wide open. "Really?"

"Yes. The butter's already softening. Do you want to invite Norah?"

"No." Landry frowns. "She's kinda being a bitch right now."

"Language."

"Fine. She's kinda being a *pain* right now. And she definitely doesn't deserve cookies."

"Fair enough. Get dressed."

My little sister might be in charge of the actual cooking—and she might force an unnatural number of vegetables upon us in that endeavor—but *I* am the cookie connoisseur of the family. I mean, it's not like I do anything fancy. But I'm incredibly adequate at turning a bunch of flour and sugar into pretty much any drop cookie you can imagine.

"What's the plan?" Landry asks as she pads into the kitchen barefoot half an hour later, in one of my baggy sweaters. I'm wearing her apron, so I decide to call us even on the clothes-borrowing front.

"Chocolate chip and salted caramel." I hold up a canister of large-grain salt and a bag of caramel chips. "We're going to consume our weight in sugar today."

She sits on her knees on one of the bar stools. "Can we skip the baking and just eat the dough?"

"No. Raw eggs. But we can eat the cookies right out of the oven. While they're all melty and gooey."

Landry laughs. "Clearly those are technical culinary terms."

For the next hour and a half, everything feels normal. Penn comes home, sweaty from his run, as we're pulling the second baking sheet out of the oven, and he joins us at the island, eating cookies straight off the pan. Gasping because they're way too hot, as chocolate drips down our chins.

I want to live in this moment forever. I want to scoop us up, kitchen and all, and slap a glass globe over us and store us on the shelf in some museum of perfect moments. Because we deserve this one.

We eat fresh cookies for lunch.

That afternoon, with the taste of chocolate still sweet on my tongue, Sophia Nelson and I head over to Dunley's Funeral Home and do the most depressing thing in the entire world.

We select a casket for a baby.

Landry wanted to come, but I drew the line at letting her help plan the funeral. Instead, Penn took her to pick out a Christmas tree from the lot set up in front of the Walmart in Daley.

Mr. Dunley is very accommodating, and I can't tell whether that's because he knows that the world will be watching Lullaby Doe's funeral, or because Sophia basically tells him that cost is no issue. In a couple of hours, we have the whole thing planned for the afternoon of the twenty-fourth—Christmas Eve—and he assures us that three days is plenty of time to pull the whole thing together.

After the funeral home, we pick out a plot. I don't think the cemetery has ever dealt with teenagers before, but the man who shows us our options is very nice. I'm not sure it matters which plot we pick, but Sophia is worried about which way the sun will glare on the attendees and how far people will have to walk from their cars.

I think that putting so much fuss into a funeral is a bit like spending all your time worrying about your wedding and none thinking about the actual marriage. It's just one day. After the crowd has gone home, with any luck Lullaby's secret relatives will be able to visit her in peace and privacy, and I doubt they'll care about the sun shining in their faces.

*God, please let someone claim her, even if only in private.*

"So, why couldn't Amira come today?" Sophia asks as we head back to our cars after picking out the funeral plot.

I shrug. "I didn't ask her to."

She stops walking and lifts one brow at me. "Why not? Did you guys have a fight?"

I'm not going to tell her about my suspicions, but I feel like Amira's suspicions about me are fair game. "Kinda. She thought I was the baby's mother."

"I'm sorry," Sophia says. "I don't think I realized how hard this must be for you until last night. Until that crowd practically came after you with torches and pitchforks."

"They think I'm lying about not being the mother. But you don't, do you? How are you so sure everyone else is wrong about me?"

I realized last night that Sophia would never have given me a speech about how the town of Clifford needs to heal if she thought she was talking to the mother of a dead baby. Is it because *she's* the baby's mother? Am I just starting to suspect *everyone* now? Have I officially lost my mind?

Sophia shrugs as we start walking again. "I have no reason to think you're lying. And I think people deserve the benefit of the doubt."

Well, that's refreshing.

She brushes her hair over her shoulder, exposing the name brand of her expensive down jacket. "I should have listened to you about the vigil, though. I don't think that helped anyone heal."

"You were just trying to do something nice." Misguided though it was.

"Still, you were right." She clicks the button on her fob to unlock her car door. "The vigil was a bad idea, considering the negative attention this has been getting. But the funeral isn't. The headstone and the grave aren't. Those are for the baby. They're the least we owe her." She opens her door and slides behind the wheel. "For failing to notice."

Sophia gives me a sad smile as she closes her door. Then she starts her car and pulls down the narrow cemetery path and through the gates.

---

Mom's car is in the driveway when I get home, and the front curtains are open. For a second, I sit in my car, looking through the window at all the smiles as my mother, brother, and sister string lights around the tree.

I thought this would be more of a bittersweet holiday, since it's our first Christmas without Dad. But for once, I would be happy to be proven wrong.

I hear the music the second I open the front door. *The Grinch*. Someone's dug out our collection of Christmas DVDs, and the marathon has begun. Usually, Dad would recite the narrator's lines, making faces as he and Penn strung lights around the top of the tree, where none of the rest of us can reach. Then Dad would drop his voice into bullfrog range and sing the Grinch song.

Tonight, Penn is singing, and I'm stunned by how much he sounds like my father. By how he can reach the top of the tree without even going up on his toes.

"Hey!" Landry beams at me, a strand of lights looped over her arm. "Shut the door! It's cold!"

I shove the door closed and nearly trip over the couch in its new position, which made room for the tree in front of the window. "That's a nice one!"

"It was on sale because the branches at the bottom were basically dead, but we just trimmed those off with Dad's hedge trimmers," Landry informs me.

"There's hot cider in the kitchen," my mom says. "Are you hungry?"

"I'll grab a cookie," I tell her. And I can't stop staring. "Why is everyone in such a good mood?"

"It's Christmas!" Landry grabs a Santa hat from the coffee table and props it on her head, so that the point with the little white ball flops over her right ear.

Mom smiles. Then she nods for me to join her in the kitchen. "Penn's test results came back," she whispers as she ladles steaming apple cider into a mug for me from the Crock-Pot where it's being kept warm. "He's not the father."

"Well, that certainly explains *his* good mood." He couldn't possibly have been sure, in the same way a woman would be. "So that means Amira . . . ?"

"If she's the mother, it's a huge coincidence," Mom says. "And it has nothing to do with Penn."

Then I owe her a huge apology.

"What's wrong?" I ask. Because my mother is still smiling, but her eyes aren't crinkling. Or shining.

"Nothing. It's just . . . There's a lot of pressure for us to identify that baby, and we've just hit another dead end."

That's not it. There's more. But she's not going to tell me. Not when tonight is so wonderful. So . . . normal.

Mom makes nachos for dinner, and we eat them on the couch, staring up at the Christmas tree while *Miracle on 34th Street* plays on the television. Penn even smiles at me. Twice.

---

The next day, I take a plate of leftover cookies to Amira's house, but I have to ring three times before she answers the door. Her parents' cars aren't in the driveway, but hers is. Still, I guess she could have gone with one of—

The door opens. "Please stop ringing the bell, Beckett."

"I have cookies." I hold up the plate, but she doesn't even look at it. "And an apology."

Amira leans against the right side of her door frame and crosses her arms, evidently waiting for me to go on.

"I'm sorry I didn't believe you about the baby. I, of all people, should know how shitty it feels not to be believed. The only excuse I can make for myself is that I really need to get to the truth. That feels like the only way I can clear my own name. Since someone smart stopped me from baring my stretch-mark-free belly to the entire school."

Finally, she smiles. "I'm starting to think that was the right impulse after all. Maybe that would have put an end to this a week ago."

"It wouldn't have. You were right; people believe what they want to believe. So until someone comes forward and claims that baby—until someone gives them a story they'd rather believe—I'm stuck with these rumors." And, possibly, the death threats.

Amira steps back to clear the doorway. "Come in. And bring the cookies."

I step inside and close the door, then I follow her into the kitchen. "Would those be good with hot chocolate?" she asks.

"Yes. Thanks." I set the plate on her counter and lean back against one of the cabinets while she makes us each a mug of hot chocolate from little white packets printed with an outline of the Swiss Alps.

"So." She sets a mug in front of me. It's shaped like a cat, with pointed ears sticking up and a tail for a handle. "What made you decide I was telling the truth?"

I asked Sophia that same question yesterday, and she didn't seem to have as much trouble answering it as I am. I take a sip of hot chocolate from between the cat ears to buy time to think.

Amira gives me a look. "I take it you didn't spontaneously come to your senses."

"I think we both know that if there's any way to misinterpret the situation, I'm going to find it."

She snorts into her plain blue mug. "When we were kids, you always took the winding path to any goal, be it the swings or an invitation to a sleepover."

"My dad called it the—"

"—the scenic route. I remember." She takes a long sip. "He told me once that being your friend would never be easy."

I set my mug down and stare at her. "He did? Really?"

"Yeah. When we were around twelve. I had come over to stay the night, and you and I got into a fight. Your mom was upstairs talking to you, and your dad gave me a soda in the kitchen. He said that being your friend would never be easy, because you were always going to trust yourself more than you trusted anyone else. He said you were just like your mother in that way."

It's strange hearing something about my dad that I didn't know. Something I'm willing to believe, anyway. Something that makes me sad in a *good* way.

"I pretended I knew what that meant," Amira says. "But I didn't really. I don't think I truly understood what he was saying until just now."

I pull the plastic wrap from the plate I brought and take a cookie from the pile. "Well, maybe you can explain it to me."

"I think he meant that you're never going to be good with faith. In other people, or in anything else. And he's right. It's not that you don't believe what other people tell you. It's that you can only truly trust things you find out for yourself."

"Great. I *am* just like my mother."

"I don't know her well enough to say that. But your dad was right about you." Amira takes a cookie. "So, what did you find out for yourself that made you believe me?"

"Wow. When you put it like that, I sound like a real jerk."

She shrugs and takes a bite.

"Penn's paternity test came back negative."

Amira frowns. "That doesn't mean it couldn't be my baby. Just that it isn't his."

"I know. But the only reason I thought it might be yours was that you slept with him, and Lullaby Doe was found wrapped in his shirt. So there's nothing left linking you to the baby."

"Well, as long as *you're* satisfied," she says, brushing crumbs from the front of her shirt.

"Like I said. I'm a jerk." And she has every right to stay mad at me.

"At one point or another, we each suspected the other of the same thing. So why don't we call it even and just move on?"

"Yes. Thank you." I break another cookie in half and hand her one of the pieces. "I've missed you this year."

She takes a bite, then she covers her mouth as she speaks around it. "You had Jake."

Hopefully I still have Jake. Hopefully I haven't *quite* screwed that up beyond repair. "Yeah. But that's not the same."

Amira had Sophia and Cabrini, and it may be selfish of me, but I hope that wasn't the same for her either. I hope she missed me.

I take another sip from my mug, and my gaze falls on a family portrait on Amira's living room wall. Her dad looks the part of a middle school principal—which he is—and for the first time, I wonder what he's like here in his home. Away from all the teachers, and students, and parents. I wonder what he's like as a father.

I bet he's . . . normal. I bet he asks her about her homework and knows the names of all her teachers. And that he's always in bed asleep by ten p.m., with a half-read crime novel on his nightstand.

# SIXTEEN

I leave Amira's house so quickly that I forget my plate in my rush to race home and ask my mom what on earth the Crimson Cryer could be talking about.

So far, that anonymous asshole's information has been so accurate, according to my mother, that the police think someone in the department is leaking information. But there's one exception.

Me.

Twice now, the Cryer has either implied or announced that I am Lullaby Doe's mother, and obviously that's been wrong, both times. Yet a few days ago, the Cryer also came to my defense, asking people to leave me alone and reserve judgment.

Why the change of heart? Why the transition from fact-based—if leaked or stolen—information to flat-out lies about me?

I park on the curb in front of the house, because Penn's already claimed the second spot in the driveway, and I stomp across the yard, ready to demand answers from my mother. But when I throw open the door, Landry stumbles to a startled halt in the middle of the living room, on her way to the kitchen.

"Beckett! Come on! We're doing gingerbread!" She holds up the Bluetooth speaker Mom gave her for her thirteenth birthday, which she's evidently just retrieved from her room.

"It's kind of crazy. My dad just . . . doesn't make any sense."

"Okay. I'll bite." Amira holds up her cookie and grins over her stupid pun. But her smile fades with one look at my face.

"He . . . I just can't understand how the man who wrote bedtime songs for me and flew Landry around like an airplane when she was a toddler could be the same man who popped pain pills like they should have come out of a gumball machine. How can the soldier who served several tours in Afghanistan and put out fires for a living be the same man who practically melted into the couch there at the end? Who never wanted to leave the house?"

Those pieces of the puzzle that was my father don't seem to have come from the same box. It's like the factory mixed up two puzzles and gave us a few pieces of someone else's dad. And someone else got the missing pieces of *my* dad.

And that has to be it, because *we* certainly didn't get those last few pieces.

"Nobody's only one thing, Beckett."

"I know. But how can one person have been so many *different* things? So many different people?"

"Addiction is an illness." Amira looks distinctly uncomfortable with the platitude. As if she doesn't know what else to say. How to help me understand.

"Everyone says that, but what other illnesses do people *choose* to have?"

She sets her mug down and watches me. She's sitting very still. "You think he *chose* to get hooked on pain pills?"

"No. But I think that at some point, he made a decision, right? Isn't that what really happened? At some point he *must* have consciously decided that he liked being high better than he liked being with us. Or being alive. Every pill he swallowed was a choice. Every drink he took—same thing."

"I don't think it's ever that simple. I don't think addicts see it as an either/or kind of situation. I don't think he chose to die, Beckett. I can't imagine him wanting to leave you guys."

"Penn thinks he did."

She's quiet for a moment, and I understand that I shouldn't have said his name. *Finally*, I realize that she's not over my brother. Even though they've hardly spoken in seven months.

"I know," she says at last. "He said that, in his car that day."

In *my* car. The day my brother and my best friend had sex in *my* car.

*Not the point, Beckett.*

"But I don't think it's true," she adds.

"Why would it be? I mean, he had a family! A good one! Mom loved him, and their marriage was good, until the Oxy. Landry— She *worshipped* him. Penn's killing himself right now, trying to turn himself into our dad. To be a better version of him. And I'm not sure whether to applaud him or slap him silly for that. For wanting to be like the man who abandoned us. Or for believing that he can do a better job of it.

"He was in the newspaper once, did you know? The *Dallas Morning News*. My dad's unit was sent out to Texas, for hurricane relief, and a reporter snapped a picture of him saving a dog from floodwater. My mom still has, like, ten copies of—"

Amira's phone beeps, and before she can pick it up, I see that it's an alert. My hand clenches around what's left of my cookie.

The Crimson Cryer has tweeted again.

**CRIMSON CRYER**
@crimsoncryer · 2h

Finally @CliffordTNpd has evidence that @BeckettBergen TRULY IS #LullabyDoe's mother.

#JusticeForLullaby

 1058    2477    3057

*Doing* gingerbread?

I close the front door and follow my sister into the kitchen, where my mother and brother are gathered around our small island, huddled over something. Landry sets the speaker on the counter and plugs it in, because the stupid thing has never been able to hold a charge. She taps something on her phone, and Christmas music starts playing over the speaker.

"Hey!" My mother stands with a tube of icing in one hand and a big, square cookie in the other, and suddenly I understand.

They're making a gingerbread house.

Or rather, they're putting together a premade gingerbread house, from a kit.

"They were on clearance!" Landry announces as she steals a piece of candy-coated chocolate—a generic M&M—from a bowl on the end of the island. "Even though it's still three days until Christmas!"

"Wrapping paper and lights were on sale too," Penn says around a chunk of something sticky. There's an empty candy wrapper on the counter next to him.

"When I was a kid, my parents always bought clearance wrapping paper and lights the week after Christmas," my mom says. "But now the stores put everything on clearance a week before the actual holiday, assuming everyone's already done decorating for the year. *Boy*, have they underestimated the Bergen family's willingness to procrastinate!"

"Hey, can you hold this?" Penn nods at the gingerbread wall he's propped into place. "So I can glue it?"

I hold the wall—another big, square cookie—while he squirts thick white frosting on one edge, then I place it where he shows me, pressing the frosted edge against another big cookie to form the corner of this super-basic gingerbread house.

We used to do this for real. Mom and I used to make home-made gingerbread dough, while Dad and Penn sketched out a design for the house. Then we'd roll out the dough and measure and cut the pieces, while Landry danced around in Christmas pajamas and a Santa hat, because she was too little to help, until we got to the part where she could glue on pieces of candy.

She used to eat as much as she put on the house.

We haven't done that in three years now. Dad was deployed three Christmases ago, and it didn't feel right to make a ginger-bread house without him. The Christmas after that, he was in rehab. And last Christmas, he was "sick."

But now . . .

It's not the same. The picture on the box is of a very simple square house, decorated with the very basic collection of candy that came with the kit. But Landry's smiling as she helps Mom glue on a section of roof. Penn's biting his lip while he uses a can of green beans to support the piece I just helped him glue on, while the frosting hardens.

It's not the same. But it's close enough that I can't ruin this by asking Mom about that tweet. So I grab a slab of gingerbread and join in.

Penn remembers how to make icicles hang from the edge of the roof by squirting a small glob of frosting, then pulling the tip straight down, to stretch the glob into the shape of a tiny little ice spear. He makes a million of them, all the way around the roof.

Mom squirts frosting on Landry's nose and tries to make a

piece of candy stick to it. She fails repeatedly, but she laughs over every effort. She's relentlessly cheerful tonight. Maybe she's making up for lost time, or for time she plans to lose in the near future. Maybe she has to go in early tomorrow, so she's capitalizing on this night at home.

I wish I could trust her cheer.

At some point, Landry remembers her Santa hat, and while she's in her room, digging around for it, a beep from her phone interrupts a beautiful rendition of "White Christmas" playing over the Bluetooth speaker.

I grab her phone in time to see an alert for the Crimson Cryer's tweet, from the app I caught her scrolling through the other day.

"Delete that," my mother whispers, staring over my shoulder, and I jump. I had no idea she was there.

I swipe left to delete the notification before it disappears from Landry's lock screen, and the music starts playing again. Mom's smile is gone, until the moment my sister walks back into the room in her Santa hat. Then her merriment blooms anew, brighter than ever. And finally I understand her tenacious cheer.

She's already seen the tweet. Maybe Penn has too. They're shielding Landry, as much as they can. Trying to give her a good holiday in the middle of the shit storm hounding our family like the cloud of dust that follows that kid from the *Charlie Brown Christmas* movie.

Maybe they're onto something. Maybe my questions can wait.

An hour and a half later, we stand back to look at our creation. I have to admit that for a store-bought kit, it's pretty cute.

Landry tiled the roof with sections from a box of stale wafer cookies, and Mom sprinkled powdered sugar over the whole thing, to look like a light dusting of snow.

"I've had enough sugar for an entire lifetime," Penn announces as he swipes empty candy wrappers from the island into the trash can.

"For a week at least," Landry agrees. "I wish Dad could see this. I think he'd like it."

Penn snorts. "He'd tell us that our joints aren't at ninety-degree angles and our door is off-center."

"And he'd be right," Mom says. "But he'd still like it. Flaws and all."

Fact-Check Rating: One hundred percent true. Because no one understood more about flaws than my dad.

———————————

"Beckett." Someone grabs my shoulder and shakes me. "Beck, honey, wake up."

I blink into the dark and see my mother's silhouette leaning over me. "I'm awake." Almost.

"I need to talk to you," she whispers. My bedside lamp clicks, and light floods my room. "I'm sorry it's so late."

"S'okay. What's wrong?" I blink sleep from my eyes.

"Shhh . . ." She nods toward the hallway. "In the kitchen."

My mother is no longer smiling.

I've only been asleep for two hours, because I watched *It's A Wonderful Life* over FaceTime with Jake until nearly midnight. But I throw back the covers and shiver as I step into my fuzzy green Grinch slippers—a gift from my dad last Christmas. At least, his name was on the tag, but I'm not sure how much shopping he did himself.

"What's going on, Mom?" I ask again as I follow her into the kitchen. Her eyes are red from crying, and I can smell wine on her breath, but she's not drunk. Her gaze is very, very focused. If teary.

"Do you want some cider? I can stick a mug in the microwave."

I shrug as I settle onto one of the bar stools. "I kind of feel like that's the least you owe me, after waking me up at two in the morning."

"I'm sorry." She pulls a plastic carton of apple cider from the fridge and half fills a mug, then she sticks it into the microwave and sets the timer for thirty seconds. And for that entire thirty seconds, I wait for her to say something.

Twice, she starts to. But then she closes her mouth again and bites at that hangnail on her thumb. Both times.

I eat a white-chocolate-covered pretzel that's fallen from its position as part of the fence around our gingerbread house.

When the microwave beeps, we both jump. My mother opens the door and pulls out the mug, then she grabs a shaker of cinnamon from the spice rack and sprinkles a little on top of my cider.

"What's going on?" I ask again as she sets the mug in front of me.

She settles onto the stool at the other end of the island, leaving the one between us empty. "Beckett, I have to ask you a question again, and I really need you to tell me the truth this time." She takes a deep breath, and dread churns in my stomach. "Is Lullaby Doe your baby?"

"*What?*"

"Please just answer the question."

"I've already answered that question a million times. No, she's not mine. I've never been pregnant. Why are you asking me this again, at two in the morning?"

"I . . ." She shrugs. But my mother *never* shrugs. She's always certain, if not of the answer, then at least of the question. Of the fact that she should be asking it. "Some new evidence has come to light, and—"

"What evidence?" This doesn't feel right. Cops ask questions about evidence, but Mom's not wearing her badge. Not even psychologically. She's been drinking. And crying. And it's two o'clock in the morning. "Is this about that tweet? Because it's a lie. I never—"

Wait. Mom was upset before tonight. "Last night, when we were decorating the tree, I could tell something was wrong." She should have been as relieved as Penn was about his test results. But she wasn't. "You said it was just the pressure to identify Lullaby Doe, but that wasn't it, was it?"

"No. I'm sorry, Beckett. I wasn't ready to tell you yet. Hell, I wasn't ready to process it for myself yet."

"But now you've processed it?" Whatever *it* is?

"Not really. But with all three of you out of school for the next two weeks, this is the only chance I really have to catch you alone, when I'm not working."

And she's definitely not working. This is not the bearing, or the phrasing, or the approach of a cop. "What's the evidence, Mom?"

"Beckett, did you have a baby?"

240

"No! I've already told you! That baby is not mine."

"Lower your voice, please. I need you . . ." She inhales deeply, then she exhales slowly. "I need you to have an exam."

I push my cider back, untouched. "What kind of exam?" But I think I already know, and the answer makes me feel sick.

"I need to take you to see my gynecologist."

For several seconds, I can't think of what to say. I can't even form clear thoughts. "I can't— I can't *believe* you! You want a doctor to tell you I've never had a baby?" I shove my stool away from the island and storm into the living room. I'm halfway to the hall when she catches up to me and grabs my arm.

"Beckett, come back and hear me out."

"Let go!"

"Shhh," she hisses. "*Please* come back and hear me out, and if you still don't want the exam after that . . . that's fine."

I go with her not because I have any real interest in hearing her out, but because I'm almost as curious as I am pissed off. What kind of evidence could make her think it's my baby, just as she finds out it isn't Penn's?

And how did the Crimson Cryer get ahold of that intel before I did?

"Tell me everything," I say as I sink back onto the bar stool and pick up a mug that has grown cold. "*All* of it. Right now. Or I'm going back to bed."

"Okay. You have a right to know anyway. I was just waiting for the right time to tell you. In private. Because I didn't want to upset Penn and Landry."

She looks like she wants to be holding a wineglass. Instead, she grabs a glass from the top rack of the dishwasher and fills it with water from the tap. Her hands are shaking as she sits on the last bar stool again.

"So, I told you that Penn's paternity test was negative, but the truth is that it's not quite that simple. Paternity tests don't just say 'yes' or 'no.' They give a percentage of DNA shared by the child and the potential father, along with the likelihood that the man tested is the father of the child in question."

"Okay. And Penn's test said he can't be the father, right?"

"Yes. He doesn't share enough DNA with Lullaby Doe to be her father."

"Enough? He doesn't share *enough* DNA? So he shares *some*?"

"Around twenty-five percent." My mother takes a long sip from her glass, and I'm surprised she can get any water into her mouth, with how hard her hand is still shaking.

"What does that mean? The baby is, like, a cousin?" But we don't have any other relatives in Clifford, other than my paternal grandmother.

"According to the lab tech who sent me the results, it means that Lullaby Doe is almost certainly either Penn's niece—or his half sister."

"Oh my god." I gulp my cooling cider, to give myself time to think. "And I'm guessing *you're* not her mother . . ."

"No." My mom's voice breaks on that one syllable.

"I'm not either. Which means Dad—" I pull my phone from the pocket of my pajama pants and open the calendar.

"What are you doing?"

"Counting back thirty weeks from last Friday."

"I've already done that at least fifty times," my mother says. "The math never changes."

"But he died thirty-two weeks ago, and you said Lullaby Doe was at thirty weeks' gestation when she was born a week ago. She's a week too young. She can't be his baby."

"Thirty weeks was just an estimate, Beckett. That baby could have been conceived within a couple of weeks of your father's death, in either direction, and still be within the margin of error of her gestational development."

Those are just a bunch of fancy words—of doctor-speak—for "Lullaby Doe could be your sister, Beckett." She could be *my father's illegitimate child.*

"Oh my god. Oh my *god!*"

"Shhh."

"Is that why . . . Mom, do you think he knew? Do you think he did it on purpose? Did he kill himself because he knew about the baby?" The seat beneath me suddenly feels unsteady, as if it could fall out from under me at any moment. Or maybe that's the whole world.

My *whole world* is crumbling.

"I don't think so, hon."

But I can't get that thought out of my head. What if Penn was right? What if my dad's death wasn't an accident? What if he knew what this baby would do to my mother—to *all* of us—and he took the only way out that he could think of?

"No, Beckett." My mom scoots onto the bar stool next to mine and grabs my hand. Because evidently she can read my mind now. "Even if the baby is his"—and I can see how much it costs her just to say those words aloud—"the pregnancy wouldn't have been far enough along for him to know about it. For anyone to know about it. Even the mother."

The mother.

If Lullaby Doe is my dad's baby, who's the mother?

"Oh my god." I'm repeating myself, but I can't help it. "Mom, who is she? Does she go to my—"

"No!" my mother snaps, and her grip on my hand starts to hurt. The look in her eyes is fierce, in spite of the red ringing them. The veins standing out among the whites of her eyes like bloody little tree branches. "I can't— Don't say whatever you were going to say. We don't know that yet, and I can't think about . . ."

—*school.*

I think the word anyway. Because how can I not?

Why would my dead father's dead baby be born in my school, unless the mother went to school there too?

"Maybe it's a teacher." I give my mother this hypothetical gift because it's so damn close to Christmas. Because neither of us can stand to think that my father might have cheated on my mother at all, much less with a *teenager.* "Mom, Lullaby Doe's mother could be a teacher."

She blinks at me, and relief floods her face. That clearly hadn't occurred to her, and in this moment, I understand how much like my mother I truly am. We both need answers at any cost, and the worst possible scenario is guaranteed to burrow its way into each of our brains, as if an earworm were an *actual* thing that could get into your gray matter and chew and chew and chew, until there's nothing left to think but *this one thought.*

*My father might have been a pedophile.*

"It has to be a teacher," I tell her. "I know you thought Lullaby Doe's mother must have been a student, because an adult wouldn't have had any reason to hide the pregnancy, but *this* could be the reason. An affair."

An affair with a married man.

An affair with a married man who has three children and an addiction to alcohol and pain pills.

The more I think about it, the worse it all sounds.

"Yeah. It could be a teacher." She lets go of my hand, and slowly the feeling starts to return to my fingers.

And the truth is that even if it is a student, he could have slept with a seventeen- or eighteen-year-old. That feels like a horrible thing to be relieved about, but I'm grasping at straws here, and eighteen-year-olds are technically adults. And seventeen-year-olds are old enough to legally consent. So I will hold on to this straw until it falls apart in my hand, because the alternative would be to *lose my mind.*

"Beckett, I still, um . . . I still need you to have that exam. *Please.*"

"What? Why? It's not my baby, Mom."

"I just . . . I need to exhaust all the other possibilities before I can let myself go down this path, mentally. *Please*, Beckett. Dr. Baker said she can see you at seven tomorrow morning. Seven *this* morning, I guess," my mother corrects herself with a glance at the clock on the microwave.

"She's open that early?"

"No, this is more of a favor. You need to go anyway. You're sixteen, and that's about when a girl should have her first gyne-cological exam, so we can just call it that. Our insurance will even cover it."

So, she wants to get me up at the crack of dawn to go for my very first, perfectly normal gyno checkup, on the Monday before Christmas. Before the doctor's office even truly opens.

It's ridiculous. It's insulting. But I can't say no, because as much as this is obviously going to suck for me, my mother needs this proof, just like I needed proof that the baby wasn't Amira's.

"Okay, but why can't you just run a DNA test on me, like you did with Penn?"

"Because we're no longer looking for the next of kin. The coroner has released the body for burial. The Clifford PD's part in this has ended. And if that weren't true, the results of your DNA test would become part of the official evidence, and I'm not sure I want that, no matter what the outcome is."

I don't want that either. Not that it matters anymore. This is no longer a police matter. It's personal now. "Fine. I'll go."

My mother's sob of relief echoes in my head on my walk back through the living room and into the hall. It follows me all the way into my room and under the covers.

But I already know, as I turn out my lamp, even though there's zero chance of me getting any more sleep tonight, that this isn't going to end like it did when I suspected Amira of being the mother. There won't be cookies and hot chocolate, and relief that also feels a little bit like resentment. Like a lack of trust.

Because proving to my mom that Lullaby Doe wasn't my baby won't solve my mother's problems. It will just expose another secret that could tear this family apart.

# SEVENTEEN

The table is cold. The instruments are even colder.

My mom agreed to wait in the lobby, but even without her here, this is the most humiliating moment of my life.

"Almost done," Dr. Baker says. "You might feel a little bit of a pinch."

I lay my forearm over my eyes and hum the theme song from *How the Grinch Stole Christmas*, until finally the doctor pushes her stool back.

"You can get dressed now. There are some tissues on the counter if you need them. When you're ready, just open the door."

I don't thank her. I'm not trying to be rude. I'm just not feeling very thankful.

I use the tissues, then I pull on my clothes and leave the hospital-style gown on the bed. Right at the end, between the stirrups. Then I open the door and sit in one of the two chairs against the wall.

My mother follows Dr. Baker into the exam room and closes the door, even though there's no one else in the office yet. Not even a nurse or a receptionist.

"Beckett, do I have your permission to share your medical information with your mother?"

I shrug. "That's what we're here for." And I'm a little

surprised that she asked. I'm not sure whether she's being polite or she's legally obligated.

"Well, everything looks fine," Dr. Baker says as she sinks onto her rolling stool. My mother just stands there in the middle of the room, looking like she's about to be shot. "Normally, we would have the results of the pap smear in a couple of days, but with the holiday coming up, it may be a week. But I don't anticipate any problems there." The doctor sets my chart down and looks up at my mother. "Beckett has not recently given birth, and I see no sign that she's ever been pregnant. However, considering that she *is* sexually active—"

I hold my head high.

"—I'm going to recommend that we start her on—"

"Yes. Call in a prescription. I'll pick it up this afternoon."

Evidently I'm going on birth control. I didn't ask for that, but I'm not going to turn it down either.

This is the strangest moment of my life.

---

"Mom," I say as we head toward her car. A truck is pulling into the lot, with a woman behind the wheel. Dr. Baker's office opens in half an hour, though she'll be closed starting tomorrow for Christmas.

"Please, Beckett. I'm tired and I need coffee." She tugs her blazer closed against the cold wind and crosses her arms over it. "Can we talk about this later?"

"Yeah." But we won't. I already know we won't, because there's nothing left to say. She'll bring home the pills, and I'll start taking them, and I may or may not sleep with Jake again.

But none of that will change the fact that I'm not Lullaby

248

Doe's mother. And I don't quite know how to feel about the realization that my mom is really, really upset about that.

———————

Mom drops me off in the driveway with a whispered apology, then she heads straight to work, and for a couple of minutes, I just stand there on the porch, shivering. I want to call her back. To convince her to talk to me. I have the completely irrational urge to apologize for not getting pregnant in high school.

I head inside to go back to bed, but the aroma of coffee draws me into the kitchen instead, where I find Penn on the center bar stool, hunched over the old, second-gen iPad we all share. He's holding a steaming mug and his earbuds are in, so at first I think he's watching a movie. But when I get close enough to see over his shoulder, I realize he's staring at his West Point application.

"Hey," I say, and he jumps, so badly startled that he sloshes coffee onto the screen.

"Damn it, Beckett!"

"Shh . . ." I lurch for the roll of paper towels next to the microwave and toss them to him. "I need to talk to you before Landry wakes up."

"I already got her a new cookbook. A nice, hardback one." He rips a paper towel from the roll and blots at the screen with it. "If you want in on that, your half is eleven dollars."

"No, it's—" I shrug. "Okay, sure. Thanks." I've been so distracted by the disaster my life has become, of late, that I've hardly even thought about Christmas shopping. "But that's not what I wanted to talk about."

"Well, whatever it is, can it wait? The deadline on this application is—"

"No." I pull a mug down from the cabinet over the micro-wave and half fill it with coffee. "It can't wait, Penn."

He frowns at me. "Why are you up so early? And already dressed? And why are you drinking coffee?"

I've always loved the scent, but hated the taste, a fact I try to fix by dumping powdered creamer into my mug until my coffee is the color of melted vanilla ice cream.

"I didn't get any sleep." I take a sip and grimace at the taste. Still bitter. "And Mom dragged me to the gynecologist at seven this morning."

"Okay, I don't need to know that."

"Yes, you do." I grab the sugar bowl and scoop several spoon-fuls into my coffee. "Because now that Mom knows for sure that I'm not Lullaby Doe's mother . . . she's pretty sure Dad is—was—her father. The baby's, I mean."

I shake my head and try my coffee again. Not bad.

"Sorry. I'm too tired to make much sense. Did you follow any of that?"

"Not a word." Penn pushes the iPad back and snags a chocolate-covered pretzel from the gingerbread house fence. "In your sleep-deprived delirium, you almost made it sound like Dad was Lullaby Doe's father."

I take my mug and sit next to him. "That's how it's starting to look."

Penn blinks at me. "What the hell are you talking about?"

I take another sip, and this stuff really isn't too bad now. Maybe a half-and-half mix with hot chocolate . . ."Did you ever hear anything bad about Dad? Like, at school?"

He sets his own mug down and swivels on his stool to face

me. There's a weary kind of dread playing over his features. "Beckett, none of that matters anymore. Can't we just let him rest in peace? Can't we just remember him the way he was before?"

"That's not . . . I'm not talking about the pills, Penn. I'm talking about an affair."

The word tastes bitter. It sounds ridiculous. Yet this is where we are now.

"Did you ever hear anything like that? Right before he died, maybe?"

"No. No, Beckett, there was never anything like that, that I know of. There's no way he's that baby's father."

"How do you know?"

"With all the crap people were saying about him by the end, I definitely would have heard something about an affair. About a *baby*."

"Maybe not, if it was too new. He would have died before the pregnancy was far enough along for anyone to know about it."

"Then why are you asking what I heard?"

Good point. I shrug. "I thought that if he cheated, this might not have been the first time."

"No, I never heard anything like that." Penn drains his mug, then he gets up to pour himself another cup of coffee.

"What *did* you hear?"

"Beck—"

"Please. Tell me what you know, and I'll tell you why Mom thinks Lullaby Doe was our sister."

Penn groans. Then he scoops sugar into his mug and returns to his bar stool. "Fine. But I'm only dragging our father through the mud posthumously under duress."

"Noted."

"Okay. Beckett, Dad had issues."

I huff. "I am aware. Because of Afghanistan, that last time."

Penn nods. "I mean, a seed can't grow where the soil isn't fertile, so I doubt that was the *very* start of it, but as far as I know, Dad really had his shit together until then. But after that last deployment . . . I mean, he saw three of his friends die. He nearly died himself."

"You don't have to defend him, Penn. I know what he went through."

"But you're mad at him. He's been dead for seven months, and you're *still* mad at him. And that has nothing to do with Lullaby Doe."

I have to think about that for a second. It never occurred to me that you could be mad at someone who isn't even alive anymore. I mean, it's not like he just ran to the store, and I can yell at him when he gets back.

He's not coming back. Ever.

But I think Penn's right. I think I *am* mad at my dad. I think I'm *pissed* at him, and that I've been pissed at him for a long time. And I think I'm pissed that I never got a chance to *tell* him I'm pissed, because he died, and you can't yell at someone who's dead. You can't say bad things to or about someone who's dead. You can't be mad at someone who's dead.

Yet that's exactly what I am.

"Okay. You might be right." I take another sip from my mug. "But I'm not mad at him for having problems. Or for taking Oxy in the first place. I *know* he was in a lot of pain."

"Not all of it physical."

"Yes! That's it, exactly. And he *knew* that pills and alcohol can't make that kind of pain go away. But he took them anyway. What I'm mad about is the fact that we weren't enough to make him stop."

"What do you mean?"

"I mean . . . how could he see us every day? How could he see Mom and Landry *every day*, and decide to keep taking pills? To keep buying whiskey? How could we not be enough to make him *try harder*?"

"I don't have that answer, Beck. I'm sorry."

"Don't be. Just tell me about the rumors. Please."

"Most of what I heard was about the pills. Our third baseman's dad is a doctor. He said Dad went to several doctors at the same time, including his father, to get multiple prescriptions. Evidently there's some kind of database that doctors can use to check for stuff like that, if the patient is suspicious."

My father was suspicious. Great.

"I also heard that he stole drugs from the hospital. But the worst of it was people saying he was arrested, a couple of months before he died, for forging a prescription. Arrests are public record. It was in the paper, Beck. In print and online. I checked."

So, Dad was in the paper for saving dogs during a hurricane *and* for forging a prescription. Maybe my father was one of those jigsaw puzzles that has a different picture on each side. Maybe that's how he could be both a soldier and a criminal, at once. A father and an addict.

"I heard he stole a prescription pad from one of the doctors at the hospital."

Penn shrugs. "I heard he tried it with an online pharmacy. Either way, I know he was never prosecuted."

"Why?"

"No idea. But I don't think it had anything to do with Mom, no matter what you heard."

I wish I could believe that. But I *know* how much she loved him. I'm not sure there was anything she wouldn't have done for him, or for any of us.

"Is that it? Is that all you heard?"

Another shrug. "Yeah. I mean, those are the only ones I thought might actually be true, other than the *actual* true ones. That he went into rehab. That he lost his job at the firehouse. Once I heard that he'd been dishonorably discharged, which is *not* true. And there was one asshole who claimed that Dad killed those three men who were in the jeep with him in Afghanistan."

"What is *wrong* with people?"

"I don't know. Obviously that was a flat-out lie. So why shouldn't I believe that some rumor about Dad being Lullaby Doe's father is just another lie?"

"Because this isn't just some rumor we heard at school. Mom didn't tell you the whole truth about your paternity test. It does say you're not the father, but it also says that you share around twenty-five percent of your genes with Lullaby Doe. Mom says that means she's related to you. Probably either your niece or your half sister."

"Wait, seriously? Shit." Penn pushes his bar stool back, his coffee forgotten. "That's why she took you to the doctor. Because if the baby isn't yours . . ."

"She has to be Dad's." I give him a second to process that. "I don't think Mom's ready to deal with that." Not that I can blame her. "But your test results are an official part of the police's attempt to ID Lullaby, so I don't think this is going to stay quiet for very long."

"Shit. That's what the Crimson Cryer was talking about. Somehow, that asshole got ahold of my test results and thinks that means you must be the mother."

"I guess so." Honestly, I'd forgotten about that tweet after my mom's bombshell.

"I can't believe he would cheat on her. I *can't*."

I shrug. "Things were tense there at the end."

"Because he was *using*, not because he was cheating."

"We don't know that, Penn."

"Well, if he was, Mom didn't know about it."

"Or she didn't want to admit she knew about it. Even to herself." My coffee has grown cold, but I drink it anyway.

Penn frowns, and I can practically see his train of thought derailing, as his hand clenches around his mug handle. "So, if Dad is Lullaby Doe's father . . . who's the mother?"

"That's the million-dollar question. I told Mom that it was probably a teacher, rather than a student. That she might have hidden the pregnancy, because of the affair. But I'm not sure that really holds water. If she's married, she could have told her husband the baby was his. If she's not . . . no one would really care who the father was. At least, no one would come right out and ask. And even if she were hiding the pregnancy, why would she give birth in the locker room? Why not call an ambulance or drive herself to the hospital?"

"Also, someone would have noticed if a teacher just disappeared in the middle of the school day." Yet Penn still looks unconvinced. "If Dad was sleeping with a high school student, there definitely would have been rumors."

I can only shrug. "There weren't any rumors about a pregnant student, other than Lilly." I groan with a sudden realization. "Penn, they're going to start asking questions. They'll probably start with our friends." I fold my arms on the island and lay my forehead on them. "The police are going to ask my *friends* if they ever slept with my *dad*! Not that I have many friends left . . ."

Penn puts one hand on my shoulder. "No they won't. The investigation is over. They've released the body, so the police are no longer looking for a next of kin. Which means that as messed up as this is for us, chances are good that no one else will ever know."

"I *really* hope you're right."

"What's wrong?" Landry asks, and I pop up from my bar stool to find her standing in the kitchen doorway in green plaid leggings and a baggy red nightshirt, the same Christmas pajamas she's worn for the past two years.

"Nothing."

Fact-Check Rating: Lying through my teeth.

"Want some coffee?" I ask her.

"Yuck, no." She pads into the kitchen in fuzzy red socks and heads straight for the fridge. "Why are you guys up so early?"

"West Point application. It's due by midnight." Penn pulls the iPad close again and wakes up the screen.

"I woke up to pee and realized I haven't done any Christmas shopping."

Landry turns away from the open refrigerator, eyes wide. "Me neither!"

"Great. You whip us up some french toast while I take a quick shower, then you and I can go shopping in Daley while Penn finishes part one of his diabolical plan to become an American supersoldier and leave us all behind."

Penn rolls his eyes at me. Landry grabs a carton of eggs from the fridge and a loaf of bread from the counter.

"You have fifteen minutes to shower," she says.

---

"I *have* to find a real job," I groan as I set our bags on the coffee table. It took us two hours and the entirety of my savings— except the eleven dollars I now owe my brother for half of Landry's new cookbook—to get gifts for Mom and Penn. I couldn't afford anything nice for Jake and Amira, so I got ingredients for another batch of cookies, hoping that my time and the willpower it will take me to resist eating them all myself will qualify as giftworthy. Because I'm now broke.

Of course, no one's going to hire the #babykiller, and if I'd had a real job before, they probably would have asked me to stop coming in, just like my babysitting clients did when the world decided I was small-town Tennessee's version of the Antichrist.

"What'd you get me?" Penn emerges from the kitchen with the iPad in one hand and a huge smile on his face.

"Hey!" Landry plants herself in front of our bags so he can't see them.

"I take it you finished your application?"

"I did." And while his relief is real and obvious, I can't help noticing that his smile looks a little forced. Like my mom's has for the past couple of days.

Finding out your dad might have fathered a baby with one of your classmates can do that to you.

"Let's have some lunch. Jake's going to be here in an hour to help us string up Christmas lights."

"You invited him?"

"More like I begged for an extra set of hands." Penn's smile finally reaches his eyes. "But I doubt he's doing it for me."

Landry and I hide our gifts in my room, then we make sandwiches. Jake rings the doorbell as we're loading the dishwasher after lunch, and he's holding a staple gun.

"Does your dad know you borrowed that?" I ask as I let him in.

"Yes. But it's *possible* he doesn't know which friend I'm helping out today."

"Thank you." I hug him, and I don't want to let him go. "I'm sorry your parents hate me."

"They don't hate you," he whispers into my hair as his arms wrap around me. "They just don't want my name associated with a scandal."

I roll my eyes as I shrug out of his embrace. "They think I sullied their precious angel, and that grudge predates Lullaby Doe."

Jake's brows arch as he pulls me close again. "Want me to tell them that any sullying *definitely* went both ways?"

"That'd be great, thanks."

He laughs, and when my brother and sister emerge from the kitchen, he finally lets me go.

Penn pulls a cardboard box of Christmas lights from the garage, and we spend about an hour sorting through them, plugging them all in to check for outages. Between the old lights that are still functioning and the new ones Penn got on clearance, I think we have enough to string along the front edge of the roof, and maybe enough to wrap the trunk of the tree in our front yard.

We haven't put up lights in a few years, because Dad was either deployed, in rehab, or not feeling up to it. But Penn used to help him decorate, and Jake helps his father every year, so I feel like we're pretty well prepared for the challenge. Except that we only have one ladder.

We give Landry one of the new strings and assign her the tree trunk, while Jake, Penn, and I take turns on the ladder, stapling strands of white lights in as straight a line as we can manage. After about an hour, we're halfway done, but Landry's hardly made it a foot up the tree trunk.

When I turn to find her on her phone again, I whisper to Penn, while he holds the ladder steady for Jake. "What's going on with Landry?"

Penn glances at her. "She and Norah are having another fight."

"Really? She didn't say anything." I'd offered to let Norah come shopping with us, and when Landry didn't seem to want that, I'd assumed she was going to be buying something for her best friend.

But now I realize she didn't get a thing for Norah. Come to think of it, I can't remember Norah and Fletcher coming over to finish their extra credit project either.

"Landry," I call as I cross the yard, zipping my coat against the cold. "What's wrong?"

"Nothing." She looks up and angles her phone away from me as she types. Then she shoves it into her pocket and picks up the strand of lights she's supposed to be winding around the trunk. "Norah's just being a . . . pain."

"I'm sorry. Need help with the lights?"

She rolls her eyes at me. "I think I can handle winding a string of lights around a tree trunk."

"The evidence does not support your conclusion," I tell her, my hands propped on my hips.

"Ha ha."

"You sure you're okay?" I ask as she resumes winding the unlit strand around the tree.

"I'm fine."

So I take her at her word and I go back to help Jake and Penn.

Half an hour later, I hear a muted buzz. I turn to see Landry reading something on her phone, but then she returns it to her pocket without replying. She finishes the tree trunk and heads toward the garage for an extension cord, but in the driveway, she stops and looks at another message. Then, again, she pockets her phone without replying.

I follow her into the garage, and she doesn't hear me as she rummages through a plastic storage tub, pushing aside a small spade and a broken hose nozzle, evidently unconcerned that she's looking in Mom's gardening supplies instead of Dad's box full of spare cords and wires.

Her phone buzzes again, and this time I snatch it from her hand before she can slide it back into her pocket.

"Hey!" Landry spins around, angry for a second, until she sees that it's me. Then she suddenly looks *terrified*. She grabs for her phone, and I backpedal until I hit a broken bicycle and send it crashing into the box she *should* have been searching for the outdoor extension cord. "Give me my phone, Beckett."

Instead, I read the text thread on her screen.

Landry: delete it. NOW!

Norah: no!

Landry: its gone too far. delete the account!

Landry: your going to get us in SO much trouble!

Norah: stop being paranoid

Norah: come over. we got another DM from that reporter.

Norah: if you dont come over i'm gonna answer her

"Oh my god." My hand clenches around her phone, and it creaks in my grip. "You're the Crimson Cryer. You and Norah are the *fucking* Crimson Cryer!" I don't mean to shout. The last thing I want is for anyone to hear me. But this is . . . This is . . .

"How—?" I can't make the rest of the question come out. I can't remember how words work. There's nothing left inside me right now but so much anger that I'm afraid that if I move a single muscle, I'll kill my sister.

"Inside," I say though clenched teeth. "Now."

# EIGHTEEN

Landry heads for the door into the kitchen, and on the way through the garage, she holds her hand out. For her *phone.* "Can I—"

"Do *not* finish that question."

When the kitchen door closes behind her, I count to ten, mumbling through clenched teeth. Then I turn to the open bay door and shout into the yard. "Penn! Inside! Now!" And I follow Landry into the house.

She's sitting on the couch with her hands in her lap. Staring at the Christmas tree. Her foot is tapping on the floor, rapidly bouncing her right knee.

"How—?"

The front door flies open, and Penn appears in the doorway. "Beckett? What's wrong?"

"Come in and close the door."

Penn glances from me to Landry, who won't look at him. Then he steps inside. Jake follows him in. "Everything okay?" he asks. "Should I go?"

"You may as well stay," I tell him. "This kind of involves you."

So Jake closes the front door.

"What about the latest tweet?" I demand. "Is Norah the one who lied about the police having evidence that I'm the mother?"

"That wasn't a lie, exactly," Landry says, staring at the coffee table. "Just a misinterpretation. Some doctor texted Mom about Penn's paternity test results, saying that he might be the baby's uncle. And Norah just kind of jumped to that conclusion."

"Why would you show her that?" I can't seem to stop shouting. I can't believe this is happening. I can't believe my own sister would—

"Because she's my friend!" Landry sobs. "You tell your friends things. Especially when you can't tell anyone else."

"Some friend," I snap. "She used you to get Twitter-famous."

"Beckett."

Penn gives me a look. But screw him. *I'm* the one getting death threats.

He turns back to Landry. "We have to explain something to you. About those test results."

I groan when I realize he's right. We can't keep hiding things from her; her efforts to find information on her own are what led to the Crimson Cryer destroying my life.

I sink onto the love seat, on the side nearest the couch, and Jake sits with me. "Should I go?" he whispers.

"No." I take his hand. "But promise me you won't tell anyone any of this."

"Of course not."

"What's going on?" My sister swipes her fingers across her cheeks again, wiping away more tears.

Penn takes a deep breath. "Landry, the baby being my niece was only one of the possibilities. The other reason Lullaby and

"What's going on?" Penn looks nervous, probably because of how pissed I obviously am.

I hand him our sister's phone, which hasn't auto-locked because I keep touching the screen. "Landry and Norah are the Crimson Cryer."

Penn looks skeptical for a second. Then he starts scrolling through the texts, while Jake reads over his shoulder, and his expression slowly morphs from disbelieving to angry. "What the hell were you thinking? How is this even possible?" He hands the phone back to me, but he's talking to Landry. "How did you get access to all that information?"

Landry's leg bounces even faster. There are tears in her eyes. "Okay, I'll tell you, but you have to promise not to get mad."

"The hell I do!"

"Beckett." Penn takes a deep breath. Then he sits on the coffee table facing Landry, and he better be playing good cop to my bad cop, because he has almost as much right to be mad about this as I do. "Landry, just tell us what happened."

"She's not on Twitter." I scroll through her phone, and there's no Twitter app. And that third-party app I caught her on the other day won't let her post anything. "Start talking, Landry."

She glances at me, then her gaze falls back on Penn, and I can't really blame her. "Norah has a burner. She's not allowed on social media, and her parents check her phone, so she got a burner a couple of months ago. Walmart has them. You just buy them off the shelf, and—"

"Get to the point," I snap.

"Yeah. So anyway, the day you found the baby, I stayed the night at Norah's. I got a notification on my phone that our cloud storage was full, and that we should upgrade to a paid account or adjust our settings. Or something like that. So I went to see what was even on our cloud account, and I found that picture you took of the baby."

"Wait, what?" Penn spins on the coffee table to look up at me. "You took that picture? I thought it was leaked from the police."

"That's what everyone thought. But I found it in the backup of Beckett's phone." Landry shrugs. "Turns out our whole family shares a cloud account, and a lot of our information is set to back up automatically. Some of Dad's pictures are still on there too."

That feels like a punch in the gut, intended to distract me.

"Why would you take a picture of a dead baby?" Penn asks.

"Because she recognized my bag," Jake tells him. "She took the picture to show me."

"Do you have *any idea* of the damage you've caused?" I demand, and more tears fill Landry's eyes.

"Just let her finish." Penn spins around on the coffee table again to face the couch. "Where did the rest of the information come from?"

Landry shrugs. "Mom's texts back up to the cloud too. Including the ones from work."

"Jesus, Landry." I lean back against the wall, trying to wrap my mind around it all, while the Christmas tree blinks in glaring shades of red and green on the edge of my vision. "So, you had the intel, and Norah had the Twitter account? And you just gave her all that information and let her post it? *Completely* out of context?"

"No! At first, we did it together. Anna Weston was on the high school newspaper staff her freshman year, which is we got the name, and—"

"Why?" I demand. "Why would you even start some like that?"

"Because there was a dead baby!" She sniffles and tears from her eyes as they spill over. "I found the pictu showed Norah, and we . . . Well, we thought people know about her. We thought the world should get to s To know that she existed."

"It doesn't sound like they meant to hurt anyone," Per

"But they *did* hurt someone! Why would you drag me Why would you accuse me of being the mother? That's a lie! I'm getting death threats, Landry! Our school got threat! Penn got fired from his job, and no one's ever goir me babysit again!"

"I didn't get fired," he interjects. "It's a temporary absence."

"I'm sorry!" Landry cries. "I didn't mean for any of happen. And I didn't write that about you. Norah did it. account only has a couple dozen followers, but the ( Cryer got hundreds and hundreds of them, in just a fe and she figured that would all go away if we didn't keep So she just . . . made it up."

"Oh my god! Landry, lies like that can ruin someon

"I know! We had a huge fight about it, and she never to do that again. Then I used the account to tell leave you alone."

Well, that explains the contradictory nature of th posts about me.

I could share nearly a quarter of our genetic material—the only reason that still makes sense—is if she were my half sister. *Our half sister.*"

Landry blinks, and I can see her trying to puzzle through that. "But Mom didn't—"

"Not Mom," I tell her.

"*Dad?*" She shakes her head. "You think Dad cheated on Mom? He didn't. He *wouldn't.* And anyway, he was already dead before the baby . . . I mean, wasn't he?"

"There's a possibility the baby could have been conceived up to two weeks before he died," I explain.

"No," she says. Penn and I just look at her, waiting for her to process what she's hearing. Jake squeezes my hand. "So . . . she's our family?" Landry says at last.

Penn nods. "Looks that way."

"So then, *we're* her next of kin. We can claim her . . . body."

I glance at Penn. Somehow, neither of us has thought of that. Not that it matters. "It's too late for that," I explain. "The coroner released her yesterday. She's at Dunley's Funeral Home now."

"Oh. Well—"

Landry's phone buzzes in my hand—the one not currently clutching Jake's. I'd forgotten I was holding it. There's a new text from Norah.

landry i can see that you've read my texts

I reply.

come over. bring the burner. front doors open

"Norah's on her way over with that phone," I say.

Landry's eyes go wide and scared again. "Just let me talk to her."

"I think you've done enough of that," I snap, and Penn gives me another look. "I'm just going to get the phone from her and delete the account."

"You're not going to tell anyone?" Landry asks.

"Of course not." The last thing I want is another news alert about the Bergen family of Clifford, Tennessee. Especially knowing what we now know about my dad.

The front door opens, and Norah steps into the living room. She freezes, her hand still on the knob, when she sees all of us waiting for her.

"They found out we're the Crimson Cryer," Landry explains before I can even make it off the love seat.

Norah tosses white-blond hair over her shoulder and gives me a defiant look as I approach her. "Give me the burner."

"No! It's mine. I'll delete the account, but—"

"Give me the phone now, or I'll go next door and tell your parents—"

"No!" Landry and Norah both shout. "Just give it to her," Landry says. "Please."

Finally, Norah digs a cheap smartphone from her pocket and slaps it into my palm. "We didn't mean any harm," she says, and out of the corner of my eye, I see Landry shake her head. Telling Norah to shut up.

Smart kid. They're both in enough trouble without digging that hole any deeper.

"Password?" I hold out the phone, and Norah taps four digits into the lock screen.

"Don't touch anything but—"

I look up, and it must not be holiday cheer Norah sees in my eyes, because her jaw snaps shut.

While she watches, I open her Twitter app and delete not only the Crimson Cryer account, but her personal, secret account too. But I'm too late to stop the Cryer from tweeting about Lullaby Doe's funeral. Which means we can probably expect another media circus.

With both of Norah's accounts deleted, I delete her Twitter app as well. A scroll through her screens shows me that she's also on a couple of other social media sites, but I'm not her mom. I resist the urge to delete them all, out of revenge. "If the Crimson Cryer makes another appearance, on any social media platform, I'll know who to come looking for. Understood?"

Norah nods. She looks over at Landry, then back at me. "Is that it?"

"What more would there be?"

"I don't know." She glances at Landry again. Then back at me. "Just . . . Can I go?"

"Please do," Penn says.

Norah snatches her burner from me and flees out the front door.

"Are you . . . Are you going to tell Mom?" Landry asks as the slamming of the door echoes in my head.

I look at Penn, and he shrugs. "I don't see any reason to add to what she's going through right now," I say.

"Works for me." Penn stands and brushes his palms on his jeans, and suddenly he looks so much like our dad that I feel like someone just punched me in the chest. "It's getting dark," he says.

"Let's plug in all those lights we just hung and scrounge up some holiday joy. Who wants the honors?"

---

"The Crimson Cryer deleted his account," my mother says. "Or maybe Twitter finally got around to processing our requests to have it removed." She stands in my bedroom doorway, watching as I tuck the hourglass pendant into my black blouse. It's the same shirt I wore to my dad's funeral, though I wore a skirt with it then. Today, I'm wearing slacks.

"I saw. But his last tweet was a link to the funeral announcement. So we're expecting a crowd."

"The Clifford PD has been informed." My mother's wearing dark slacks too, but not for the funeral. She's dressed for work, in a wine-colored button-down blouse and a gray blazer, with her badge on her hip, as usual. "We can't keep reporters out of the cemetery, but they're generally pretty respectful at funerals. But there may be more protesters."

I can't imagine what today must be like for her. How can you ever *truly* be ready to protect and serve—to keep the peace, in case of protesters—at a funeral for your dead husband's illegitimate child?

Lullaby Doe was evidently my half sister. But to my mother, she was a tragedy and a police matter, who became proof that the *last bit* of faith she'd had in her husband was misplaced.

I don't know how she's handling this so well.

Wait, yes I do. She's wearing the badge. She's not a widow or a mother today. Not really. She's Detective Julie Bergen.

I wish I had a badge. Or better yet, a shield.

"Mom?" I sit on the edge of my bed to step into the black flats we bought for my dad's funeral. It's weird to be wearing them again, especially for another funeral. Especially for *this* funeral.

"Yes?"

"Was Dad a thief?"

"What?" She frowns, clearly caught off guard. "Why would you ask that?"

"I know he was arrested a couple of months before he died. Penn told me. It was in the paper."

My mother sighs as she steps into the room and leans against the top of my dresser, arms crossed over her chest. "Prescription drug fraud. He was arrested for asking two different doctors to prescribe the same painkiller within a thirty-day period, without disclosing the first prescription to the second doctor."

"That's it? He didn't forge a prescription? Steal a doctor's pad, or something?"

"No. He asked an emergency room physician to write him a prescription for pills his general practitioner had already pre-scribed. Which shouldn't have happened in the first place. The ER doctor checked with the GP, then she called the police. But the charges were dropped."

"Why?"

My mother holds my gaze. "Ask me what you really want to know, Beckett. I'm sure you've heard the rumors."

I exhale slowly. "Did you do it? Did you get the charges dropped?"

"Did I break the law to help your father? No. I couldn't have, even if I'd wanted to. And the truth is that I *did* want to. There were times when I would have done *anything* to help him, if

271

I could. But I had nothing to do with that. The DA dropped the charges because they were for a Class A misdemeanor, and his plate was full of felonies. And because he's a vet, himself. He knew what your father went through. What he was still going through. And because your dad promised to go back into rehab. He never got a chance, though. There was a waiting list at the only one we could afford, so he tried to get clean on his own. And I tried to help. But . . ."

"But it was too hard."

"Yeah. I guess that's as good an explanation as any."

"And it's more than we're ever going to get about the rest of this," I say with a glance down at my funeral clothes.

"With any luck, it's almost over. The case is closed. That poor baby is about to get a proper burial. Maybe we can all move on."

She's not just talking about Lullaby Doe. She's talking about my father. Maybe we can all move on from Dad and from the ripple effect his decisions have had in our lives, even seven months after he died.

"But don't . . . Don't you want to know?" Because *I* want to know. "Who she is, I mean? The mother?"

My mom sighs. "Beck, there will *always* be a part of me that wants to know. Because regardless of how she got pregnant and what that had to do with my husband, we've failed her. She went through pregnancy and labor all alone, and she lost her child. And that's not fair. It's not *right*. But she obviously doesn't want to open up to anyone about that. She probably especially doesn't want to open up to anyone in *this* family. And I can't say I blame her. So we're going to let her move on. We're going to hope she comes to the funeral to say goodbye, and that she feels comfortable visiting the grave, once the headstone comes in, if that's something that will help her. Then we're going to let her put it behind her, just like we're going to put it behind us. Because that's really our only option now."

"Okay."

"Beckett. I'm serious. You have to let this go."

"I know. I will." But she clearly doesn't believe me, and I can't really blame her. "I'll try. I promise." And I guess that must be good enough, because she nods as she backs toward the door.

"Keep an eye on Landry."

"I always do."

---

After the catastrophe that was Lullaby Doe's candlelight vigil, Sophia agreed with me that the funeral should include only a graveside service, to minimize the number of opportunities for any more protests. So instead of filing into a church, like we did for my dad, even though he didn't go to church, for Lullaby Doe's funeral, Landry and I meet Sophia and the rest of the Key Club behind Dunley's Funeral Home.

The hearse is idling beneath the portico when we get there, and a line of cars has already formed behind it. I recognize several of the drivers as Key Club members, their cars full of other classmates dressed up in church clothes.

Today everyone's wearing dresses or slacks, including Jake, who usually wears jeans to church. He heads my way as I pull into the line.

I roll down my window, letting a gust of cold air into the car. "I didn't think your parents would let you come."

He leans in with a somber smile, his arms folded in my open window. "I didn't ask them. Can I ride with you?"

"Yeah. Get in." He looks really good in slacks and a green button-down. Broad shoulders. Strong jawline. I know that's not what I should be thinking about right now, but it's true.

Landry climbs into the back seat without a word, so Jake can sit up front with me. She's been quiet all morning, and I'm afraid she's going to freeze to death during the service, because she refused to wear her coat. It's pink, and she insisted that wasn't appropriate for a funeral, so she borrowed a long-sleeved black sweater from me to go over her black jeans. The sweater's big on her, and as she settles into the back seat, she seems to be trying to shrink into it. To let it swallow her.

I should have insisted she stay at home. But now that she knows about Dad's connection to the baby—about our whole family's connection—I can't keep her out of this. I don't think I can keep her out of anything anymore.

Landry was the only one who didn't know Dad was using. She'd just started sixth grade when he came home from Afghanistan with a shattered leg. He died at the end of her seventh-grade year. She'd just turned thirteen.

All she really understood was that he'd gotten hurt and he was in a lot of pain, and the medication the doctors prescribed made him too tired to do much of anything except sit on the couch with her and watch cooking shows. I think he spent more time with Landry, back then, than with any of us. And in a way, I think she knew him best by the end.

Yet somehow, she also knew the least about what was really going on. Because she was just a kid.

But maybe that's not true. Maybe *none* of us knew what was really going on. This funeral seems to be proof of that.

While we wait, a police car pulls into the parking lot. Doug Chalmers gets out of it and talks to the driver of the hearse. He's our police escort for the processional, and he's telling the driver that he's ready to go. I know, because he did the same thing at my dad's funeral. Only this time, there's no family car to follow the hearse.

Well, I guess that's not entirely true. My car is the family car, but no one knows that. And anyone who suspects it is right for the wrong reason; they still think I'm Lullaby Doe's mother.

Doug gets back into his car and turns on the flashing lights. He pulls slowly out of the parking lot, and the hearse follows him. Sophia's car is behind the hearse, then Cameron Mitchell's, with Cabrini in his passenger seat. Half a dozen more cars follow Cameron's before I can pull forward, but Penn's truck is not among them. He and Daniela are meeting us at the cemetery.

I follow the processional out of the parking lot, and there are six or seven cars behind me. By the time we get to the cemetery, there are at least twenty. I don't know when they joined us.

The road in front of the cemetery is lined with even more cars, but a police officer waves us through the gate and directs us to pull all the way to Lullaby's plot, where a tent has been set up with three rows of chairs beneath it. The coffin hasn't even arrived, but the second and third rows of chairs are full.

The first row has been roped off. It was Sophia's idea that the empty chairs be reserved for Lullaby Doe's family, even though no one came forward to claim her. What I didn't realize, when I agreed to that, was that *we* were the family that never came forward to claim her.

But we aren't the only ones. That poor baby had a mother too.

There are at least two hundred people gathered around the square of green material that covers the open grave and the small pile of dirt that came out of it. More cars are still pouring into the cemetery. More people are coming from every direction, stepping carefully around other headstones in long dark coats. The women walk on their toes to keep their heels from sinking into the grass. Most of them carry flowers or little teddy bears.

I wish I'd thought of that.

On the perimeter, several reporters have set up cameras and are filming the crowd. Taking photos of the arrangements of flowers, and the tent, and the hearse, and the people.

Brother Bill stands in front of the tent, speaking quietly with the preacher from First Baptist, where Sophia and Jake go to church. Their pastor agreed to perform the service. He performed my father's funeral too, but I can't remember his name.

I don't remember much about that service, actually, beyond flashes of memory. The scent of the flowers. The buzz of a bee around my head. That fake green material that is supposed to look like grass but isn't fooling anyone.

I remember the flag. And the honor guard from my dad's reserve battalion. And the six men in uniform who carried his coffin. Afterward, they folded the flag into a formal triangle and gave it to my mother. But I don't know where she put it.

As Jake, Landry, and I take a place on the left edge of the crowd, I can feel gazes on us. I can hear the whispers. I'm recognizable from my interview with Audrey Taylor, and anyone who took the Crimson Cryer's link to my Twitter profile would have seen the pictures I've uploaded. Everyone knows who I am, and the locals recognize Jake as well.

I can't hear what they're whispering, but I know. And the longer this goes on, the harder it is to pretend I don't care what they're saying. What they're thinking.

White trash. Teen pregnancy. Addict. Crooked cop.

It doesn't matter. I *know* it doesn't matter.

Fact-Check Rating: False.

It *matters*, no matter how badly I want it not to.

Amira appears just as the hearse finally opens, and she gives me a small smile as she squeezes in on Jake's other side.

Cameron Mitchell and Matt Umbridge pull out the little white coffin Sophia and I picked out. It's small enough that one person could have carried it. But there are two handles.

Jake and I should be the ones carrying that casket. We should have volunteered.

People sniffle as Cameron and Matt carry the small casket from the hearse toward the covered plot. Brother Bill shows them where to set it down, then they step back into the crowd with their girlfriends, who each carry small pink teddy bears.

Penn catches my eye, approaching from the opposite direction with Daniela. He must have had to park way off. They blend into the crowd on the opposite end of the coffin, just as Brother Bill begins to speak, and the whispers fade into a formal, uncomfortable silence.

"Thank you all so much for coming. I think it speaks volumes about this community that we've come out in such numbers to rally around one of our own. One whom none of us ever got to know. Or even to meet. But though we did not know Lullaby Doe in life, we all know her in death. We are all here to say goodbye, to usher her on from this world, though none of us could be there to welcome her when she came into it."

Sniffles echo all around me. Women clutch at teddy bears held close to their hearts. Even the men look red-eyed. And just as my mother said they would, the media is keeping a respectful distance. But the crowd of mourners continues to grow, people quietly crossing the cemetery to join the assembly as Brother Bill talks about the value of life and the responsibility of a community.

When he's finished, he steps back, and the pastor from First Baptist begins a formal funeral service.

I don't pay attention to much of what he says, but I recognize enough of it to know that it's basically the same thing he said at my father's funeral. The words are kind. They are somber but hopeful, and full of platitudes about how long Lullaby Doe's afterlife will be, though her life here on earth was so very short.

On my left, Landry sniffles. She wipes her eyes, then swipes her hand beneath her nose. On the other side of the casket, Daniela's nose is red from the cold, her eyes shiny with unshed tears. No one is unaffected.

Jake takes my right hand, and the look he gives me feels like a glimpse right into my soul. This wasn't our baby. Lullaby Doe had nothing to do with us. Yet I feel connected to her in a way I can't quite describe. I feel like I let her down, in a much more personal way than everyone else here feels.

Because I found her? Because we're family? Because everyone here thinks I'm responsible for her death? Whatever the reason, as the pastor finally bends his head to pray over the tiny casket, I find my own eyes damp with tears.

After the prayer, the preacher introduces Cabrini Ellis, who steps forward to sing an a cappella version of "Brahms's Lullaby." Which turns out to be the "Lullaby and Goodnight" song that plays in just about every music box ever made.

I don't even know all the words, but it seems especially appropriate for a baby the internet has named Lullaby Doe.

No, wait. The internet didn't name her. Landry did. My *sister* named this baby, in the guise of the Crimson Cryer. How have I not realized that before?

I turn to look at Landry, just as she bursts into hysterical sobs. I put my arm around her, and she looks up at me, tears streaming down her face. Agony shining in her eyes. And suddenly I realize that this is more than the vicarious grief the rest of us are feeling.

My entire existence narrows into this one devastating moment of epiphany, and I see what's been right there in front of me the whole time.

Lullaby Doe *was* my brother's niece. Because Landry is her mother.

"Oh my god," I whisper.

Then my sister turns and runs away from the graveside service, her long dark hair flying out behind her.

# NINETEEN

I race after Landry, and the freezing air stabs at my lungs like icicles shoved all the way through my body.

How could I not have seen it? How could I not have known?

Because she's thirteen years old. That's how. She's just a *kid*. We were trying to hide all the bad things from her, and she was—

"Landry!" I call softly, trying to get her to stop without shouting over Cabrini's voice as she sings the lullaby that sent my sister into hysterics. Maybe no one else knows why she ran. Maybe they think she's just sad, like everyone else is. Or that she's sad because her niece—*my* baby—is in that box.

God, please don't let anyone else have figured it out.

"Landry," I call again, and she finally stops. Not because I've asked her to, but because she's out of breath. It's difficult to cry and run at the same time.

I stumble to a stop next to her and pull her into a hug, and all I can do is hold her while she sobs into my shoulder. I don't know where my mom is. I didn't see her at the grave, so she's probably with Doug at the cemetery entrance, ready to help direct traffic when the ceremony is over. Even though she's not a patrolman.

Landry's tears soak through my blouse. Her snot smears my

shoulder. I stroke one hand down her hair, trying to calm her enough so that I can walk her back to the car.

Footsteps pound behind me, and I twist us around to see Penn headed our way at a brisk walk. Jake is on his heels.

"What happened?" Penn asks.

I can't believe he hasn't figured it out, because suddenly it seems to make so much sense. The Cryer account. His baffling paternity test results. The baggy sweaters Landry's been "borrowing" from me.

"She's the mother," I whisper over her head as Jake jogs to a stop next to me.

"Is she okay?" he asks, and I can tell with one look at him that he hasn't figured it out either.

"She's fine," I say, and Penn only stares at me, shock shining in his eyes while he tries to process what I've just said.

He shakes his head slowly—denial? confusion?—and I can only blink at him.

"I'm going to take her home. Can you give Jake a ride, please?"

"Don't worry about me. I'll ride with Cameron," Jake says. "Call me later?"

I nod, and he gives Landry one more sympathetic look, then he heads back to the service, where I can see people filing past the coffin now. Leaving flowers and teddy bears.

Penn hovers behind Landry, like he's not sure what to do for her. His hand rises, as if he'll pat her shoulder, but then he lowers it again and gives me a helpless look. "I have to drop Daniela off," he says at last. "Then I'll meet you at home."

"Can you call Mom on the way?"

"No!" Landry pulls away from me, aiming a terrified, teary look at us both. "You can't tell her."

"Lan, we're way past that. We have to tell her." I take her by the shoulders while she wipes tears from her cheeks. "She thinks Dad cheated on her with a teenager. We have to tell her the truth."

"She'll be so upset," Landry sobs.

"She's *already* upset," Penn says. "But it's going to be fine," he adds when I give him a look. "Just go home with Beckett, and we'll figure this out there."

Landry gives him a teary nod. Then I lead her the long way around the cemetery, hoping that no one stops us to ask if she's okay. Or if I'll give them an interview. On the way, I pass two different reporters talking to my classmates, asking them why they decided to come to the funeral for a baby they never met. A baby no one's even identified yet.

"Because no one was there for her when she was alive," Abby Winegarden says. "The world failed this poor baby. The least we can do is be here for her now."

Landry bursts into fresh tears as we pass, and I hurry her toward my car.

She sniffles all the way home, but we don't talk. I have a million questions, but I don't know where to start. I'm *so mad* at her. For so many reasons. But I also feel guilty. She's just a kid. I don't know how this happened, but it shouldn't have gone unnoticed.

Not by me.

At home, I park in the driveway, and Landry follows me inside, where she curls up on the couch with her knees tucked to her chest, her arms wrapped around them. "Do you want some hot chocolate?" I ask, but she only shakes her head. So I make a pot of coffee.

I'm starting to kind of like it, as long as my mug is half-full of milk and there's enough sugar to settle into a thick syrup at the bottom.

Penn makes it home first, but Mom's right behind him. The way she races down the driveway and then bursts into the house makes me think she misses the days when she drove a patrol car, so she could turn on the blue lights and go as fast as she wanted.

I've never seen the look that's in her eyes as she shoves the front door closed and drops onto the couch next to Landry to pull her into a hug. It's fear, but it's also . . . guilt. It's terror, and grief, and sympathy, and then finally, it's just tears. It's chest-heaving, hiccuping sobs, which Landry matches.

Which I'm having a hard time resisting myself.

But finally, when the tears have been exhausted, my mother lets her go and grabs a tissue to blot black streaks of makeup from her cheeks.

"Coffee?" I ask as I cradle my own mug.

"Please," my mother says over Landry's head. "Black."

So I pour a cup for my mother, which Penn takes to the living room while I reclaim my own mug. He sinks into the big chair to the left of the couch, and I perch on the arm next to him.

"Landry." My mother strokes one hand down the back of my sister's head and over her long, dark hair, but Landry still has her face buried in Mom's shoulder. "What happened, honey? I need you to sit up and take a deep breath. Then I need you to tell me what happened."

"I— I had a baby. But she wasn't breathing." She sniffles into Mom's shirt, and Penn grabs a box of tissues from the end table and leans forward to poke her with one corner of it. Landry finally looks up. She takes a tissue and wipes her nose, but she won't look at us. She's staring at the coffee table.

"We did everything the internet said to do, but she wasn't breathing. And she was so little. She just . . . she never *breathed*."

"Okay. That's a good start," my mother says. "Now I'm going to ask you some very important questions. First of all, who's 'we'?"

"Norah," I say while Landry blots her eyes. There's mascara running down her face. "Right? Norah knew?" That's the only thing that makes sense, considering that they shared the Crimson Cryer account.

My sister gives me a miserable nod as she centers herself on the middle couch cushion, tucking her knees up to her chest again. Trying to compose herself. "She was excited. I wanted to tell you guys, but Norah said I'd only be making everything worse, and everything was already so bad. She said I shouldn't tell anyone. She said the baby could be our secret, until she could get pregnant too, so we could do this together."

Oh my god.

"I told her that was crazy, but she wanted . . ." Landry sniffles again and blots her running nose, smearing mascara across it from her wadded-up tissue. "She said she could get Fletcher to do it, so our babies could be siblings."

Oh my *god*.

"But—"

"Fletcher Anderson?" Penn says. "He's the father?"

*Father.* I can't quite make sense of that word, in this context.

Fathers are adults. Like my dad. They make mistakes, like everyone else. Sometimes they make a lot of really big mistakes. But a father is someone Landry's supposed to *have*, not someone she's supposed to make out of some kid in her class.

How is it possible that the more answers I get, the less I seem to understand?

"Yes," Landry says at last. "It's Fletcher. But he doesn't know. He doesn't know about *any* of this. You can't tell him!" she cries.

Penn is clearly ready to rip someone's head off, but my mother looks . . . relieved. That takes me a second to understand.

Fletcher Anderson is fourteen years old. He's in the eighth grade, with Landry. He and my sister made a huge, stupid mistake, but they're just kids. They're *both* just kids.

The alternative—Landry getting pregnant by someone who *isn't* her age—would have been infinitely worse.

But it's already pretty bad.

"Fletcher. But he was just over here the other day. Are you two still together?" I ask.

Landry gives me a teary head shake. "We were never really together. It just . . . happened. Then I felt bad, because Norah really likes him. I don't really talk to him anymore. I didn't know he was coming over the other day. She just invited him to join our project."

Of course she did. Norah *knew* he was Lullaby Doe's father, and she invited him to our house. Without even warning Landry!

"Okay, we'll figure out what to tell Fletcher and his parents later. For now, just tell *us* what happened. You need to tell us *everything*. Norah wanted to have a baby too? Do you have any idea why she would want that?" Mom asks.

I wonder if this is how she sounds when she questions other people's children. Calm and rational. As if her entire world isn't falling apart around her.

"She said it was so I wouldn't be doing this by myself. So that if people were mad, they'd have to be mad at both of us. She said it was for me. Because she's my best friend."

But that's not it. Not really. Norah Weston needs attention like most people need food and air. If she wanted to have a baby, it was to keep Landry from getting all the attention. If she wanted that baby to be Fletcher Anderson's, it was because she didn't want Landry to have all of Fletcher's attention.

Norah's had a crush on him forever. It must have *killed* her to find out he liked Landry.

"I tried to talk her out of it," my sister says. "I told her one baby would be hard enough. And finally she said she wouldn't do it if I . . . If I let her help me raise my baby. She said it could be our secret. I mean, not forever, but for a little while, at least."

I want to wring Norah Weston's skinny little neck.

Landry shrugs. "I know that sounds stupid. But I was *so* scared. So we had a secret. We . . . learned things. We read things online and watched videos. I started taking vitamins and cooking a lot of vegetables. I read about cloth diapers and Lamaze breathing techniques. And I wanted to tell you all, but the longer I went *without* telling you, the harder telling you seemed. Until suddenly I was six months pregnant." Landry sniffles again, and Penn gives her a clean tissue. "I had a little pooch by then, so I started wearing baggier clothes. Borrowing Beckett's sweaters. I knew I'd have to tell you all soon. And I was going to. But then the baby came early. And she wasn't breathing."

Landry breaks into heaving sobs again, and Mom pulls her into a hug. I don't know what to do, so I get up for more coffee, even though I don't really want any. I just want to hold a warm mug.

Landry is hiccuping when I get back into the living room. Trying to get control of her tears. I sit on her other side this time, sandwiching her on the couch between my mother and me.

"Okay, let's back up a little," Mom says. "Why were you at the high school that day?"

"For the eighth-grade tour," Landry says. "Because we're going to go to school there next year. They take half of us for a tour in December, and half in February. Norah and I were in the first half." She frowns up at our mom. "You signed the permission form."

Mom's eyes close and she takes a deep breath. She hasn't touched her coffee yet. "Of course I did. And then I promptly forgot what day the trip was." She opens her eyes. "I'm so sorry, hon."

My mother forgot about the trip, and I never even knew about it, because I took a mental health day that Friday. I have no idea what Penn's excuse is.

"So, they took you to the high school on a school bus?" Mom says, gently urging her to continue.

Landry nods. "During second period. We were supposed to tour the school and have lunch in the cafeteria, before the high school kids have their lunch. But my back had been hurting all night, the night before. Then my stomach started cramping early that morning. A lot. I didn't realize it might be labor until we were already at the high school, but it was too early. I hadn't told anyone yet. So I couldn't call an ambulance."

"Oh, Landry," my mother says. "You should have called me."

"I couldn't! I was scared! So Norah and I snuck into the locker room. No one was supposed to be in there, because of the fresh paint. We thought someone would come looking for us. We thought we'd get caught. But no one came." Landry shrugs. "There were forty kids in our group. I guess no one noticed two missing."

Mom looks like she's going to be sick. "So you were all alone, going through that."

"No. I had Norah. She watched videos and talked me through it, but mostly we just tried to be quiet. The internet said it could take all day, but it only took about five hours."

Though it sounded like her contractions actually started long before she realized she was in labor.

"But something went wrong. She wasn't breathing. She never opened her eyes or cried, and I don't know what I did wrong!"

Penn's hand is clenched around the other arm of the chair. I'm staring at my sister through a sea of unshed tears.

"You didn't do anything wrong," my mother tells her. "Sometimes babies just don't make it."

"But if I'd gone to the hospital—"

"We don't know that," I tell her, just like Mom told me last week. "That might not have changed anything."

Landry gives me a teary nod.

"So, when you realized there was nothing you could do for her?" Mom says. "What did you do then?"

"Norah helped me get cleaned up. She had Tylenol in her purse, and there was a pad dispenser on the wall of the locker room. We'd used towels we found on a shelf, and she put them in a garbage bag she found with some cleaning supplies in a closet. She sprayed out the shower—that's where it all happened—then she took that trash bag . . . somewhere. Outside. A dumpster, maybe. Or maybe she just hid it. I didn't ask. I just let her take care of everything while I . . . I held the baby." Landry's eyes fill with fresh tears, but she blinks them back. "We'd wrapped her in a shirt we found in Penn's duffel bag."

"Why did you have my bag?" Penn asks.

"The zipper on my backpack broke, and you'd left your duffel in the kitchen for a few days, so I figured you didn't want it anymore, so . . ." She shrugs. "I thought I'd save Mom some money and use your old bag instead of asking for a new one. I'd been carrying it for about a week, before that day."

Only . . ."Landry, that was Jake's bag," I tell her.

"Then why was Penn's shirt in it?"

Penn shrugs. "I must have mistaken his duffel for mine. I didn't realize I'd left my shirt in it." He frowns. "I thought Mom threw out the shirt after I ripped the underarm seam."

But Mom hadn't known about the ripped seam. Or the backpack. Or the eighth-grade tour. Or Fletcher Anderson.

I hadn't known any of that either.

"We didn't know what to do with the baby," Landry says, staring at the coffee table again. Her gaze is unfocused. Her words sound . . . distant. "The internet said that you can take a baby you don't want—or one you can't take care of—to any hospital or fire station, and they can't ask you any questions. But I didn't think that would work for one that wasn't breathing. And we couldn't just get on the bus with her. And I was afraid . . . I was scared that we'd get in trouble. So I made a cradle for her, out of

Penn's bag. At least, I thought it was his bag. And I kissed her on her forehead. Then Norah and I went outside and waited on a bench until the tour ended and the rest of the kids came outside. We just got back in line with them and got on the bus back to the middle school. Then Anna came to pick her up, and they gave me a ride home. And I—"

"You spent the night at Norah's . . . ," I say, remembering that I had forgotten to pick her up that day, because I'd found the baby. Because I'd been interviewed by the police. Because I'd become the subject of the most malicious rumor ever to circulate through Clifford High School.

"I said you could stay with her and have pizza, because I didn't want you to hear too much about the dead baby." An irony that feels especially bitter now.

Landry nods. "I mostly slept a lot. And cried. Norah brought me pads, and frozen peas to sit on, and she gave me more Tylenol. She kept reading instructions online. She took care of me."

While my mother and I were each consumed with identifying the baby I'd found, my little sister was recovering from unattended childbirth next door. And we had no idea.

"Then I got that notice about our cloud account," Landry continues. "It just popped up on my phone."

"What notice?" Mom frowns.

"Did you know that some of the information on our phones is backed up to our family cloud storage account automatically?" I ask her.

Mom shakes her head. "Your dad must have set that up. I don't know anything about the cloud."

"Me neither," I admit. "But that night, Landry found the picture I'd taken of the baby, on our cloud backup. That's why she and Norah started the Crimson Cryer account."

"You—?" Mom turns on her, truly surprised for the first time since I can remember. "That was you?"

"It was Norah's idea." Landry wipes at her eyes again, smearing more mascara. "She started it so we could . . . um . . . She called it 'controlling the narrative.' She said that if we told the story we wanted people to believe, no one would find out the truth. I didn't think it would work. I thought someone would figure out she was mine, because of the shirt and the bag. But that just never happened."

"Because Norah told everyone the baby was mine!"

"I'm so sorry!" Landry cries. "I was so mad at her for that. And she promised she wouldn't do it again. And I tried to fix it. But she was really excited by all the new followers we got every time we posted, and every time that started to slow down, she had to post something new. To keep the story alive. To keep people interested." Another tear rolls down her cheek. "And people really seemed to care about her. About Lullaby. I got to *name* her on Twitter, and there were so many messages, and it started to feel like she hadn't really died. Like she was still *alive*, as long as people remembered her. So I let it go too far, and I'm so sorry."

She let *Norah* take it too far. And Norah didn't care about Lullaby's memory. She only wanted the attention, even if no one knew she was the one pulling the strings.

"Norah and I started fighting. I'd get mad about something she posted, and she'd apologize, and we'd make up. But then *she* started getting mad. Because I got to help with the candles, at Sophia's house, and she didn't. Then I went to the vigil without her. She said I was leaving her out. Leaving her behind." Landry leans forward and drops both of her used tissues onto the coffee table next to my mother's untouched mug. "Then, yesterday, Beckett figured out about the Cryer, and she deleted the account. So, I think . . . I think this is over now." She exhales, and her shoulders slump with the motion.

"Landry, I am so sorry," my mother breathes.

My sister shakes her head. "It isn't your—"

"Yes, it is," Mom insists. "I should have known . . . I should have seen . . . I should have noticed that something was wrong."

"*Everything* was wrong," Penn tells her. "It's hard to notice one extra drop of water in the ocean."

"Until that drop becomes a tsunami." Mom tears up. "Your dad used to say that."

"I'm sorry I became a tsunami," Landry whispers.

"No, honey. You're not a tsunami. We're going to talk about all of this at length. But first, we're going to get you to the doctor." Mom snatches her phone from the coffee table and starts texting.

"But it's Christmas Eve."

"Doctor Baker is a friend. She'll see you if I tell her it's an emergency."

Landry looks terrified. "But it's not an—"

"Landry." My mother takes her hand, and now she's wearing her no-nonsense face. "You gave birth a week and a half ago. You have to see a doctor. And we are *not* waiting until after the holiday. So it's Dr. Baker this afternoon, or we spend Christmas Eve in the ER."

"Fine. Dr. Baker."

"She's nice," I assure Landry. But I get why she's scared. My first gyn appointment—just yesterday—was terrifying. I can't imagine going through that postchildbirth. Though I guess most women would have had a bunch of those appointments by now if they'd just had a baby.

Mom's phone beeps, and she looks relieved when she reads the text. "Go put your shoes and your coat on. She's going to meet us at her office in half an hour."

Landry stands, wringing her fingers so hard they look like they might break off. "But what if someone sees me there?"

"No one will see you. Her office is closed."

Landry reluctantly heads to her room, and my mother grabs her mug. I follow her into the kitchen, where she dumps the coffee into the sink. She stands there for a minute, leaning with both hands on the counter, staring out the window. Then she hangs her head. "I can't believe I didn't see it. I can't believe I wasn't *watching* her."

"You were grieving."

"We were *all* grieving!" she whispers fiercely as she turns from the window. Her eyes are ringed in bright red, yet despite the tears standing in them, she looks *angry*. "She lost her father. You all did, but she was just a kid. And instead of being there for her, I disappeared. She basically lost *both* parents, and I let her stumble into the biggest decision of her youth, without a single word of caution or advice. Without telling her she was *too damn young*. Without even knowing she was thinking about sex. Or that she was hanging out with Fletcher alone. And then . . . For *seven months* . . ."

She's angry at herself.

"You worked. You *had* to work. No one blames you for this, Mom."

"Well, they should. You *all* should." She turns back to the window, her arms crossed tightly over her chest. "I should have been there."

Yeah. She should have.

I tap her on the shoulder, and when she turns, I hug her. A full embrace. I can't remember the last time I did that. Not since Dad died, anyway.

She sniffles, and her whole body hitches against me. "I can't believe I thought that your father . . . That he would *ever* do that. He had problems. I know that. And he made a lot of bad decisions near the end. But he was a good man, Beckett. I need you to know that. I need you to believe that, no matter what you hear."

"I do," I assure her. "People are going to believe what they want about him, just like they will about the rest of us. And you were right. There's nothing we can do about that but learn to live with it."

Fact-Check Rating: Insufficient evidence. I'm willing to test this theory, and I hope someday I can prove it wrong.

She nods and pulls away. Then her eyes widen as she takes a step back, looking me over from head to toe. "You've outgrown me." My mother laughs and swipes moisture from beneath her eyes. "I don't know when that happened."

"Me neither."

"I'm ready," Landry calls from the living room, and I turn to see her wearing her pink coat over my black sweater and her own

"And I can't do that, because I love you." And because this is my fault, at least a little.

*Please watch your sister.*

Landry and I shared a room for years. We aren't just siblings; we're *sisters*. If there was anyone she would have listened to about sex, it was me.

If there was anyone she should have felt comfortable confiding in . . . Anyone who should have noticed the changes in her . . .

"Beckett. Get out." Finally Landry sits up to show me her tear-streaked face.

"Nope. Give me your coat."

She hesitates for a second, then she shrugs out of her pink coat and kicks off her sneakers.

I toss her coat over the back of the only chair in the room, then I sink into it. "It's going to be okay. I know it feels like it won't be, right now, but it will."

"How do you know?"

Fair point. For the first time, what she's going through isn't something I've already done. I have no experience-based wisdom to impart. And while life has taught me many lessons over the past year, "it's going to be okay" has not been among them.

"Mom called the Andersons?" Landry asks when I can't offer a meaningful follow-up to my pointless platitude.

"Yeah. I think they're coming over."

"Oh my god, *why?*" Landry throws herself facedown onto her pillow. "Why does she have to tell them? It's all over now. Why can't she just let this go away?"

I hesitate, again, because that's another fair question. "Don't you think they have a right to know?" I ask at last.

black jeans. "Well, that's not true. But I'm ready to get this over with."

Mom grabs her purse from the coffee table and digs in it for her keys. Then she turns to Penn and me. "While we're gone, why don't you two decide what you want to do for dinner?"

"It's Christmas Eve. Can we have dumplings and egg rolls, like we used to?" Landry asks.

That was Dad's idea, several years ago. He said that by the time the holidays were over, everyone would be sick of turkey and ham and dressing, and that we should just pick up Chinese take-out for Christmas Eve. So we've done that every year since. Even last year, when he was "sick."

Mom digs through her purse. "I don't have any cash."

"It's on me," Penn tells her. "I have a little left from my last paycheck."

"Thank you." Mom puts one hand on the side of his face and smiles up at him.

He outgrew her too. Years ago.

# TWENTY

While Landry and Mom are gone, I head into my room to finish wrapping my presents. Landry's appointment takes longer than mine did, and by the time Mom's car pulls into the driveway, Penn and I are on the couch, pretending to pay attention to that Christmas movie that plays over and over every year. The one with the little blond boy in the pink bunny suit.

I hear the car door slam, and a second later, the front door opens on a frigid gust of wind. Landry stomps inside without a word and heads straight for her room.

"She's fine," Mom says as she closes the door. "Physically, anyway. She has a follow-up with Dr. Baker in a month and a referral for counseling." She crosses into the kitchen and sets her purse on the counter, then pulls off her coat. "You haven't gone for food yet, have you?"

"No, we didn't want it to get cold," Penn says as we follow her into the kitchen.

"Okay, good. We're going to need to wait a couple of hours, I think."

"Wait for what?" I ask.

Instead of answering, my mother digs her phone from her pocket and makes a call. After three rings, an unfamiliar voice answers. "Hello?"

"Hello. Mrs. Anderson?" My mother's frown lines are deeper than I've ever seen them.

"Yes?" the other voice says.

"This is Julie Bergen. I got your phone number from my daughter, Landry. I'm not sure if you know her, but she's a classmate of your son Fletcher."

"Yes, of course, Landry's been over here several times," Mrs. Anderson says, and my mother looks like she's just been slapped in the face by this new bit of information. "She's a sweetheart. What . . . ? Is there something I can do for you, Mrs. Bergen? It's Christmas, and we're about to—"

"I'm sorry to bother you on the holiday. Please understand that I wouldn't be calling if this were not very important. That said, would it be possible for you and your husband to bring Fletcher over. We . . . Well, we really need to speak to all three of you."

"Right now? Are you serious?" Mrs. Anderson says. "We were about to sit down to dinner. What is this about?"

"I— I would really rather discuss this in person, and I think you'll understand why . . ."

I head into the living room and fold up the snowman-themed throw blanket, and when I turn off the television, I hear quiet sobs echoing from down the hall. I follow them to Landry's room, where I hesitate for a second before knocking.

The sign on her door rattles. She sniffles from inside. "Go away."

Instead, I open the door. "Hey."

Landry is lying facedown on her bed, still wearing her coat and shoes. "I said go away," she mumbles into her rumpled comforter.

Landry sits up, her brows deeply furrowed. "No! Why would they have that right? It's *my* body. It was *my* baby. My mistakes. My consequences. I would have had to tell everyone if the baby had lived, but she didn't, and now . . ." Fresh tears slide down my sister's cheeks. "How am I ever supposed to face Fletcher after this?"

"Why wouldn't you be able to face him? Landry, this is a mistake and a tragedy that you're *both* responsible for. Don't you think he should share that responsibility? Don't you think he should know that his actions had consequences?"

"I guess. But, I mean, he didn't lie. He didn't hide a pregnancy. He didn't leave his baby in the locker room . . ."

"That doesn't mean he doesn't share—"

The doorbell rings, and Landry jumps. Her eyes widen, and her hands begin to shake. "I can't do it. I can't tell him. I can't look at his parents and tell them what I did. That it's my fault they never got a chance to see their grandchild. I—"

"Yes, you can." My entire body aches in sympathy for her. Dragging her into the living room—into this confession—feels like the opposite of watching out for her. But Lullaby Doe doesn't belong to just her anymore. In fact, that was never really true in the first place. "Come on. Mom, Penn, and I will be right here with you." I give her my hand, and she takes it as she climbs out of the bed.

I wrap my arms around her trembling shoulders as I lead her down the hall.

Mom lets the Andersons in as we step into the living room. Either Fletcher is an only child or they've left his siblings at home, because it's just him and his parents. Thank goodness.

His mother and father look very, very worried about whatever has earned them this call on Christmas Eve, but Fletcher looks *terrified*. He steps over the threshold with his hands in his pockets and his shoulders hunched up to his ears beneath his thick gray coat. His gaze is on the floor, then he finally looks up, and his eyes widen when he sees Landry's tearstained face.

"Mrs. Bergen." Mr. Anderson closes our front door at his back, and for once I decide not to comment on her title. My mom isn't a cop tonight. "Maybe you should just tell us what this is about."

"Yes." Mom rubs her palms on the front of her jeans. "Would you like to sit?"

Mrs. Anderson starts toward the sofa, but then her husband clears his throat pointedly. "We're fine," he says, while Fletcher scuffs the toe of his left sneaker in our carpet. "What's going on?"

My mother pulls Landry into a side hug, keeping her arm protectively around my sister's waist. "Well, there's no easy way to start this conversation. But I assume you've all heard about Lullaby Doe, the baby found at the high school."

"Of course. But what—?" Mrs. Anderson's hands fly up to cover her mouth and nose, while her gaze flicks between my sister and her son. "No . . ."

Fletcher looks up again, and it's clear from his confused frown that he hasn't made the connection. "Wait, what? I thought . . ."

I don't know what he thought. That he was in trouble for not finishing the extra credit project? Or maybe that my mother found out, seven months late, that he and Landry had sex. Maybe he thought this was going to be some kind of a middle-school abstinence intervention.

Landry bursts into fresh, quiet tears, and a look of utter shock washes over Fletcher.

"Oh my *god*," Mrs. Anderson whispers.

"What did you *do?*" Mr. Anderson grabs Fletcher's arm and practically jerks him off his feet. "What the *hell* did you *do?*"

"He didn't know," my mother insists, letting go of Landry so she can hold both hands out, deescalating the situation out of habit, evidently. "Landry was afraid to tell anyone until this afternoon. But now that we know, I suggest we all just sit down and—"

The doorbell rings again, and my mother frowns with a glance out the window, where there's just enough light left in the sky for her to see whoever has pulled up in front of our house. "Beckett." She gestures for me to answer the door. "Take it to your room, please."

I don't understand until I open the door and see Jake standing there. "What are you doing here?" I whisper, well aware that everyone's staring at us now.

"*Beckett*," my mother repeats.

I glance from Landry's tear-filled eyes to Jake's bewildered expression, then back. "Just go," my sister says. So I reluctantly grab Jake's arm and haul him inside, then all the way to my room. I don't want to leave Landry, but Penn and Mom are both there for her, and Jake's . . .

I don't know what Jake's doing here.

"What's wrong?" I ask as I close my bedroom door.

301

"That's what I was going to ask you. You're not answering your phone. I was worried. Because of the death threats."

"My . . . ?" I pat my back pocket and find it empty. Because my phone is lying on my bed, where I must have left it when I was wrapping presents. I pick it up and see seven messages and two missed calls from Jake. "Sorry. We're having a rough day. But I'm fine."

"What's going on? Why are the Andersons here on Christmas Eve?" he asks as he sinks onto the end of my bed.

"You know the Andersons?" They don't have any kids in high school. Yet.

He shrugs. "They go to my church."

Of course they do. But I don't know how to answer his question. It's not my place to tell him—

"Was Landry crying?" He glances toward the living room, as if he can see through the wall. "Still, or again?"

"Still, mostly. The funeral hit her hard." Which he knows, because he was there for her breakdown.

"Is she okay? What's . . . ?" Jake asks, and I can only watch in horror as understanding washes over his features. He stands. "Oh my god. It's *her* baby? Not your dad's?"

"Jake—"

"I left my duffel here." He paces across my room, then suddenly he turns back to look at me, still putting the pieces together. "And the shirt. Was it Penn's?"

"Yes. She just told us all this after the funeral. We're still processing."

"Landry and *Fletcher Anderson?*" His voice drops into a conspiratorial whisper. "They're still in middle school!"

"I know—"

"What the hell was she even doing at the high school? This is crazy. This is . . ." His suddenly somber focus narrows on me. "This is so sad."

"Yeah." I pull him back down onto the edge of the bed. "The Andersons are just now finding out, and this pretty much sucks for everyone. Her life is basically ruined, and that's kind of my fault."

"Wait, what?" Jake frowns as he takes my hand. "How is any of that your fault?"

I exhale, breathing through an overwhelming pressure mounting around me, as if the air in my room is starting to solidify. "We've heard all week long how Clifford failed both Lullaby Doe and her mother. I just said that to Sophia the other day. I told her that someone should have known. Someone should have seen what was going on. It turns out *I'm* that someone. I left Landry on her own when she was the most vulnerable, right after my dad died, and this is what happened." I shrug miserably. "After that, I just kept *not noticing*. Not seeing what she was going through. Not asking the right questions. Not listening—not *really* listening—to the answers she did give." I swallow past the raw, swollen feeling in my throat. "I had *so* many opportunities to help her, and I failed *every single time*."

"No, Beck, this isn't your fault. Landry also has a mother and a brother, and friends, and teachers, and—"

"And my mother should have been there. I know. But I *was* there, once things got back to 'normal' around here. I was usually the one picking her up from school and hanging out with her while she made dinner. I had every opportunity in the world to see what was going on. To help her. And I didn't do it." Tears burn the backs of my eyes. "And it's not the first time."

Jake frowns. "What are you talking about?"

I swipe at my eyes and look up at him. "Do you ever wish you could have a real-world do-over? That you could just, like, press rewind on *life?*"

If I could choose one superpower, that's what it would be: the ability to undo a mistake. Screw flight or invisibility. I wish I could fix the things I've messed up. I wish I could just *take it all ba*—

Pain fires through my chest, and I pop up from the bed, rubbing at my sternum.

*Whiskey on the end table.*

*Pill bottle wedged between the couch cushions.*

"Beckett?"

"Something's wrong," I gasp, fighting to make my lungs expand. "I can't get a deep breath." And the harder I try, the more difficult breathing becomes. The more desperate I get to just make my lungs relax. To talk my rib cage out of this brutal lockdown.

"You're okay." Jake stands and pulls me into a hug as I gasp, sucking in short, sharp little breaths. "You *are* breathing. Just slow down and—"

*Childproof cap on the carpet.*

*Dad, lying still on the floor.*

"Something's wrong!" My head is spinning, and the edges of my vision look dark and smudgy.

"I know. You're having a panic attack. This happened after your father died. Remember? We were lying in your bed, and you woke up from a nightmare, and you said you felt like your whole body was in a vise. No, wait, you said something about a full-body corset."

I do remember that. The full-body corset. That's how I feel now too. Like there's something constricting my lungs. My entire chest.

"Take it slow." Jake rubs one hand up and down my back while I clutch at his sweater, my face pressed into his shoulder. While I suck in breath after breath through the loose weave. "In and out. You're fine."

I close my eyes and fight to slow everything down. To breathe evenly, despite the panicked insistence from my brain that I suck in as much air as possible, as quickly as possible. And gradually, the world returns to normal. The room steadies around me. The dark smudges fade.

My chest still feels bruised, as if it's had to work too hard for too long. But he's right. I'm fine.

Fact-Check Rating: Nothing could be further from the truth.

"Come sit." Jake leads me back to my bed, where he settles next to me. And for a couple of minutes, we just sit there, his arm around my waist. My head on his shoulder. "Can you tell me what you were talking about?" he says at last, whispering into my hair. "Are you ready to let it out?"

"I saw the pills." Saying the words feels like jumping off a cliff, waiting to feel my body smash on the rocks.

Telling the truth is supposed to feel good, isn't it? Liberating? This doesn't feel like that *at all*.

"What pills? Beckett, what are you talking about?"

"The night my dad died. I saw the pills before I went to bed. I *saw* the *bottle*. I knew what they were, and I knew he wasn't supposed to have them. But I didn't do anything. I didn't say anything. I could have grabbed them and flushed them. I could have told my mom. I could have actually called my dad on his bullshit, right to his face. *Any* of that could have changed that entire night. I could have saved his life, Jake."

He's already shaking his head. "No, you—"

"But I was a coward. I was afraid that if I said anything, I'd be starting another fight between him and my mom. Or that Landry would hear, and she'd figure out he was using. Or that he would . . . that he would be mad at me. I was afraid of making things worse. So I did nothing. And two hours later, I woke up and found him dead on the floor."

Jake blinks at me. He looks really, really worried. "Beck, that doesn't make it your—"

"Don't. Don't say it's not my fault. I didn't get the Oxy for him. I didn't get him hooked. I didn't put the damn pills in his mouth, and I didn't make him wash them down with whiskey. I know all of that. I'm not absolving my father for what he did. But he needed help, and I had a chance to help him. But I didn't do it. Just like with Landry."

Jake takes me by both arms and looks right into my eyes. "Beckett, he was your father. He was a firefighter and a soldier. You could live that night over and over for the next year and it still wouldn't be your fault for not telling a grown-ass adult how to live his own life. That's on *him*."

"But—"

"Listen to me. Please. Landry's a kid, and a lot of people should have seen what was going on with her. Including you. Including me—I've spent a lot of time here too this year. Hell,

I was probably the distraction that kept you from noticing what was going on with her. But your father is another issue entirely. You were not in control of his decisions. You're not in control of *anyone* else's choices, and you can't blame yourself for failing to prevent an adult's mistakes.

"You can be there for people when they ask for help, but you can't *make* them ask, Beckett. You can't make them accept help they don't want. And you can't blame yourself for not being able to read minds. To see the future. Down that path lies madness." His expression softens into the beginnings of a grin. "And panic attacks."

My laugh is half sob.

I let my forehead fall onto his shoulder as my arms wind around his neck. "Why are you so good to me?"

He pulls back enough so that I have to look at him. "Because I love you, Beckett."

Suddenly my chest feels tight again, and this is an entirely new kind of panic.

He's serious.

I mean, he's said that several times before, and I've even said it back. But this time, he *means* it.

Maybe he's always meant it.

"I—" I have no idea what to say. Fortunately, at that super-convenient moment (it's not convenient), his phone beeps, and he pulls it out of his pocket. "Your mom?" I ask. She's probably pissed that he's here with me on Christmas Eve.

But then Jake flips his phone over, facedown on my comforter, and irritation whooshes like fire through my veins.

"Seriously?" I launch myself off the bed, fighting whiplash

from the sudden emotional one-eighty. "You're still doing that? You *just* said you love me, and you're hiding texts again. How am I supposed to trust you, if you—"

"Beckett, I'm not cheating."

"Then show me! Show me the damn text, Jake! Otherwise, I can't—"

He exhales as he picks up his phone. Then he tosses it to me underhanded, like a softball pitch. I catch it, and my heart pounds while I stare at the darkened screen. "Really?" I didn't think he'd actually show me.

He shrugs, looking miserable. "You're just going to dump me again if I don't. And there's no point in me hiding it from you if I don't even have you."

I groan. "You couldn't have thought of *that* a week ago?"

Another shrug. So I tap the screen to wake it. The text alert is still there.

Happy Holidays from all of us at Texas Tech. We're really hoping you'll grant our Christmas wish and reconsider our offer.

I roll my eyes at him. I can't help it. "You do *not* want to play baseball with Cameron Mitchell at Clifford County Community College." Jake has good grades, decent scores, and endless talent. He works hard, and he deserves so much more. "Are you . . . Are you scared?"

"No." Yet the doubt creasing his forehead says otherwise. "But Beckett, I'm not Penn. I don't need to conquer the world, and I don't have anything to prove. And I'm not sure I want to be out there all alone."

"Okay, then." I squeeze his hand again. "Be honest, at least with yourself. If you don't want to go, that's fine. But don't use me as an excuse for giving up this chance. That's not fair to either of us."

"You're not an excuse. You're a reason." He pulls me close, trying to distract me with a kiss. "I'd miss the hell out of you."

"I'll miss you too. But what do you have to lose from trying it?" I shrug. "If you don't like it, you can always come back. Or transfer. To Knoxville, *not* to CCCC."

Jake blinks at me, staring straight into my eyes. "You really think I'm cut out for this?"

"I do. And so does the Texas Tech coach, obviously. And that's exactly what I would have told you three weeks ago, if you hadn't started hiding texts from me." I punch him in the shoulder. "I can't believe you did that! And you let your parents blame me for this!" I frown up at him. "You have to tell them I talked you into reconsidering the scholarship."

"I'm not sure I'm reconsidering. Yet. But they did invite me for a campus visit next month. Come with me?"

"To Lubbock? My mom will never—"

"Use one of your college days. We can take a road trip." He shrugs. "Who knows. Maybe *you'll* like Texas Tech."

# TWENTY-ONE

The pounding in my chest feels like those dinosaur footsteps in *Jurassic Park*. Like my whole world is quaking. I read the text again. "What does this mean? What offer?"

Jake sighs. "You know what it means, Beck."

What I know about Texas Tech, in three bullet points:

- They have one of the top five college baseball teams in the country.
- They're a Division I school and a member of the Big 12 Conference.
- They've been Jake's second-choice college—behind Vanderbilt—since he was twelve years old.

"You got a scholarship? That's great!" I smile so wide it hurts. "Why didn't you tell me?"

But he isn't smiling.

"Jake?" And suddenly the rest of it sinks in. "Reconsider. Why would you need to reconsider?"

He shoves his hands into his pockets and blinks at me.

"You turned it down." My hand clenches around his phone. "Why *on earth* would you do that?" And he'd been hiding texts from me for a couple of weeks before we broke up, which means he turned it down at least three weeks ago.

He holds his hand out for his phone, before I can crush it, and I almost throw it at him. "Say something, Jake! Baseball is all you ever talk about! This is your dream! Why would you turn that down?"

"Because I'm staying here." He pries the phone from my grip and slides it into his back pocket.

"The hell you are."

"Lubbock is too far away. Vanderbilt would be one thing. Or even Knoxville. But Texas Tech—"

"Bullshit. It's your number two pick."

"Yes, but you're my number one pick." He reaches for me, and I backpedal, horrified by this new understanding.

"No. Don't do that. Don't say that." I back farther away, as if I can distance myself from this guilt. Over something I didn't even *know* about. "You are *not* staying here for me. Do your parents know you turned it down?"

He doesn't have to answer. I can see it on his face.

No wonder they hate me.

"Oh my *god*, Jake! I can't be the reason you give up your dream! Don't put that on me!"

"I'm staying *for* you. For *us*."

He reaches for me, but I push him away. "Don't be an idiot. You're going to college. On scholarship. You're going to pitch for Texas Tech, and you're going to get a degree, and you're going to get far away from this place. You're going to do *anything* you want."

"I'm not leaving you here."

"What makes you think I'm staying?" I demand, throwing my hands in the air. "I have dreams too, you know!"

I mean, I certainly *plan* to have dreams. Yes, right now it feels like I'm the only member of the junior class who has no idea what she wants to do or who she wants to be, but where does it say I have to have my whole life planned out at sixteen?

I'll figure it out.

"I just . . ." Jake runs one hand through his hair. "I don't want to leave you here alone. Penn will be in New York—I *know* he'll get into West Point—and your mom's never really here, and . . ." He shrugs. "You have nightmares. And panic attacks."

"I've had two panic attacks in seven months. That's not exactly a chronic condition. And I haven't had nightmares in a long time. Look, as sweet as it is that you want to be here for me—like, melt-my-insides sweet—I'm a big girl, Jake. I'm going to be *fine*. And even if that's not true, you need to listen to your own advice. It's not up to you to take care of me."

Like it wasn't up to me to take care of my dad.

Though I, of all people, understand why it may feel that way.

"But now you're getting death threats," he insists. "I'm not going to abandon you with all that going on."

"Going to college isn't abandoning me. Besides, you won't even be leaving for eight more months. This will blow over long before then." Especially now that Lullaby Doe is buried and we've shut down the Crimson Cryer.

I take his hand and tug him down onto the bed next to me again. "What's this actually about?" Because it isn't about me. Not really.

"Nothing. I just . . . I don't want to leave you, and I don't even know that I want to live in Texas. I'm just going to go local. I can commute from home and save money on housing. That's what Cameron's doing. We can both play for CCCC."

"I'll ask my mom." I still don't think she'll say yes, but crazier things have happened. "Next week. When things have died down a bit around here. Speaking of which."

"I know. My mom's going to kill me as it is." He stands and tugs me up. "We're supposed to be opening one present each tonight while we watch Christmas movies."

"Sounds like fun. I'll walk you out."

To my surprise, the living room is empty, and when I walk Jake to his Camry, I see that the Andersons' car is gone. As is Penn's truck. He must have gone for dinner.

"Talk tomorrow?" Jake says as he unlocks his door.

"Maybe even later tonight." I go up on my toes to kiss him. "But only if you redeem me in your parents' eyes."

"I will do my best," he promises. "Merry Christmas."

"Merry Christmas." I shiver while I watch him drive off, reindeer antlers bobbing in the wind. Then I head back inside, where I find Mom and Landry in the kitchen.

"That was quick," I say as I slide onto the bar stool next to my sister, pleased to see that my mother is making a pot of real hot chocolate. On the stove, with milk, sugar, and cocoa powder.

"Yeah. Turns out there's not really much to say after 'Sorry I had your son's baby without telling you. Happy holidays!'" Landry mimes a wave with a half-hysterical laugh.

"They have a lot to think about," Mom says, stirring the pot with a whisk. "And a lot to talk about."

Landry moans. "Fletcher's dad's going to kill him."

"No he won't," I assure her. "It was a mistake and a tragedy. But you were right. It's all over now, and—"

"And now everything's ruined." Landry's chin quivers.

"No. Now everything's *different*," I tell her. "Not gonna lie.

I don't think you can go back from this. But you can move forward. And we'll be right here beside you."

"Beckett's right." Mom pulls two mugs down from the cabinet and turns off the stove. "I'm sorry I wasn't there before." She leans over the island and takes both of Landry's hands. "Sorrier than you'll ever possibly understand. But I will be from now on, and I need you to start trusting me. Talking to me. Even if that's just to tell me that I'm totally screwing up this single-parenting thing."

"You're not—" I begin, but my mother shushes me as she stands to pour the cocoa.

"Things have to change around here. So we're going to have a nice, peaceful Christmas. Just the four of us. Then I'm going to lay down some new rules."

I frown into the mug she sets in front of me. "I think that may be an overreaction."

"It isn't. There are going to be far fewer unsupervised study sessions and closed bedroom doors when you have company."

I groan.

"And there will be more family meals."

"Does that mean you'll be home for dinner?" Landry asks.

Mom grins at her. "I may even cook occasionally."

My sister rolls her eyes. "Frozen pizza doesn't count."

"Noted. But you will be expected to talk at these family dinners. I want to hear what's going on in your life. Good or bad. I want to know who you are these days." She reaches out and tucks a strand of Landry's hair behind her ears. "And we're not going to have any more secrets, okay? That doesn't mean no more privacy," she adds when I open my mouth to object. "But no more secrets. And that's not up for discussion. Got it?"

Landry nods, and though she's frowning, trying to appear irritated, the look in her eyes is pure relief. I think she's done with secrets for a while. For a long, long time, I hope.

"Because like it or not," Mom continues, blinking back the sudden shine in her eyes, "you're still a child."

*God, please let her have some childhood left.*

The front door opens, letting in another cold gust, and Penn appears in the kitchen. "Hot chocolate and pork dumplings?" he says, eyeing our mugs and the pot on the stove. He frowns as he sets the takeout bag on the island. "That's weird."

"What says our resident culinary expert?" I arch one brow in Landry's direction.

She grins. "I'll allow it."

I take the steam-damp bag and set a series of takeout boxes on the coffee table, where multicolored lights reflect on it as the Christmas tree blinks. Mom grabs four plastic cups and a two-liter bottle of Coke from the fridge, while Penn turns on *How the Grinch Stole Christmas* in the living room.

We gather around the coffee table, Penn in the armchair, the rest of us on the couch, and reach over one another to grab egg rolls, wontons, and dumplings from open containers. We don't talk. No one's really smiling. But we're together, and the food is good.

Tomorrow's going to be hard, because Dad isn't here. Because we're not the same family we were when he was alive. Before he got sick. Because in some ways, we hardly even know each other anymore.

But I don't think it's too late for us, just yet.

# EPILOGUE

The sun beats down on my scalp, and I wipe sweat from my forehead. July in Tennessee feels like breathing through a warm, wet rag.

"Did you put those there?" I nod at the fresh flowers in the marble vase built into the base of Lullaby Doe's headstone. It's beautiful, especially now that the grass has filled in around it.

Landry shakes her head as she bends to add her own pink rose to the arrangement. "People keep leaving them. I thought they would forget, but someone keeps visiting."

And as nice as it is for Lullaby that the community hasn't forgotten her, it's even better for my sister. Because if there are other regular visitors, she won't look suspicious coming here on occasion.

It took nearly a month to get her here. Her therapist kept encouraging gently, but ultimately, it had to be Landry's decision. That first time, back in January, she cried for a solid half hour.

She's come twice since then. Once with me, and once with the whole family, on the anniversary of my father's death, in May. Because we were visiting him anyway. Landry never says much at the grave site. I never do either. But this place is peaceful, and I think having a grave to visit has helped her.

She stands and kisses her fingers, then presses them to the top of the headstone. "Sleep well, baby girl," she whispers. Then she follows me over three rows and down one, to where Mom and Penn stand in front of Dad's headstone.

"Hey, Dad," I say, while my brother scoots over to make room for us. "I guess Penn told you tomorrow's the day." But he didn't, of course. Penn doesn't talk to Dad. Not out loud, anyway. "He's trading in his running shoes for boots and a rifle." And more physics and calculus than anyone would ever take on a volunteer basis.

Penn reports to West Point in five days, and we're all taking him. We're making a family trip out of it: a three-day drive, then a day and a half in New York City, right before we drop him off.

I mean, we can only afford to stay in New Jersey, but we'll get to *see* New York.

"He'd be so proud," my mom says, wrapping her arm around Penn's shoulders. "As I am."

We all are. Penn's going to get his dream. He's going to work really, really hard for it, but he's going to get it.

A month after we get back from New York, Jake leaves for Lubbock. He met several of his new teammates when he went down for freshman orientation last week, and he seems to like them.

I'm not sure he and I have forever in our future, but I'm sure we're going to try. I mean, a guy who doesn't give up on you even after you accuse him of getting some other girl pregnant . . . ? He might just be worth fighting for.

School starts for Landry and me that same week. She's going to be a freshman, and like all the other freshmen, she's going to have to change for PE in the girls' locker room. I'm not sure she's ready to go in there again. The therapist says she may have issues, so Mom and I are kind of preparing for the worst. But hoping for the best.

On the bright side, the media has long since moved on from Lullaby Doe. Someone online mentions her from time to time, along with a few other "unsolved mysteries." But suspicion and outrage are exhausting, and people have mostly moved on from the #babykiller obsession as well. Online, anyway.

Here in town? They'll probably always give me strange looks. Some of them will probably always think I got away with something horrible, because the only way to clear my name would be to drag my sister's through the mud, and I'm not going to do that.

As hard as it is for me to accept, sometimes, that people are always going to believe a lie about me, the truth is none of their business.

My *life* is none of their business.

In one month, I'll be a senior. I've even—finally—signed up for the ACT. I'm thinking about UT Knoxville. About maybe rooming with Amira. About meeting some people who've never heard of Beckett Bergen, the #babykiller.

I still don't know exactly what I want to do with my life. But for the first time in a long time, there is *nothing* holding me back.

# AUTHOR'S NOTE

Dear Reader,

This story is not autobiographical, but it is without doubt the most personal thing I've ever written, and parts of it were inspired by events from my own life. I really had a pregnant teenage sister. But unlike Landry, she was fifteen, and her pregnancy was the exact opposite of a secret. It was also not a rarity, in my small Tennessee hometown. Fortunately, my sister's baby lived, and he grew up to be my amazing, kind, compassionate nephew.

I also really did grow up with a parent who was addicted to painkillers, though we didn't know anything about an "opioid epidemic," back then. The origin of the addiction was an entirely legal prescription for a real medical condition, though I didn't know any of that at the time. In fact, I was much less in the know about the situation than Beckett. I knew something was wrong. I knew things weren't adding up. I knew there were rumors, and that my mother had lost a series of jobs with no explanation that made sense. The scene in the book where Beckett describes calling her father's boss? That really happened. I actually made that call, but it was at Christmas, not Thanksgiving. It broke my heart. It changed my perspective in a brutal way.

However, I am happy to say that my mother not only survived her opioid addiction, she kicked its teeth in. Not quickly. Not easily. But soundly.

Several other parts of this story were inspired by real events. My husband served honorably in the military and retired after twenty years of service in the U.S. Air Force. He was in the desert several times. He was in Saudi Arabia when our daughter took her first steps.

That daughter grew up and applied to West Point, as well as to the other service academies. The application process alone is grueling and prolonged, and waiting for an acceptance or a rejection was the most nerve-racking thing I've ever gone through. And I wasn't even the one applying. So it made perfect sense to me that Penn would channel his grief into an obsession with getting into the United States Military Academy, especially considering his dad's history as a vet.

The inspiration for the most prominent event in the story was a rumor from my high school days, when a girl I went to school with was pilloried much like Beckett was in the book. Fortunately, those were the pre-internet days, so the rest of the world did not get involved. Equally fortunately, the baby rumored to have died at birth—or been killed—wasn't actually found in the school. I have no idea if it was ever even real. But the *rumors* were real, and the former students I mentioned them to as I was writing this book still remembered them, twenty-seven years later. Everyone told me a different version of the rumors they remembered—how and where the baby was found, and who the father was.

According to the version I heard when I was in high school,

the father of the dead baby was the boy I was dating at the time. I didn't have the nerve to ask him if it was true. To say that the rumor stuck with me is an understatement. Unfortunately, I suspect it also stuck with the girl rumored to be the mother.

I *really* wish I could say I never repeated that rumor.

I am not Beckett Bergen. She's much stronger and smarter than I ever was. Much more determined and resilient. She is who I wish I could have been, and I hope she's found a place in your heart.

*Rachel Vincent*

### Findtreatment.gov

An extension of the Substance Abuse and Mental Health Services Administration (SAMHSA), this federally funded site offers resources for better understanding addiction, finding treatment, and understanding the correlation between addiction and mental health. Their website also has the ability to search for local resources using your zip code or city.

findtreatment.gov

### Help and Resources—National Opioids Crisis

Backed by the U.S. Department of Health and Human Services, this site offers information to understand the opioid epidemic from a wider perspective, as well as specific links for help with prevention, treatment, and recovery—for individuals struggling with addiction as well as their loved ones.

hhs.gov/opioids

### Make the Connection

For veterans and their families, Make the Connection offers information, resources, and solutions to the issues affecting their lives, including PTSD. Their website also has the ability to search for local resources using your zip code.

maketheconnection.net

# RESOURCES

The following resources offer additional information or assistance on the topics covered in this book.

## American Pregnancy Association—Teen Pregnancy Helpline

Available 24/7, this helpline is a safe place for pregnant teens to talk about their options. The corresponding article offers a comprehensive list of all the different aspects of being a pregnant teen, and also includes additional resources for more in-depth information.

**1-800-672-2296**

**americanpregnancy.org/unplanned-pregnancy/pregnant-teen**

## National Alliance on Mental Illness (NAMI)

For those struggling with mental illness, such as PTSD or depression, the National Alliance on Mental Illness site includes information on different illnesses, ways to find support or treatment, as well as coping mechanisms you can begin at home. Their website also has the ability to search for local resources using your zip code or city.

**NAMI Helpline: 1-800-950-NAMI (Mon.–Fri. 9 a.m.–6 p.m. EST)**

**Text NAMI to 741-741 for 24/7 crisis support via text message**

**nami.org**

# ACKNOWLEDGMENTS

This story is very personal for me, and many of the details were inspired by events from my own past, but *Every Single Lie* could not exist without the input and efforts of many others. With that in mind, I would like to thank the following people:

Infinite thanks go to Maegan Chaney-Bouis, MD, for answering my medical questions about teen pregnancy and delivery. Any mistakes made are my own.

Thanks also to Clayton Westbrooks, for answering my frequent and specific questions about small-town police procedure. Again, any mistakes are my own.

Thanks, as always, to Jennifer Lynn Barnes, my frequent lunch and writing buddy, for all the suggestions and advice. I hope to see you again, when this pandemic finally ends.

Thanks to my daughter, whose stressful experience applying to West Point made such an impression on me that it became Penn's obsession and coping mechanism.

Thank you, of course, to my agent, Ginger Clark, for all the things a literary agent handles, not the least of which involve hand-holding and talking me off ledges.

Thanks to the amazing production team at Bloomsbury,

including Claire Stetzer, for all the work that went into *Every Single Lie*, at every single level. (See what I did there?!?)

And finally, all of my gratitude goes to Cindy Loh, my editor, for taking a chance on this book. On me, and on a story that gutted me with every word I wrote. This book would not exist without you, your patience, your enthusiasm, and your invaluable input.